A Garland Series

Foundations of the Novel

Representative Early Eighteenth-Century Fiction

A collection of 100 rare titles
reprinted in photo-facsimile in 71 volumes

Foundations of the Novel

compiled and edited by

Michael F. Shugrue
Secretary for English for the M.L.A.

with New Introductions for each volume by

Michael Shugrue, *City College of C.U.N.Y.*
Malcolm J. Bosse, *City College of C.U.N.Y.*
William Graves, *N.Y. Institute of Technology*
Josephine Grieder, *Rutgers University, Newark*

Letters
from the Marchioness de M* * *
to the Count de R* * *

by

Claude Prosper Jolyot de Crébillon *fils*

with a new introduction
for the Garland Edition by
Josephine Grieder

Garland Publishing, Inc., New York & London

1972

Bibliographical note:

This facsimile has been made from a copy in the Yale University Library (Hfd29 144f)

Library of Congress Cataloging in Publication Data

Crébillon, Claude Prosper Jolyot de, 1707-1777.
Letters from the marchioness de M*** to the count de R***.

(Foundations of the novel)
Translation of Lettres de la marquise de M*** au comte de R***.
Reprint of the 1735 ed.
I. Title. II. Series.
PQ1971.C6A6713 1972 843'.5 [B] 72-170590
ISBN 0-8240-0572-4

Printed in the United States of America

Introduction

The reader acquainted with the epistolary novel only through Pamela, Clarissa, or Sir Charles Grandison may be tempted to assume that the form sprang full blown like Athena from the brow of Samuel Richardson. Such is not the case, as Robert Adams Day thoroughly demonstrates in Told in Letters; and the Letters from the Marchioness de M***, to the Count de R*** (1735) by Crébillon fils is a good example of an earlier effort in the genre.[1] The title page, in its quotation from the Journal Littéraire, indicates the work's immediate antecedents, the Lettres portugaises (1669) and the Lettres galantes du Chevalier d'Her** by Fontenelle (1683 and 1687); but Crébillon creates a heroine more sentimental and worldly than the passionate Portuguese nun and focuses less on satirical portraits of the beau monde, Fontenelle's chief interest, than on the Marchioness' inner joys and torments.

The technical problems involved in the composition of an epistolary novel – how to present differing points of view; how to provide the characters with enough motivation, leisure, paper, and ink to write – are here reduced to the minimum. The sole correspondent is the Marchioness. The sole recipient is the Count, whose alternating assiduity and indifference to his mistress occasion her correspondence. Short billets, generally *setting assignations, contrast with longer letters concerning her emotions; she enlivens her pages with gossip about friends, her husband, and other suitors. Sometimes she writes to request his help in an amorous affair; sometimes to assure him of her feelings; and very frequently to reproach him for his coldness or inconstancy.*

But Crébillon, in employing the epistolary form, seized on its essential virtue: because the reader sees without an intermediary the feelings of the Marchioness, he is directly engaged emotionally with her. The translator, Samuel Humphreys, makes this clear in his preface.[2] *He anticipates that those ladies "who pretend to be devoted to the severest Sanctity" will no doubt disapprove of the work, but "The amiable and generous Part of the Sex, will be soften'd into Compassion, for the Frailties of a Lady who was too lovely to be exempted from the Ensnarements that result from blooming Beauty, and shining Wit." The Marchioness indeed deviates from virtue, but a consideration of circumstances "shall easily permit our Constructions of her Conduct to be moderated by the Sentiments of Humanity." And particularly on reading of her death, "we intermix our Tears with hers; we intreat Heaven to be propitious to her . . . and wish to see her wafted, by Angels, to those blissful Regions where all Sorrows shall for ever cease, and where the Infirmities inseparable from the present State of human Nature, will no more be repeated" (no pp.). Such participation on the part of the reader is particularly necessary in a story where sentiment is the chief interest and morality depends rather on nuances of feeling than on rigid interpretation of actions.*

The Marchioness is, as we first see her, a delightful, witty coquette, intrigued by the Count's passion. Men's "Follies contribute to my Amusement," (p. 10), she declares; though she is not "insensible" to his charms, she suggests that he "endeavour to refine your Heart from this unavailing Passion" (p. 15) and try elsewhere. Besides, her idea of love as "a mutual Confidence, an untainted Friendship and a perpetual Sollicitude to please" does not correspond to the modern idea; "That Passion, as it is now conducted, is no more than a frail Intercourse formed by Caprice; cherished awhile, by a Cast of Mind, still more contemptible; and, at last, extinguished by both" (p. 22).

Nevertheless, little by little, passion makes inroads on this confidence. She finds in herself "something more lively than Friendship" (p. 27). In response to his reproaches on her sarcasm, she tergiversates: "How do you know but that the Vivacity you complain of, may be my only Expedient to conceal half your Happiness from you, and to preserve me from the Confusion of declaring that I love you?" (p. 37). She becomes seriously annoyed at his apparent infidelity and exclaims, "Good God! can I be weak enough to wish you may be able to justify yourself!" (p. 49). Finally, conscious of being led into "a dreadful Abyss . . . the fatal Gulph" (p. 51), she admits the force of her feelings: "O Heavens! whither shall I fly from such a

Combination of fatal Foes! My Sighs and Tears, and even my strongest Oppositions, give new Vigour to my unhappy Passion" (p. 52).

Assured of her love, the Count urges her, as we learn indirectly, to grant the "last favours." She is caught in the inextricable female dilemma: "How happy is your Sex, in their Prerogative to pursue their Inclinations without the Checks of Shame and Confusion! whilst we, who are under the Tyranny of injust Laws, are compell'd to conquer the Impulse of Nature, who has implanted, in our Hearts, the same Desires that predominate in yours, and are so much the more unfortunate as we are obliged to oppose your Sollicitations and our own Frailty" (p. 58). Nevertheless, she marshalls the usual prudent arguments against such a step. First, man's nature is inevitably inconstant; and she is "persuaded it would be better to lose a Lover who is dissatisfied with our Cruelty, than one who is satiated with our Favours" (p. 63). Second, she fears her conscience. The Count's discretion might be able to conceal their arrangement, "but alas! who would have the Power to screen me from the Remorse of my own Heart?" (p. 67). She temporarily concludes that "the Emotions of the Heart are not subordinate to the Judgment: But, surely, I have the Ability to be virtuous; and we never cease to be so, against our Inclinations" (p. 67).

Does the Marchioness actually capitulate? Her Letter XXVII informs the Count that "your impatient Ardours had almost surprized me into an absolute Insensibility *of my Duty" (p. 106) when the arrival of her husband fortunately saved her virtue, and she swears never to have another such interview with him. But relenting, "You see the Perplexity in which I am involved," she declares; "your Lordship in one Scale, and Virtue in the other: How difficult is it to adjust the Ballance! (P. 109). Two quick billets follow, the second arranging an assignation; "Some Letters are here suppress'd" (p. 111), the editor informs us. And in the next letter, the Marchioness reproaches R*** for too warm a declaration of his affection in public. Crébillon originally wrote at this point, "Voulez-vous faire deviner à tout le monde que vous m'aimez, et qu'il ne manque rien à votre bonheur?" Mr. Humphreys chooses to translate this ambiguously: "Would you have all the World suspect your Passion for me; and are you desirous they should believe you want nothing to render your Happiness compleat . . .?" (p. 113).*

Whatever the English reader may choose to decide, the Marchioness knows from this point on all the worries that a mistress is subject to. In order to keep him interested, she gives him frequent cause for jealousy because "I have observed that it is good to awaken your Passion" (p. 129); satirical portraits of amorous tax collectors, an old marquis, her philosophy professor, a fop, and a prince enliven her letters. She is concerned about her reputation – "From the first moment I lov'd you, every Instance of my Conduct has been a Deviation from my Duty" (p. 169) – but her husband troubles her less as a watchdog than as a person whose justifiable amorous solicitations prove troublesome to her passion. She is continually in dread of the Count's inconstancy and reproaches him for it, though she asks him to "Pity me, in some tender Moments; for I cannot presume to require, from you, any Sentiments that are more ardent" (p. 230). Hoping by her coldness to revive his interest, she declares to him that "I once lov'd you to Adoration, and my Passion was incapable of a Moment's Insincerity; but you have, at last, caus'd it to expire" (p. 258).

An unexpected event – her husband's promotion to a post abroad – triggers the denouement: the Marchioness' death from anguish at being obliged to part from the Count. All her guilty feelings now come forward to torment her: "I am constantly haunted by the most criminal Ideas, and find it impossible to chase them from my Remembrance" (p. 297). She is repentant – and yet she loves. "It is no longer the frail Person enslav'd by a fatal Passion, who writes to you now. It is an unfortunate Creature, who repents of all her Crimes; who reviews them with Horror; who is sensible of all their Weight, and who yet is unable to refuse you new Proofs of her Tenderness" (p. 302). She is, in fact, more concerned about the Count's despair at her death than about her own situation and urges him to be steadfast. At the end, she neither loses dignity nor recants her love. "I am now come to the last Period of my Days, and am preparing to end them with Fortitude. Adieu! Adieu! Adieu! for ever!" (p. 304).

The ordinary reader will see in these letters the

progress of feminine sensibility from coquetry to a tender and sincere passion. The perspicacious reader will see as well a comment on woman's ambiguous position in contemporary society. The novel presents, in effect, a ménage à trois. *But the husband is impossible: free to engage in the amours which please him; delighted to retail to her the history of his conquests; yet out of boredom capricious and demanding of his marital rights. The much-loved Count is scarcely less agreeable on close inspection. He parades his mistresses before the Marchioness; he brags to others of his inconstancy; he neglects her "with no other View than to satisfy your Curiosity whether the Loss of you will affect me" (p. 253); he neglects her for no reason whatever. But the Marchioness tacitly accepts the current code and lives as honorably as possible with it. Unlike later heroines who lament and repent at length their fall from virtue, she has no recriminations until the moment of her death. This perhaps makes her technically "immoral"; that she continues faithful and tender in such a situation makes her, however, extremely admirable and even lovable.*

Josephine Grieder

INTRODUCTION

NOTES

[1]*The complete title of Mr. Day's work is* Told in Letters: Epistolary Fiction before Richardson *(Ann Arbor: University of Michigan Press, 1966); a brief discussion of the* Letters *will be found in pages 107-109.*

[2]*Humphreys (1698?-1738) was a poet and a respected, if minor, figure in the world of letters: he provided the texts to several of Handel's most celebrated oratorios; and he did translations from Italian and French, including Gueulette's* Peruvian Letters *(1734) and pieces from La Fontaine.*

LETTERS

FROM THE

Marchioneſs de *M****,

TO THE

Count de *R****

Tranſlated from the Original *French*,

By Mr. *HUMPHREYS*.

" *If any* Love-Letters *may be rank'd with the* " *celebrated ones of* Abelard *and* Eloiſa; thoſe *of a Reli-* " *gious* Portugueſe *Lady, and* thoſe *of the Chevalier* de " Her——; *They are* Theſe *of the Marchioneſs* de M— " *to the Count* de R—. *They have the* Fire, *the* Turn, " *the* Spirit, *and* eaſy Air *of* Thoſe *we have men-* " *tion'd*: *They furniſh us beſides with this uſeful Leſſon,* " *That* Guilty Love muſt expect to meet with unhappy " Conſequences. *Journ. Liter.* 1734.

LONDON:

Printed for J. Wilford, at the *Three Flower-de-Luces*, behind the *Chapter-houſe*, in *St. Paul's Church-yard.* M DCC XXXV.

[Price Three Shillings.]

The TRANSLATOR's PREFACE.

HE following Letters have received such uncommon Applause, in several Parts of Europe, *that there was some Reason to believe they would not be unacceptable to the Publick, in an* English *Translation.*

They paint, in the warmest Colours, the Progress of an unfortunate Passion, from its seducing Birth, to its fatal Period; and represent an amiable Mind variously agitated by the Impressions of Tenderness, and the Dictates of Duty.

 The

The beauteous Marchioneſs had frequent Recourſe to the Aids of Virtue, and the ſtricteſt Sentiments of Honour: She diſtruſted the natural Softneſs of her Soul, and neglected no Endeavours to extinguiſh a Flame from whoſe Prevalence ſhe had Reaſon to be apprehenſive of ſuch unhappy Events. Her Breaſt was, perhaps, a Scene of the ſharpeſt Conflict that was ever ſuſtain'd by Love and Innocence; and if this latter had not the Glory of being victorious, it was becauſe the other had the Fatality to be invincible.

Thoſe of the Fair Sex, who pretend to be devoted to the ſevereſt Sanctity, and have refin'd themſelves into ſuch Ideal Perfection as to be inexorable to every Inſtance of human Weakneſs, will doubtleſs be as uncandid to this unfortunate Lady, as they are partial to themſelves. Let them rejoice then, in the Steadineſs of their unaſſaulted Virtue, and boaſt their Inſenſibility of Temptations they never experienced; let the cold Purity of a Breaſt, which no one ever

ever wiſhed to kindle, be miſtaken, by them, for a Series of untainted Chaſtity; but let them know, at the ſame time, to their eternal Mortification, that ſollicited Beauty never ſuffers from the Spleen of Prudery, or the ſolemn Cenſoriouſneſs of grey Virginity.

The amiable and generous Part of the Sex, will be ſoften'd into Compaſſion, for the Frailties of a Lady who was too lovely to be exempted from the Enſnarements that reſult from blooming Beauty, and ſhining Wit. It was her Misfortune to be betray'd into a Deviation from Virtue, by a Paſſion ſhe was unable to elude; but, if the ſeveral Circumſtances of her unhappy Situation be impartially conſider'd, we ſhall eaſily permit our Conſtructions of her Conduct to be moderated by the Sentiments of Humanity. We ſhall then repreſent to our Imagination, the Injuſtice ſhe ſuſtain'd by a Marriage of Compulſion, in her early Flower of Youth; we ſhall reflect, with Indignation, on the ungenerous Treatment ſhe

received

received from a Husband of that Indelicacy, as to have no Taste for the Treasure he possessed, and who prostituted, in a Length of degrading Amours, all the Tenderness that was so justly due to his charming Spouse; we shall consider, with Astonishment, that uncomplaining Softness of Soul, with which she so long sustain'd his Barbarity, and will find it difficult to suppress our Impatience to behold her awaken'd into Resentment, at her unmerited Wrongs; we shall think it natural for the Brutality of a Husband to open her Eyes to the Assiduities of a youthful Lover, adorn'd with every pleasing Quality that could possibly tempt her to listen to the Language of his Addresses; we shall be candid to the Intercourse they afterwards maintain'd: And, tho' we acknowledge her Example to be no proper Model for her Sex, even in her Circumstances of Life, yet we shall find ourselves obliged to confess that she well deserv'd to be immaculate, since she had so much Reluctance to be otherwise. But,

when

when we at laſt trace her in the Pangs of Death, and read the moving Flow of her agonizing Penitence; every Inſtance of her former Frailties diſappears from our View; we intermix our Tears with hers; we intreat Heaven to be propitious to her, in her laſt Moments of Mortality, and wiſh to ſee her wafted, by Angels, to thoſe bliſsful Regions where all Sorrows ſhall for ever ceaſe, and where the Infirmities inſeparable from the preſent State of human Nature, will be no more repeated.

I am almoſt perſuaded that ſome of theſe Impreſſions, at leaſt, will be experienced by the generality of thoſe who read the Letters. I have attempted to tranſlate: But, as I have been pleading for Candour to the fair Marchioneſs, I muſt likewiſe take this Opportunity to ſollicit the ſame Favour for myſelf. I am ſufficiently ſenſible of my Incapacity to transfuſe into my Verſion, all the delicate Livelineſs of Wit, and the full Glow of Rapture that

animate

animate the Original, and are as amiable as any that ever flowed from a Lover's Pen: If my Copy be not condemn'd for an absolute Unlikeness, I shall be very well satisfied with that Instance of Complaisance from the Publick.

LETTERS

LETTERS

FROM

The Marchioneſs de *M****,

TO

The Count de *R****

An Extract of a LETTER *from Madam de *** to M. de ***.*

I HAVE lately made a very agreeable Diſcovery; for I found, among the Papers that belonged to the Count of *R***, a Collection of Letters written by the Marchioneſs of *M****, and was charmed to ſee the only Remains of a Perſon illuſtrious by her Birth, and equally celebrated for her Wit and Beauty. I have read them with a peculiar Delight, and they may poſſibly prove as entertaining to you. For my part, I ſhould not be diſpleaſed, if they were communicated to the Publick. Perhaps, they may not preſent you with that Accuracy of Style, in which our Writers place ſo conſiderable a Part of their Merit; but the little Negligences of a Woman of Wit have that amiable Air, which might be difficult, even for your fine Genius to imitate: However, if they are accommodated to your Taſte, I ſhall not deſpair of their Succeſs. I muſt confeſs indeed, it would have been very ſatisfactory to me to have diſcovered more Traces of Virtue in theſe Letters; but the Marchioneſs was in Love: This was the original Misfortune, and all the reſt are, in ſome meaſure, the inevitable Conſequences of ſuch a Cauſe. I am ſenſible, that a diſtant Lover ſeems to make no dangerous Appearance, and we imagine our Virtue very ſafe in his Converſation; but the Aſpect of Things is changed, in proportion to his Approach, and thoſe Perſons muſt be unacquainted with the Diſpoſition of the Heart, who believe it incapable of Weakneſs. I could amuſe you with ſeveral Particulars on this Subject; but I am a Woman, and you may poſſibly ſuſpect that I am not entirely diſintereſted in my Obſervations: But let us return to the Letters. I have only tranſmitted thoſe to you, which I imagined worthy to be read; and tho' I have ſelected no more than ſeventy, ty, out of five hundred which are in my Poſſeſſion, you are not to conclude that the reſt are inferior to theſe; but Lovers frequently write things that are of ſmall importance to any but themſelves. I may likewiſe add, that I found my ſelf a little diſguſted at the exceſſive Warmth that glows in ſome of theſe Letters, and it ſeem'd, to me, ridiculous to indulge ſo much Weakneſs for a Man. I have likewiſe rejected ſeveral others, out of Regard to the ſtrict Rules of Decency; but, at the ſame time, I have endeavoured to diſconcert, as little as poſſible, the Order in which they were written; and yet, after all my Caution, you will ſometimes find the Connection interrupted. When you are diſpoſed to paſs ſome Time in this place, you may then judge whether I have acted with Diſcretion, in not parting with the whole Collection; and, as amiable as theſe amorous Epiſtles may appear, I am perſuaded you will not condemn my Proceeding. The ſame Expreſſions are frequently repeated in them; the ſame Situation of Circumſtances is as often preſented, and the ſame Object perpetually riſes to the Reader's View. Little Diſſatisfactions, Reconciliations, Flights of Caprice, warm Reſentments and flowing Tears, Joys, Jealouſies and Apprehenſions, Fears, impatient Wiſhes and Deſpair, are liberally diffused; and tho' these Emotions are varied in the Description, yet Love is the only Cause from whence they derive their Existence and receive their Extinction; Love still appears in this Diversity of Shapes, and the Uniformity of the Subject must infallibly be disagreeable, notwithstanding the Variety of the Sentiments; but, to give you the compleatest Reason of all, it was my Pleasure Things should be as you find them, and now I am persuaded you believe I have justified my self in the best manner imaginable.

LETTER I

I AM not certain whether you remember that we have only engaged our selves in an Intercourse of Friendship; but I have promised you mine, with a sincere Intention to be punctual; and it would give me no little Disquietude, should your desiring what I am unable to grant, oblige me to deny you what I am in a Condition to bestow. As young as I am, you may venture to believe, that I have not been destitute of proper Instructions; and that a Husband must certainly have given me a tolerable Idea of a Lover. My own particular Reflections, the Examples of others, and the Admonitions

monitions of ſome judicious Perſons, have furniſhed me with that Knowledge which others only obtain by Experience; and I have acquired all this, without the Mortification of owing it to any Experiments of my own. I may juſtly affirm then, that I am well acquainted with the Diſpoſition of Lovers, and I am dreadfully afraid you are one of that Claſs. You have ſent me a Letter, but from what Motive, I am at a loſs to determine; and I think your Friendſhip has ſupplied you with ſome Expreſſions that ſeem to have an Air of Love. I may poſſibly be deceived: But your Letter was delivered to me in a very myſterious manner: You was apprehenſive leſt my Husband ſhould ſee it; your Thoughts were diſordered when you writ it, and nothing is well expreſſed in it, but what I was unwilling to underſtand. All theſe Particulars are Intimations of Love, or of your Deſire, at leaſt, to make me believe you are influenced by that Paſſion. Why are you ſo ſollicitous to be concealed from my Husband? A long Intimacy has ſubſiſted between you, and he could never be ſurpriſed at your having an Occaſion to write to me: The Action is innocent in it ſelf, and nothing but the Circumſtances of your Conduct can make it criminal. But of what Importance is it to me, after all, whether you are in Love or not, if I am perſuaded I ſhall never be ſenſible of that Paſſion for you? However, ſince I know how deſirous you are to receive ſome Conſolation, after the Inconſtancy of Lady *H****, I extremely regret my Incapacity of contributing to your Relief, and am very ſenſible how much I am honoured by your Choice of me, to reinſtate her in your Heart. But can it enter into your Thoughts, that I ſhould imagine my Happineſs conſiſts in a perpetual Fidelity to you? I am too diffident of my ſelf, ever to entertain ſuch a Sentiment, and ſhould have reaſon to be apprehenſive, that ſince you have experienced the Inconſtancy of one Woman, you would never enter into any Engagements with another, but with an Intention to gratify your Revenge. The Language of this Suſpicion is, that I ſhould think my ſelf obliged to fruſtrate your Deſign; and indeed I foreſee, that our Engagements would be attended with no extraordinary Opinion of each other's Integrity. Beſides, I never ſhall perſuade my ſelf, that Conſtancy can be ſo generous a Pleaſure as to afford us a Recompence for all the other Gratifications it debars us from enjoying. The Truth of it is, you Men are very unreaſonable; you expect our Hearts ſhould be inacceſſible to all but your

your ſelves, and think a Moment's Attention to another Object, a great Indignity to your own Merit: You are ſuch tender, faithful Creatures, that it is no Wonder you ſhould be ſo deſirous of ingroſſing all the Thoughts of a Woman. For my part, I am conſcious of my Inability to form ſuch deep Reflections; and fear I ſhould never habituate my ſelf to that Refinement of Thought, as to pay all the Regard to your Merit as might be juſtly due. You will find me very inconſiderate and ſuch an eternal Trifler, that it would be impoſſible for you to love me long, and perhaps I might be weak enough to be afflicted at your Indifference. It is poſſible too, that Love might deprive me of my natural Gaiety of Mind; for, it ſeems, a melancholy Caſt of Thought is moſt conſiſtent with the Dignity of that Paſſion; at leaſt you open your Part in it with a very lamentable Air, and I ſhould be obliged to aſſume your Mien. One may diſpenſe with much Fondneſs for a Husband, but a Lover makes it a very grave Affair; one muſt conform to every Article of his Caprice; appear diſquieted when he is diſpoſed to be ſo; never ſmile without his Permiſſion, nor preſume to caſt a Glance on any Perſon but himſelf: But I muſt acquaint you beforehand, that I am very apt to make Uſe of my Eyes, have ſeve-

ral

ral little Fancies, am a mortal Enemy to Conſtraint, and am allowed, by my Husband, to indulge my ſelf in as much Liberty as I deſire. This laſt Article is very diſagreeable to a Lover, and he can never bear that Diſpoſition to Artifice and Curioſity, which Reſtraint naturally inſpires. You ſee my Arguments are very ſtrong againſt yours; but I had no Occaſion to draw them out to ſuch a Length; two Words would have been as ſignificant as all I have written. And it would have coſt me nothing to ſay, *I am reſolved not to love*; and indeed this is the only Anſwer I ought to have returned to your Letter: But I happened to have nothing to do when I received it, and was therefore willing to amuſe my ſelf with writing to you. Adieu, my Lord; I ſhall not be at the Opera this Evening, I am indiſpoſed, and keep my Chamber; from whence you may conclude, I have no Inclination to ſee Company; and indeed, Solitude ſeems ſo agreeable to me, at preſent, that I am not certain when I ſhall have any Curioſity to appear in Publick. I confeſs, Abſence muſt needs be a very ſevere Puniſhment to a Heart ſo much inflamed as yours. But if I did not begin with ſome Inſtances of Cruelty, the firſt Part of our Intercourſe would be too languiſhing. But I remember, in good Time, that

that you intreated me to let you know if you might be permitted to hope. I have consulted my Heart, on this Occasion, and am of Opinion, you must not.

LETTER II.

YES, my Lord, my Husband is an unworthy perfidious Man; I freely acknowledge it, and no one can enter into the Intention of your Reasonings better than my self. I ought to avenge my Wrongs; but I happen not to be of an implacable Disposition, and can assure you that I have not the least Need of any Consolation. I generously forgive my Ingrate all his licentious Conduct; and if I suffer any Dissatisfaction, it is because you interest your self so much in what relates to me. You are too much afflicted at the Misfortunes of others, and I sincerely pity you if you are as much chagrin'd at the Calamities of your other Friends, as you seem to be at mine. I say mine, to oblige you; because you are positive in your Opinion, that I am afflicted; and you conclude from thence, that I cannot alleviate my Grief better, than by imparting to my Husband, the same Inquietudes he gives me. But I must inform you, that I am perfectly acquainted with his Disposition:

poſition: He is a Philoſopher, and never ſuffers himſelf to be diſcompoſed at any thing; and tho' I ſhould rack my Invention to puniſh him, I ſhould ſtill have the Mortification to find him inſenſible of my Severity. Some Tempers are ſo perverſe, that it is impoſſible to rectify them, and his is one of that Complexion; for which reaſon, I think it moſt prudent to let him purſue his Indiſcretions; Time and a few ſedate Reflections will reſtore him to me, ſooner than we imagine. Life has ſome Moments of Inactivity, which muſt, unavoidably, be devoted to a Wife. Poor Man! I ſhould really pity him, were he conſtantly diſpoſed to pleaſe me, and had no other Recompence for that kind Intention, than ſuch an inconſiderable Toy as conjugal Affection; and indeed I have not the Injuſtice to require ſo much Complacency from him. You may poſſibly impute this Indifference of mine for my Huſband, to ſome ſecret Inclinations in Favour of another Object; but you will certainly be deceived, for he has given me a Diſguſt to all your Sex. They are not altogether my Averſion, however; but their Follies contribute to my Amuſement; and if it were not for thoſe which you diſcover, in loving me againſt my Inclinations, you would not divert me ſo much as you do at preſent. I

muſt

muſt intreat you not to be diſpleaſed at what I ſay; for you ought to conſider that it is a glorious Affair to amuſe the Perſon one loves. As to other Particulars, I am extremely concerned, that a Gentleman of your Merit ſhould laviſh, upon ſuch an ungrateful Perſon as my ſelf, that Time, which a Number of Women of my Acquaintance would undoubtedly employ much more agreeably. You will find a thouſand Ladies, who are at a Loſs how to beſtow their Hours, and would be charmed with your Perſon; for tho' I cannot prevail upon my ſelf to love you, I am not ſo ſtupid, as to be inſenſible of your Merit; and if I had nothing elſe to engage my Attention, I ſhould not be diſpleas'd to hear you ſigh for me. But my Weakneſs is very ſingular in its kind; my Huſband amuſes me; and when he has neither Time nor Opportunity to accompliſh any perfidious Action, he acquaints me with thoſe he formerly committed, and ſketches out ſuch as he flatters himſelf he may be able to favour me with hereafter. This is more entertaining to me, than all the engaging Speeches you Lovers can poſſibly premeditate. But leſt I ſhould forget the principal Intention of your Letter, I muſt obſerve, that you imagine I am diſpleaſed with you, tho' I am not able to gueſs what ſhould create that Suſpicion in

your

your Mind: I have not the leaſt Reaſon to wiſh any thing to your Diſadvantage; you are a Gentleman of Merit and Politeneſs, and apt to be a little enſnaring, if one is not conſtantly upon one's Guard. You entertain me with a thouſand Pleaſantries, which divert me extremely, when the Novelty of them prevents me from falling aſleep. Were it not for you, I ſhould never be certain that I was in Poſſeſſion of any Beauty; for all the Glimpſe I ever had of it, was in the Eyes of my Siſter-in-law, who is always out of Temper when ſhe ſees me: But that Circumſtance, alone, would not be ſufficient to convince me of my Charms; and I fancy that, in ſuch a Caſe, a Man of your Penetration is a much better Teſtimonial in my Favour, than the Jealouſy of a Woman. You ſee, by this Confeſſion of my Obligations to you, how ambitious I am to be grateful. Adieu, my Lord; no one but your ſelf would deſire any other Proof of ſuch a Diſpoſition, than the Pains I take in writing to you, but you are extremely difficult to be pleaſed. I have ſome Inclination to acquaint you, that I ſhall viſit Lady *** this Evening, and lay my Commands upon you to be there. You ought to be very well ſatisfied with me now. Bleſs me! an Aſſignation!

L E T-

LETTER III.

THE Jealousy you have lately entertained of my Husband, seems, to me, very singular, and I am extremely delighted with a Lover of such a peculiar Turn of Mind. He embraced me Yesterday, in your Presence; I said a thousand tender Things to him, and gave him many endearing Proofs of the most ardent Passion: You even heard me sigh; but I am surprised that a single Sigh should put your Imagination to the Expence of so many Conjectures. I can't possibly conceive how you could find any Ambiguity in it, and yet it has proved very injurious to your Repose. You charge me with practising the most dangerous Coquetry in the World, and declare that I am such a Proficient in it, as to love my Husband. I could be glad to know the Motive that inspires you with these extraordinary Speeches, and what Prerogative you have to utter them. Your Displeasure is not only pointed against the Marquis, but I am informed that *R**** has entirely forfeited your Esteem, because he has addressed some Verses to me, of his own composing, and they may possibly be better than those that were presented to me by your Muse. But let me desire you to imagine your ſelf in my Situation: Is it any Fault of mine, if he has an Inclination to call me *Celimene?* You tax me with Ingratitude; but I am really perplexed to know what Inſtance of it you ever received from me. Is it becauſe you tell me I am amiable, and that my Reply happens not to be agreeable to your Expectations? But is not the Pleaſure you enjoy, when you repeat ſuch fine Things to me, a ſufficent Recompence for your Trouble in inventing them? Were I to be captivated with every one who amuſes me with ſuch little Sallies of Fancy, you would ſoon begin to think me too grateful. Ought you not to be ſatisfied with my Indulgence, in permitting you to ſay thoſe Things to me, which I would never hear from any but your ſelf; and are there no Acknowledgments due to me for conquering thoſe Scruples that would diſſuade me from writing to you? Do you believe it can be conſiſtent with my Duty, to correſpond with you in this Manner? For tho' my Intentions are unblameable, they would receive a very different Conſtruction from the World; and who could I juſtly reproach for giving an unfavourable Turn to my Proceeding? You are pleaſed to ſay, you love me; you take the Liberty to write to me, and I enter into an Intercourſe of Letters with you, which, as innocent

nocent as it may be on my part, and as irreproachable as I may be inclined to think it, and hope it will prove in the Event, may yet be imputed to me as a Crime. This Consideration casts a Damp upon my Mind, and I think we ought to discontinue this trifling Correspondence, since it exposes me to a Number of Inquietudes. Resume the Friend, if that be possible, and no longer persist in your Resolution to be my Lover. Direct your Addresses to some Lady, who is better acquainted, than my self, with the Value of such a Heart as your's; I believe it to be extremely constant, and very capable of a respectful Perseverance. These are charming Qualities, but alas! I can't tell what to do with them. Were I to lose nothing but the Tranquillity of my Soul, it would give me an exquisite Pleasure to contribute to your Happiness; but you are too generous to desire any Concessions from me, that would cost me so dear. Let me intreat you, then, for the sake of your own Repose and mine, to endeavour to refine your Heart from this unavailing Passion. I have seen you sensibly afflicted at my Indifference, and I believe I sincerely pitied you. I am unwilling to familiarize my Breast to those Emotions; my Duty, and even my Inclinations oblige me, to discountenance your Addresses. You must pardon me therefore, if I determine not to receive any of your future Letters, or, at leaſt, I muſt have your Permiſſion to impart them to my Husband. You may love me as much as you pleaſe, but I ſhall be careful not to obſerve it; for ſhould I once ſuffer your Pretenſions to diſquiet me, I am apprehenſive that I ſhould, in ſome meaſure, intereſt my ſelf in what I ought to diſclaim; but this is a Weakneſs equally inconſiſtent with my Duty and Inclinations.

LETTER IV.

YOU injure me in believing I was at home Yeſterday, when you intended me a Viſit, and that I had private Reaſons not to ſee Company. Had I, really, ſhut my ſelf up in my own Appartment, and, as you are pleaſed to ſuppoſe, with a Man I love, I can't conceive that I am obliged to give you any Account of my Sentiments, or that you have a Privilege to demand any Explanations of my Conduct. It is not for me to determine, whether your Unhappineſs proceeds from the Inſenſibility that is interwoven in my Nature, or from the Prepoſſeſſion of my Heart, in favour of another. The only Particular that I can aſſure you of, with any Certainty, is, is, that I neither love you at preſent, nor ever ſhall for the future. The Chevalier *N**** whom your Jealouſy has ſelected for its Object, has as little a Share of my Favours as your ſelf; and your own Conſcience can inform you, whether you have any Reaſon to boaſt of the Treatment you have received from me. My Indifference to that Gentleman does not proceed from his want of Merit, but he never entertained me, perhaps, with an agreeable Declaration of Love, and he, very poſſibly, never had any ſuch Intention. Theſe two Circumſtances are at your Service, and you may chooſe that which appears to you moſt accommodated to your Relief. As to any other Particulars, I am not ſurpriſed at your believing me to be in private, yeſterday, with an imaginary Rival, ſince you find it more commodious to think worſe of me, than you do of your ſelf. I am willing, however, to grant you all the Juſtice you merit; you are one of the moſt amiable Men in the World; it is ſome time, ſince you firſt gave me to underſtand that you loved me, and yet your Aſſiduities make no Impreſſion upon me; you muſt certainly have Reaſon on your Side; my Inſenſibility is unnatural, and if I had not been prepoſſeſs'd with a ſtrong Paſſion for ſome other Object, I could not have ſo long retarded your Conqueſt of my Heart. But it very fortunately happens, that the Chevalier and I are not extremely conſtant, your Charms will ſoon ſupplant him; and it would be very ſurpriſing that your Sighs ſhould be unavailing, when ſuch an Effect is ſo injurious to your Merit. It has been uſual with you to receive the firſt Advances; but you have condeſcended to pay me that Compliment, and have relieved me from the Confuſion of making any Overtures inconſiſtent with the Delicacy of our Sex: You have found me a little remiſs in praiſing the Luſtre and Vivacity of your Eyes, and have vouchſafed to acquaint me that mine were not diſagreeable. You have renounced, for my ſake, all thoſe Beauties who were intereſted in your Affection; and is it poſſible that ſuch a ſingular Inſtance of your Attachment to me ſhould want ſuitable Acknowledgments? But why ſhould I reinſtate you in your Hopes? You are but too ſenſible that all my Coldneſs is affected, my Intentions are only to be convinced of the reality of your Ardours, and to render your Victory more agreeable by a little Reſiſtance. I ſeem to be more inſenſible of Conviction than the generality of my Sex; but, with all my Precautions againſt you, I ſhall find my ſelf as much deceived as they. You ought to to be tranſported at this Declaration ; it is a perfect Novelty to you, and I am perſuaded it will render me more amiable in your Imagination. Thoſe who are addicted to Inconſtancy would be too unfortunate if all Women reſembled one another ; but you muſt not think I expreſs my ſelf in this manner, becauſe I believe you incapable of a ſincere Paſſion ; I am not diſpoſed to reproach you in any Inſtance whatever, and am really perſuaded that, if ſeveral of my Sex complain of your Inconſtancy, they are more to blame than your ſelf : You was led into Engagements with them more from their Choice than your own, and they crowded their Favours upon you with ſo much Precipitation, that you had not a ſufficient Time to be amorous ; and I am not ſurpriſed at your Indifference. You ſee, my Lord, that I exceed you in Generoſity ; you charge me with indulging a Paſſion for the Chevalier, and I juſtify you againſt the ridiculous Reports that are propagated to your Diſadvantage : Can you expoſtulate with me for my Inſenſibility, after this, and is it poſſible for me to convince you how much I love you, by a more effectual Proof, than my believing you ſo worthy to be loved ? Let me conjure you, then, not to be apprehenſive that, when Chance ſhall bring us together, I ſhall have any

any Difinclination to offer you the cleareft Evidence of my Sentiments in your Favour.

LETTER V.

I DID not imagine, that I fhould ftill have a Difpofition to write to you, and always with a difobliging Air, when, by changing your Conduct towards me, you might eafily be convinced, that if I am infenfible of Love, I am, at leaft, very tender in my Friendfhip. What do you expect from me, and what Hopes can you juftly entertain? Can I liften to your Sighs, in my prefent Condition, without a manifeft Violation of my Duty? It is true, I was unable to guard my felf, yefterday, againft a tender Moment; but can you believe I will fuffer it to prevail over my better Reflections, and am I obliged to approve your Paffion, becaufe I pity your Inquietudes? But what Reafon have I to fuppofe, that you fuftain any on my Account? Am I to credit your Proteftations? And, if I fhould prevail upon my felf to be fo credulous, can I be certain, that you will love me always? Would not the fame Caprice of Imagination, which, at prefent, renders me the Object of your Vows, transfer

fer them, in a ſhort time, to another? But granting that I am not inclined to ſuſpect you capable of Perjury, and am as little diſpoſed to fortify my ſelf againſt you for the future; is it poſſible for me, when I conſider my preſent Situation, to reſign my ſelf to the Impreſſions, with which you would inſpire me? As I am under the Reſtraint of the moſt ſacred Obligations, can I permit my Heart to give any Admiſſion to thoſe Deſires, which I am prohibited to entertain; and is that Heart any longer at my diſpoſal? Could I really reſign it to you, I ſhould but offer you a tranſient Felicity, which, at preſent, you only deſire, becauſe you are not in Poſſeſſion of any Part of it; and this would open to me an eternal Source of Tears and Torments. But were it poſſible for your Love to conſtitute my Happineſs, it would prove a Happineſs for which I ſhould perpetually reproach my ſelf, and which is ever ſurrounded with Diſquietude and Remorſe. Your Paſſion would ſoon be extinguiſhed, and I ſhould have nothing left but the ſhameful Remembrance, that I had ſuffered my ſelf to be ſeduced, and perhaps the unhappy Conſciouſneſs that I ſtill continued to love you. At preſent indeed, you only deſire my Heart; but when you have once obtained it, you will inſenſibly lead me from Frailty to Frailty,

and,

and, at laſt, render me the Object of my own Averſion, as well as yours. I am not happy, but I enjoy Tranquillity; and it has coſt me dear: I have been in poſſeſſion of it but a ſhort time, and am too ſenſible of its Charms, to have any Inclination to expoſe my ſelf to the Danger of loſing them for ever.

You may boaſt of Love and its Delights as much as you pleaſe; but you will find it impoſſible to make me a Convert to ſuch Sentiments. I have frequently conſulted my Heart, with reſpect to thoſe Joys the ſofteſt Union can beſtow, and they appear, to me, to conſiſt in a mutual Confidence, an untainted Friendſhip and a perpetual Sollicitude to pleaſe: But alas! theſe are Refinements of Love, that only ſubſiſt in the Imagination, and had never any real Exiſtence. That Paſſion, as it is now conducted, is no more than a frail Intercourſe formed by Caprice; cheriſhed awhile, by a Caſt of Mind, ſtill more contemptible; and, at laſt, extinguiſhed by both. You may, poſſibly, be ſincere, but your Pretenſions to that Character muſt be confirmed by my Experience; and this, perhaps, would effectually convince me, that I was fatally deceived. You ſee I expreſs my ſelf with Calmneſs and Moderation, and I am under no Neceſſity of affecting ſo much

Compo-

Composure. I have sincerely acquainted you with what I think, and you ought to be persuaded, that I neither love you at present, nor ever shall; and my Heart confirms me in this Resolution, much more than my Reason. Adieu; I promised you a disobliging Letter, and am sorry that I am compelled to be punctual. Be so good, for the future, as to leave me to the Enjoyment of my Repose, and cease your obstinate Invasion of a Heart, which Duty as well as Inclination have fortified against your warmest Ardours. May you be happier in another Passion, and - - - - - once more Adieu; I detain you too long, since I have so little to say.

BILLET.

I am either very unfortunate, or you are extremely happy, at my having sometimes an Occasion for you, and being constantly obliged to write to you in this Manner. The Affair indeed does not deserve the Trouble I give my self; but my People are so very dull, and deliver Messages with such an ill Grace, that I find it necessary for me to write for the least Trifle. You may easily imagine how much this amuses me, who, as you are sensible, am one of the most indolent Persons in the World. This Preliminary being settled, I am *am now to acquaint you, without any Compliment, that I am obliged to be abroad, to day, upon an Affair of the greatest Importance: My Husband has thought fit to refuse me his Company, and I happen'd to imagine, at that instant, that you would treat me with more Politeness. Lady * * *, and* St. Far * * *, *took so much Pains to persuade me, that you had Leisure and Gallantry enough to afford me this little Satisfaction, that I was willing to be obliged to you for it. Your Uncle, the Governour, who is much more gouty and unintelligible in his Stammering than usual, was pleased to offer me his Hand; but he is too disagreeable to give me any Pleasure in his Civilities; and I should likewise be not a little afraid, lest he should drag me after him, in one of those Falls, that are so familiar to him; and surely, when one chooses a Gentleman, he ought at least to be able to speak, and be steady enough to support us as we walk. Besides, he is one of my professed Admirers; and tho' I could make the same Objection against you, yet I am advised by all my Friends to give you the Preference. Prepare your self, then, to wait upon me immediately; but I must desire you not to be amorous. No Sighs, or disconsolate Airs, for they will but embarrass you. However, upon second Thoughts, I must allow you some Amusement: You may put on a few Languors,*

guors, if you are ſo diſpoſed, and I give you leave to entertain all the ſeducing Reflections that can occur to you from ſuch a Favour as my permitting you to attend me; and, indeed, the Marquis has ſo provoked me, that I hardly know what I ought to refuſe you.

LETTER VI.

CAN you be ſo inconſiderate as not to know, that your Obſtinacy will, at laſt, be very diſpleaſing to me, and that we ſhall infallibly break off all Correſpondence for the future? What Methods muſt be taken to prevent you from intruding upon one's Repoſe? Was I not ſufficiently liberal of my Severities to you laſt Night; and might I not reaſonably conclude, that ſuch a Proof of my Diſpoſition would induce you to change your Conduct? But it ſeems I am deceived: Sighs and languiſhing Glances are my Evening's Entertainment, and tender Letters are preſented to me for my Amuſement in the Morning. But, in reality, I begin to be weary of theſe unpleaſing Repetitions, and were I not very cautious of giving my *Swiſs* any Opportunity to make improper Reflections, I ſhould order him not to admit your *Valet de Chambre* into the Houſe. I am quite ſatiated with always reading the ſame things, and having nothing new to anſwer. Were my Heart intereſted in any of theſe Particulars, they might amuſe me in a more engaging Manner; but it is extremely diſagreeable to be told, every Moment, that one is beloved, and yet find one's ſelf as inſenſible as ever. Our Engagement extended only to Friendſhip, and you promiſed to requeſt nothing more from me; you even aſſured me, that you would not write to me for the future, and yet the Moment I waked, I was told that *Dupré* had been waiting two Hours, and brought me a Letter from the Count. I am not diſpleaſed at your Violation of your Promiſe, ſince it furniſhes me with ſufficient Reaſons to diſregard mine. I have paſſed the Night in ſerious Reflections on the mutual Friendſhip we have promiſed to each other; but it ſeems to me very dangerous for a Woman to have ſo intimate a Friend; and I begin to be ſenſible, that this Name was only choſen to countenance a Declaration of Love. I likewiſe found, that I had Reaſon to be apprehenſive of that Confidence we repoſe in the Perſon we eſteem. A Woman eaſily habituates herſelf to unfold her Heart without Reſerve; the Friend never fails to improve thoſe Conjunctures, and very

very gravely takes upon him to be our Lover, when we little imagined he had any ſuch Intention. I am not diſpoſed to be ſurpriſed in this manner. Your firſt Endeavours have tended to inſpire me with ſomething more lively than Friendſhip; and yours had always too tender an Air, to be entitled to that Name. I might be juſtly charged with Indiſcretion, ſhould I permit you to be my Friend any longer; and yet I am unwilling to conſider you with Indifference: Can I think of no Medium then, that would relieve me from my Perplexities? I poſitively declare againſt Lovers; they give us abundance of Trouble, when we are inſenſible of their Paſſion, and grow diſſatisfied themſelves when they are convinced we love them. I have given you my Thoughts on Friendſhip; and as to Indifference, I really think it the moſt diſagreeable Situation of the Mind. You ſee, my Lord, how much you embarraſs me: Let us forbear to talk of any thing, I intreat you, till I can give you ſome fixt State in my Heart. I am going to think of it, and if I can determine on nothing better, we muſt reſolve to continue as we are. Adieu —— I would not have you give your ſelf the Trouble of paying me a Viſit this Afternoon. I have engaged my ſelf with Lady *** She has had ſome little Diſagreement with *St. Far* * * *, and he has requeſted me to ask her, why ſhe is ſo much out of Humour, as he is pleaſed to expreſs it; for my part I am perſuaded, ſhe is very excuſable, for who can be guilty of any Injuſtice to you Men? If you can find *St. Far* * * *, I ſhould be glad if you would bring him to me, he will diſcharge me from the Trouble of being his Advocate, and his Preſence will facilitate their Reconciliation. My God! how ridiculous are all Lovers! I wiſh your Lordſhip a good Morrow.

LETTER VII.

TO what purpoſe, my Lord, do you excuſe your ſelf to me, and what Offence have I to lay to your Charge at preſent? You have, at laſt, acted with the Diſcretion I have long wiſhed to ſee you diſcover, and I ſhould have preſented you with my Acknowledgments, if you had not imagined that I was diſpleaſed at your Proceeding. Let me intreat you to undeceive your ſelf; the Fact is very different, and you can never merit my Hatred, by ceaſing to torment me. I did not expect to ſee you ſo reaſonable, and am delighted to find, that in doing Juſtice to your ſelf, you

can

can likewiſe render it to me. You had no Cauſe to believe, that I had made my Husband privy to your Perſecutions ; for I never was reduced to thoſe Extremities as could make it neceſſary for me to reſort to ſuch a Remedy. The Coldneſs with which he treats you, can be imputed to none but your ſelf; you were not very ſollicitous, that the World ſhould be unacquainted with your Aſſiduities to me, and you have diſcloſed your ſelf to ſo many Confidents, that *M* *** may poſſibly have had ſome Intimations of your Conduct. You have likewiſe expoſed me to the Pleaſantries of Lady *G* ***, and I was on the Point of receiving her Congratulations, yeſterday, for the Happineſs I enjoy in your Addreſſes, and for my Senſibility of your Paſſion. This Lady ſeems to be much better acquainted with your Merit than my ſelf, and I believe ſhe conſiders me as her Rival ; but I can aſſure you, that all your Accompliſhments will never reconcile me to that Title. I ſhall therefore take it as a Favour, if you will rectify the Suſpicions, that have been created to my Diſadvantage, by ſuch falſe Inſinuations ; for as I have never countenanced your Extravagancies, it would be very diſagreeable to me to be thought capable of ſharing them ; and I flatter my ſelf, that your Honour, as a Gentleman, would not permit me to be repreſented in ſuch a Light. It is time to ſilence theſe Reports; and ſince your frequent Viſits to me are their principal Source, I muſt deſire you to diſcontinue them. It is with ſome Reluctance, that I find my ſelf obliged to come to ſuch Extremities with you; but remember that you your ſelf compell'd me to fly to this Expedient, and that inſtead of a Heart, which I neither can, nor ought to offer you, I make you the Tender of a Friendſhip, which perhaps you may juſtly think more valuable.

LETTER VIII.

SINCE you are ſo very importunate, I conſent to ſee you, and am willing to grant this Favour to the Repentance, with which you ſeem to be affected; and with a full Perſuaſion, that you will be punctual to your Promiſe, and that your Paſſion is really extinguiſhed. But why, then, ſhould you endeavour to rekindle it; and if it be true, that you formerly loved me, will the daily Sight of me induce you to forget me? I think it would be more conſiſtent with Diſcretion, if our Interviews were not ſo frequent, and you only render'd me thoſe Civilities, which your Sex uſually expreſs to a Woa Woman they esteem. I believe I can foresee, that our Friendship will have no long Continuance, and if I have any Penetration, your Cure is not so compleat as you intimate, or may possibly imagine it to be. Think of this with due Attention, and fortify your self against a Frailty, that troubles your Repose, and is fatal to the Tranquillity of my Soul. Were it possible for me to love you, can you imagine, that your Happiness would have any Increase, and that I should ever make my Duty subservient to a Caprice of Inclination, which would be the Reproach and Calamity of my Life? I am sensible that I pity you, but methinks that Pity should deprive you of all Hopes. Were I in a Disposition to be favourable to your Passion, my Disquiet would be less, for I am persuaded, your Conduct would soon incline me to be guided by my Duty, and the very possibility of creating any Suspicion of my Weakness is sufficient to guard me against it. You are, as yet, unacquainted with my Heart; it is equally delicate and imperious, and should I resign it to your Possession, I am certain, from your present Turn of Thought, that your Torments would be much superior to your Satisfactions. You have not been fated to entertain a Passion for me, by any Sentiments that were independent on your

Will;

Will; and I have never ſeen you influenced by ſuch involuntary Emotions. Gallantry alone inclined you to diſtinguiſh me by your Addreſſes; and you thought I ſhould amuſe you more agreeably than the generality of my Sex. Perhaps your Perfidy in ſome former Engagement, has left a Vacancy in your Heart, which you are deſirous to fill with another Object: But as you have found me more inflexible than other Women, you are determined to purſue me without any Intermiſſion, becauſe my Inſenſibility is an Affront to your Vanity. I may add, that your Love, with all the Humility and Submiſſion it affects to aſſume, is ſtill injurious to my Virtue; and your Attachment to me undoubtedly proceeds from your Perſuaſion, that I ſhall be conquer'd ſooner than another Object. However that may be, I permit you to ſee me ſometimes; it is in your Power to fix your ſelf in my Eſteem, and if I have ſufficient Reaſons to be averſe to your Paſſion, I have none that can induce me to refuſe you a Friendſhip, which you will merit above the reſt of your Sex, if you ſollicit me for nothing more. Adieu — Your Conduct will regulate mine.

LETTER IX.

AH poor Count! is it poſſible that you ſhould be ſick, and have Love for your Diſtemper? Your Caſe is indeed very ſingular, and my Rigour will coſt you your Life! I never imagined that I was ſo formidable; but let me intreat you not to die, ſince that Misfortune will give Poſterity ſuch an Idea of my Inſenſibility, as I may, poſſibly, not deſerve. Some malicious Poet will diſgrace your Tomb with a ridiculous Inſcription, in which I ſhall be treated with too much Severity; and I have no Inclination to furniſh Matter to the Conceits of thoſe Gentlemen. Beſides, what Recompence will you expect me to afford you, if you die for me? Would you have the Pleaſure of impoſing upon me a Tribute of Tears, which you can never be in a Condition to enjoy? But what Satisfaction would it afford you, ſhould I reſolve, amidſt my Anguiſh at your Death, to wander among the ſolitary Rocks, with a Reſolution to fatigue the Echos with my plaintive Sorrow, and expoſtulate with inexorable Fate for the Loſs of *Thyrſis*. Believe me, my Tears are unworthy the Pains you take to merit them, and our Sex is ſo extremely fickle, that perhaps I might have no Inclination to be-

wail

wail you. We forget a living Lover ſo very ſoon, that we are under no Neceſſity of beſtowing much Remembrance on the Dead. But without entring on a Detail of what other Women might do at ſuch a Juncture, I will freely confeſs to you, that none of my Sex can pretend to ſurpaſs me in Coquettry. Were I the Widow of one Lover, I ſhould immediately entertain three more for my Conſolation; for how could a leſs Number make one any Recompence for ſuch an afflictive Loſs? And therefore you, whom I cannot love, may eaſily judge how little I ſhould be affected at your Death. You, whom I cannot love! How inhuman does that Expreſſion appear! Why ſhould I indulge all this Severity, and what Riſque can I ſuſtain by ſaying, to a poor dying Creature, *You whom I love a little?* But is it therefore neceſſary, that you ſhould believe me? Why ſhould that Word coſt me ſo dear? You have utter'd it to me a thouſand times with a graceful Tenderneſs not to be deſcribed; what Inconvenience, then, can I ſuffer by repeating it, eſpecially when I conſider your preſent Situation? But what Advantage can you derive from that Word? I am apt to think, that I diſcover more Malice than Compaſſion, when I declare that I love you. As long as your Indiſpoſition continues, I ſhall make that Confeſſion

Confeſſion to you with Pleaſure. You will ſee me ſympathiſe in your Sufferings, with ſo much Senſibility, I ſhall be ſo tractable and attentive, that you will be over-whelmed with Deſpair to recover your Health at the Expence of ſo many Favours. Your Condition is more dangerous than I at firſt apprehended: How! to take to a ſick Bed, with no other View than to inſpire me with tender Impreſſions! The Idea is indeed very ſingular, and I would not adviſe you to try its Efficacy with other Women, becauſe I fear you would acquire no extraordinary Advantage from ſuch a Stratagem. It would have been very pleaſant, however, if you had plotted your ſelf into a genuine Indiſpoſition; forgive that ludicrous Thought, for, in reality, I think ſo indifferently of Mankind, that I believe there is no Artifice, which they do not practiſe, to impoſe upon our Credulity. But what can you hope from this Proceeding, and what will be the Conſequence, ſhould I diſcover that your Ilneſs is an Impoſition upon me? Nothing leſs than eternal Diſdain. But if you have acted with Sincerity, I muſt afford you a little Compaſſion, becauſe you do me the Honour to impute your Indiſpoſition to my Cruelty. You may reſt perſuaded, that I will entertain a grateful Remembrance of the Favour; but at present, I believe, the Recovery of your Health will be your discreetest Endeavour. Adieu, my Lord, and let me prevail upon you not to die. Take it for granted, that I am greatly afflicted, and entertain your self with the most pleasing Imaginations you can form. Remember to kiss my Letter, and play over all the Follies of a true Lover. I forgive you all Things at this time; but be-sure to consider, that Love alone has the Privilege to dispose of you. You were desirous that I should write to you, and, in my present Disposition to refuse you nothing, how happy am I, that you are not in a Capacity to make any other Request. Pour Count!

LETTER X.

YOUR Manner of Thinking is certainly very peculiar: I have sent you the most tender Letter in the World, and made as sincere a Confession of my Weakness as you could possibly desire; but all this is insufficient, and you are still dissatisfied. The perpetual Gaiety of my Temper drives you to Despair: Admirable Prudence, to be disquieted at such a Calamity! Ought we not, in Love, to begin with some-

ſomething, that appears a little diverting? Perhaps I ſhall conclude in a more ſerious manner than I could wiſh. How do you know but that the Vivacity you complain of, may be my only Expedient to conceal half your Happineſs from you, and to preſerve me from the Confuſion of declaring that I love you? I ſuppoſe you will fancy this to be a new Flight of Raillery; but if I ſhould be a little inſincere, would not a complaiſant Fiction be more agreeable to you than a ſevere Truth? You are ſtrangely difficult to be pleaſed; you put on Airs of Deſperation, when I tell you; that it is not in my Power to love you, and when I aſſure you that I am touched with your Paſſion, you cannot vouchſafe to believe me; what an unaccountable Diſpoſition is this! Teach me how to acquire it, and I will promiſe you to find it conſtant Employment. I am as little ſatisfied with your Averſion to Life, and ſhould be in ſome Apprehenſion for you, did we live in an Age, which made it faſhionable for Lovers to deſtroy themſelves, that they may have the Happineſs of being lamented by their fair Tyrants; but you are a Gentleman of Underſtanding, and know, as well as my ſelf, that Death is the moſt ridiculous Proof of Love that can poſſibly be given. You will tell me, perhaps, that it was not in

Celadon's Power to forbear drowning himſelf; but have you really taken him for your Model? As to other Particulars, I am charmed with the Accounts I hear of you; your Friends aſſure me, that the Conceſſions I have afforded you, contribute not a little to the Recovery of your Health: How could you be ſo malicious as to conceal this from me? Have I not ſufficiently bewail'd you? Or can you imagine, that the News of your Recovery would be indifferent to me? Ah my Lord! how little are you acquainted with my real Diſpoſition! Could you but conceive how much I am afflicted at your Illneſs, how ſincerely I wiſh for your Preſence, and with what Ardour I offer up my Vows for your Welfare; you would love me with infinitely more Tenderneſs than ever. I never knew, till now, that a Lover could be ſo entertaining. My Time has paſs'd away ſo inſipidly ſince I laſt heard you ſay, *I adore you*; I have had ſo many Diſtractions of Thought, and am changed to ſuch a Degree, that, were you to ſee me, you would be touched with as ſincere a Pity for me, as you have inſpired me with for your ſelf. I fear 'tis imprudent in me, to acquaint you with all my Follies; but my Anxiety for your Welfare would tempt me to greater Indiſcretions. However, I promiſe

miſe you nothing, and muſt deſire you not to draw any advantageous Conſequences from my Letter. I only permit you to diſcover, in it, my Affliction for the Misfortunes of my Friends; and that none of them has ſo great a Share of my Affection as your ſelf. As to my Picture, which you are pleaſed to deſire —— I was preparing to finiſh my Letter, when *St. Far* *** came into my Apartment; and, after a Number of Expoſtulations with me, on the melancholy Condition to which he pretends I have reduced you; Madam, *ſays he, with a ſerious Air*, theſe Barbarities are very ungrateful. It is altogether unreaſonable, that, becauſe you have fine Eyes, you ſhould deſtroy an unfortunate Perſon, who adores you. What will it coſt you to preſerve his Life? He only begs you would permit him to love you; and, as to the reſt, he refers himſelf to your Humanity, and the Services he is ambitious to render you. Your Severities are unnatural; it may, one Day, be your Fate to ſigh for ſome unworthy Object; and God knows, how much you will then be obliged to reproach your ſelf. As for my part, I am of Opinion, that you ought not to reject the Count; you have too much Judgment to diſregard my Advice, and nothing but the Intereſt I take in whatever relates to you, could induce me to offer it. Grant him a few ſmall Favours, and there are a thouſand, which are perfectly innocent. For Inſtance; *continued he*, that you may make him ſome Amends for your Abſence, why ſhould you not ſend him that little Picture, which lies idle upon your Toilet? You can hardly conceive, with what Gratitude, he will receive ſuch a Preſent. At theſe Words, he thought fit to take it, and carry'd it away, notwithſtanding all my Reſentment, and repeated Refuſals to entruſt you with it. I am very well perſuaded, that it is actually in your Hands at this Inſtant; but as I have no Intention to give it you, and am ſenſible, you are too much a Gentleman to keep it againſt my Inclinations, I muſt deſire you to ſend it, by *St. Far* * * *, to Lady * * * If you love me, as you would have me believe, diſpoſe your ſelf to obey me, and let not an obſtinate Reſolution to detain it, furniſh me with Reaſons to refuſe it you for ever. ——— But are you not ſurpriſed at the Aſſurance of *St. Far* * * * ?

L E T-

LETTER XI.

I AM very ſenſible you miſtake that for Love, which is only an Inſtance of Friendſhip; and I can comprehend the Extent of your Gratitude by the Ardour of your Acknowledgments: But they would be more ſatisfactory, if they did not exceed the Merit of an Obligation, which owes all its Exiſtence to your Vanity, and the Certainty you preſume to entertain of my Tenderneſs for you. I have ſent you a Letter; *St. Far**** ſeiz'd my Picture, and took the Liberty to deliver it to you; theſe, as I ſuppoſe, are the Particulars you object againſt me; and indeed they are the only Circumſtances, on which you can poſſibly found my pretended Paſſion. I confeſs indeed, that I was very inconſiderate to believe my trifling with you, could be attended with no Conſequence worth regarding. I will likewiſe acknowledge, that the natural Vivacity of my Temper, and my want of due Reflection on what you ſaid to me, as well as on what I writ to you, made me anſwer your Letter incautiouſly enough to continue you in your Error. As I wa ſure, that I had not the leaſt Paſſion for you, I was more unguarded than I ſhould have been, had my Heart been inſpired with any tender Sentiments in your Favour; and I indulged my ſelf in Expreſſions, which were contradicted by my Conduct, and never ratified by my Heart. And yet you reſolve to believe I love you. But what do I ſay! Have you not too much Reaſon to believe it? Alas! my own Imprudence has promoted that Opinion in your Mind, more than all your Vanity! Can I excuſe my ſelf for writing to you, and had I no other Expedient to prevent you from loving me? Ought I not to have been ſenſible, that my Duty oppoſed ſuch a Correſpondence, and that how little ſoever a Woman may ſay on ſuch an Occaſion, ſhe always ſays too much? To what then, can I impute my eaſy Compliance? I am conſcious, that you are not the Object of my Love; and was it poſſible for me to be deceived in that Perſuaſion? But if I have been deluded by the Diſpoſition of my Heart, how can I ever be acquainted with yours? But why do I thus diſſemble? I wiſh to love you, and you know it too well! Ah! let us no longer perſiſt in an Intercourſe, for which I reproach my ſelf as I ought, tho' the Innocence of my Intentions may render it excuſable. Return me my Letters, and that fatal Picture. Let me intreat you to ſee me no more, or, at leaſt, let not Love be your Language when we we meet. This you have promised already, and ought I not to hate you for being unfaithful to that Engagement? Let me, therefore, conjure you to speak to me no more: Not that I am apprehensive of the Impressions your Discourse may communicate to my Heart, since all the softest Powers of Insinuation, which seduce the generality of my Sex, will be unavailing with me; but, after all, it is most consistent with Discretion, to retreat from Danger; and every Woman, who depends too much on her Virtue, is sure to run the Risque of losing it. For my part, I have not that Confidence in mine, as to have any Inclination to expose it such a dangerous Trial, as the Sight of your Person, and the Attention to your ensnaring Language would prove. The Assiduities of a Lover, force those Satisfactions upon the Soul, which are irresistible; and our own Reflections rather contribute to our Ruin, than enable us to avoid it. How can I be certain, that Virtue will be victorious in the Conflict, since its Influences are too seldom efficacious in competition with Pleasure? In a word, I am determined to shun the Encounter; I will not receive any more of your Letters, and I am at a Loss to know, how I could prevail upon my self to write to you, after my last Resolution to the contrary: Nothing, but

but your Obſtinacy could make me ſo inconſiſtent with my Intentions. I fancy my Letters give a better Turn to thoſe things, which I expreſs with too much Weakneſs and Irreſolution, when I converſe with you. Your Preſence diſconcerts my Thoughts, and makes me incapable of exerting my ſelf as I ought, when I intreat you to torment me no more. Do not compel me to ſeparate my ſelf from you for ever: I have no Intention to conceal from you the Pangs I ſhould ſuſtain, were I fated to ſee you no more. When I conſider you in the Quality of a Friend, I think you the moſt amiable of Mankind; but that unhappy Title of a Lover, makes me incapable of diſcovering all the real Merit you poſſeſs; I dread to examine it with any Attention; and there are ſome Moments wherein I wiſh you were either leſs engaging, or were capable of loving me in the manner I deſire. Adieu; I have heard with exceeding Pleaſure, that you are well; but I believe that Pleaſure will be much increaſed, when you come to give me the Confirmation of that Report. Perhaps you will believe nothing of all this; but I muſt deſire you not to make your ſelf ridiculous; and, that your Satisfaction may be perfect, I permit you to ſuppoſe, that I have ſome Inclination to be a little indiſcreet.

B I I.

BILLET.

*I shall pass this Evening with the Marchioness ***; can you prevail upon your self to be there, at my Request, that we may have an Assignation in all its Forms? Be there however. I have an Inclination to devote the Evening to Pleasure, and cannot imagine why I should be always uneasy when you are absent. Perhaps it may be owing to the Satisfaction you seem to enjoy in my Company, and your Sollicitude to obtain it; or it may proceed from my Opinion, that you are more agreeable to me than any other, and that the Friendship you profess for me is entitled to some Return, for I am not ungrateful. However, let me desire you to come in a proper Disguise, for your Uncle the Governor intends to be there. It was in vain for me to tell him, that the Ball would be detrimental to his Health; he replied, that he could not owe his Death to a more amiable Cause. When I found my Persuasions had no Effect, I was obliged to let him be of the Party. He loves me; but then he is extremely jealous and can never sleep. It would mortify him extremely, should he suspect you to be one of the Company; but my Satisfaction will be as great, if I am not prevented, by his Presence, from enjoying your Conversation. Take those Precautions*

*cautions as may make you paſs undiſcovered, and reſt aſſured, that my Eyes will diſtinguiſh you in any Diſguiſe you aſſume. I ſhall be ſenſible of your Preſence the Moment you enter the Room; and as I am perſuaded you will have the ſame Penetration, I think it needleſs to give you any Deſcription of the Habit in which I intend to appear. You have no Occaſion to be under any Apprehenſions about the Governour; Lady *** has taken upon her to engroſs his whole Attention, and I ſhall not place my ſelf near him, for more Reaſons than one.*

LETTER XII.

HOW ſeaſonably did that Lady join the Company yeſterday, to convince me of your Ingratitude and Perfidy; and, that all the Proteſtations you have ſo frequently repeated to me, were but the lively Sallies of your Fancy, and not the Dictates of your Heart! I have been ſenſible, for ſome time, that you thought her amiable; and your Behaviour in her Preſence, is a Confirmation of the Particulars I have already heard. You appear'd in the utmoſt Confuſion; the Expoſtulations of her Eyes, entirely diſconcerted you, and ſeem'd to reproach you with ſome uncommon

mon Crime. When they were fixed upon you, I, from time to time, beheld them melting into Tears, which ſhe, in vain, endeavoured to ſuppreſs. I heard her ſigh, and obſerved ſeveral Inſtances of her moving Anguiſh; and as unpolite as it was in you, to leave me at that time, you choſe to be guilty of that Incivility, rather than give me an Opportunity of hearing her Reproaches. You afterwards came back to me, but extremely confuſed, and tho' you affected all the Airs of Gaiety and Eaſe, the incoherent Turn of your Diſcourſe ſufficiently diſcovered the Mortification you received from this Adventure. You eaſily preſaged the Conſequence, and might naturally imagine, that I ſhould form ſome Reflections, that would not be much to your Advantage. And would you, then, be ſo ungenerous as to deceive me! Is it from you, that I have merited ſuch a Treatment! Did I ever appear ſollicitous to be the Object of your Paſſion, and are you not the moſt perfidious of Mankind! O righteous Heavens! how deplorable muſt be the State to which I beheld that unhappy Perſon reduced, and what Calamities, ought I to expect, ſhould I ever be ſo weak as to love you! You have already ſacrificed that Lady to the Vanity of being reputed the Poſſeſſor of my Affections; but you ſhall never

never facrifice me to a frail Inclination to reinftate your felf in her Heart. It will be in vain for you to tell me, that I ought not to be apprehenfive of that Misfortune. Is there any Defect in that Lady, which can juftify your Infidelity to her? She has all the Charms of Youth and Beauty, in Conjunction with the Advantages of Wit and Birth. She once fincerely loved you, nay, I am perfuaded, fhe fincerely loves you ftill. As yet, her Conduct has not degraded her to the Level of thofe unhappy Women, who, when you are pleafed to abandon them, awake a penitent Shame within you, for having ever loved them. Her fond Paffion for you, is her only Reproach; but, at the fame time, it is a Reproach, to which fhe might, poffibly, have never been obnoxious, had not her Weaknefs been pointed out by your officious Indifcretion. And can you now imagine, that after all the apparent Reafons I have to deteft you, I fhall ever be guilty of fuch an unpardonable Infatuation, as to place my Heart, my Honour and my Repofe, in your dangerous Power? Can you believe, that I will confide in the Love you fwear my Eyes have kindled in your Soul, when every Circumftance of your Conduct makes it evident, that all the warm and tender Language, in which your Addreffes to me were deliver'd,

flow

flow'd rather from your fatal Ability to feign it, than from any Reality of Paſſion. You offer'd, yeſterday, to clear up my Suſpicions; but my Silence made you eaſily conceive the Juſtice of thoſe Reproaches I was preparing for you. Would any Intimations of Guilt have been viſible in the Air of your Behaviour, without ſome ſufficient Cauſe; and would your Impatience to juſtify your ſelf have appeared ſo uncommon, if you had not been conſcious of ſome Crime? Believe me, I was ſenſibly afflicted at what I beheld; not from any real Tenderneſs for you; but becauſe I once thought you a Man of Honour. If I may be permitted to adviſe you, let what you have already done, remain as it is; and forbear to aggravate it by any future Apologies, which will only leſſen you in my Eſtimation. Your Diſcourſe will not be ſo perſuaſive with me, as you may imagine. Falſhood is my perpetual Averſion; I have ſome Penetration; and it will undoubtedly embarraſs you a little. For which reaſon, it will be better for us to continue as we are at preſent. If, however ——. Good God! can I be weak enough to wiſh you may be able to juſtify your ſelf!

LETTER XIII.

IN what Manner would you have me expreſs my ſelf to you? I imagined you had deceived me; I was even convinced of your Guilt; and yet when I had liſten'd to your Language but a few Moments, my Heart was ſo impatient to acquit you, that it contradicted the Teſtimony of my Eyes; it even renounced its own Conviction, and entertain'd an implicit Perſuaſion of your Innocence. Yes, my Lord, I am willing to believe you worthy of my Eſteem; you deſire this Inſtance of my Complacency; and I will confeſs, that I might poſſibly have been impoſed upon by my Suſpicions. The Sentiments of my Soul are too delicate, and have betrayed me into Miſapprehenſions of your Virtue, that I ought not to have founded upon ſuch faint Probabilities. You are dearer to me than I can well expreſs, and my Friendſhip for you is ſo exquiſitely tender, that it is eaſily alarmed at every Circumſtance that bears the leaſt unfavourable Aſpect; it is jealous, and unreaſonable; and, to oblige you, I will add, that it is too ſevere, in the Reſtraints it would lay upon your Conduct: But you know I promiſed you a few Extravagancies ſometimes; and yet let me intreat

you

you not to be ſo unjuſt as to hate me. If you really love me, your own Heart will furniſh me with a Vindication of my Weakneſs. Be ſatisfied, if poſſible, with the Aſſurances I give you of a conſtant and untainted Friendſhip, and let me taſte the Pleaſure of yours, ſince this is a Bleſſing I can enjoy without any Remorſe. Let us not ſeek for Misfortunes, which, at preſent, we may eaſily elude; and, as we are ſtill in Poſſeſſion of ſome Remains of Reaſon, let us employ it to extinguiſh thoſe Inclinations, which, without its Aſſiſtance, may be reproachful to us both, and perhaps are already ſo. To what a fatal Situation do you reduce me! I am conſcious of thoſe Emotions, which I dare not examine with a due Calmneſs of Thought; I ſuffer myſelf to be inſenſibly led on by my firſt Reflections; I want Reſolution to turn my Eyes upon myſelf; and every thing conſpires to plunge me in a dreadful Abyſs. The very Sight of it fills me with Conſternation, and yet I precipitate myſelf into the fatal Gulph. I would willingly hate you, if that were poſſible; I am ſenſible that you treat me with Injuſtice, and yet I have not the Power to entertain any Reſentment againſt you. There are ſome Moments wherein you are my Averſion, becauſe you love me; and there are others wherein you would ſtill be more odious to me, if you regarded me with Indifference. Every Circumſtance intimates to me that I ought to diſregard you; but you tell me the contrary, and I bluſh to think I have not Reſolution enough to contradict you. In vain do I endeavour to conceal my Confuſion from you; every little Incident makes me ſenſible of its Impreſſions. My Inquietude in your Abſence; my Tranſports when I behold you; your Idea which is perpetually interwoven in my Soul; and my criminal Inclinations ſometimes ſuppreſs'd, and immediately reviving with a more tyrannic Power —— O Heavens! whither ſhall I fly from ſuch a Combination of fatal Foes! My Sighs and Tears, and even my ſtrongeſt Oppoſitions, give new Vigour to my unhappy Paſſion. Should not the frightful Aſpect of a Crime be a ſufficient Diſſuaſive againſt it? What can be ſo dreadful, as to find one's ſelf engaged in a Conflict, without the leaſt Hopes of Victory? Has Duty, then, ſo little Prevalence againſt the Power of Love? Ah me! Can I preſume to flatter myſelf with the languid Remains of Virtue! Have I a competent Share of it to enable me to fly, for ever, from your ſight; or do I even wiſh that I had ſuch a Power! Do not believe, however, that I love you. I have not loſt the Remembrance of myſelf to that wretched Degree; and yet I cannot anſwer

anſwer for my Conduct, ſhould I ſtill conſent to ſee you. But this Acknowledgment will be no Addition to your Happineſs, and I can impart it to you without a Crime, when I declare, at the ſame time, that we muſt now be ſeparated for ever. I ought, without doubt, to have form'd this Reſolution long ago; but I depended too much on my own Sufficiency, and did not impoſe that Silence upon you which was neceſſary to my Quiet; but I ſhall hardly relapſe into the ſame Frailty for the future. I am ſenſible, there are unguarded Moments, and I am as little exempted from them as another. I am now preparing to go far, very far from you, in ſearch of that Repoſe which perhaps I ſhall never obtain. I ſhall endeavour to eraſe you from my Remembrance, and I ought to call up all the Powers of my Soul to aid me in that Intention. Make no Attempts to ſee me; for thoſe fatal Interviews have already coſt me too many Sighs, and I ſhould conſent to truſt myſelf in your Preſence again; how can I be certain that I ſhall accompliſh my Reſolution to withdraw myſelf from you for the Remainder of my Days? I ſay, how can I, who begin to be alarm'd when you have been abſent from me but a Day, be able to bring my Paſſions into ſo much Subjection? Why is it impoſſible for me to love you without a Crime! Ah! were my Paſſion but conſiſtent with Innocence, you ſhould no longer complain of my Inſenſibility; nor ſhould the ſofteſt Ardours of my Soul then cover me with Confuſion. But ſuch is my Situation, that the very Pity I afford you is my Reproach. Did I ſay, Pity! Ah! can I be ſo infatuated, as to give that cold Name to the Emotions I experience; and could my Heart be ſo fatally tormented by ſuch a Trifle! I am now going to obtain my Huſband's Permiſſion to linger out, in the Country, thoſe Days which your Abſence will render very languiſhing and undelightful: But, whatever may be the Event, this is the only Expedient that can preſerve my Virtue, and I cannot purchaſe it too dearly. You ſollicite me to grant you an Interview; what Reply would you deſire me to make, and what Conceſſions can I afford you, wherein my Honour will not be intereſted? Let us not contrive to render ourſelves ſtill more unhappy; our Meeting will only ſoften us into new Weakneſs; and therefore endeavour to baniſh me from your Thoughts: But I fear it will be impoſſible for me to forget you, for ever; at leaſt you ſhall not be the Witneſs of my Frailty. Adieu —— I have read your Letter once more, and begin to think that I ought not to refuſe you a Moment's Audience, for the laſt Time. Take a Walk, a Walk, at nine in the Morning, in the Gardens that belong to *** perhaps you may find me there. Forgive me this Doubt; for I am in ſuch a State of Sorrow and Uncertainty, that were you to ſee me, I am ſure you would pity me.

LETTER XIV.

HOW fatal is Love to us both! I not only feel the Severity of my own Torments, but I likewiſe ſuffer thoſe which I am ſo unhappy as to create in you; and am the more to be pitied, becauſe I have no Permiſſion to afford you any Conſolation, and am unable to oppoſe my ardent Deſire to ſee you once more. Is it thus that I triumph over my Weakneſs! We have mutually ſworn never to meet again; but alas! how can I depend on thoſe Oaths, which are every Moment invalidated by your Tranſports and my Tears! Can we declare, in a more effectual manner, that we intend to perſiſt in our Paſſion to the lateſt Ghaſp? Why have you retarded my Departure, and why will you not permit me to fortify myſelf in my Duty? Perhaps, by this Time, I had defaced your Idea from my Remembrance, or, at leaſt, my Honour, as well as Intereſt, would have prompted me to that Attempt;

Attempt; and tho' it would have coſt me many tender Tears, yet, at laſt, I ſhould have obey'd the Impulſe, and might, poſſibly, have extinguiſhed a Paſſion, which your Preſence and reſiſtleſs Language are perpetually increaſing. Pity the Condition to which I am reduced, and reſolve never to ſee me more. Be guided by my Example, in the Suppreſſion of a Flame which muſt be fatal to me in the Event. Reflect on the Calamities that will be inſeparable from our Intercourſe: The Forfeiture of my Reputation, the Loſs of my Huſband's Eſteem, and perhaps ſomething worſe. As much Purity as refines our Sentiments, for I will ſuppoſe yours are conformable to mine; can you believe the World will render us the Juſtice we deſerve, and not take ſome malignant Opportunity to depreciate my Virtue? Your Merit alone would ſuffice for my Condemnation. My Sex, judging of me by themſelves, will never be perſuaded that my Converſe with you was confined to the Limits of Friendſhip. Thoſe, whoſe Actions have been the moſt exceptionable, will be the firſt to cenſure my Conduct; and I ſhall not, like them, have the Effrontery to be unaffected with ſuch injurious Diſcourſe. The only Means to free me from ſo many Fears, will be to withdraw myſelf from you; for whilſt we continue in the ſame Place, I

ſhall

ſhall ever be diffident of myſelf. Aſſiſt me, I conjure you, to vanquiſh my Weakneſs! You wiſh that I would conſent to ſee you again; but would it be prudent in me to expoſe myſelf to ſo much Danger; and will not this Interview be as unſucceſsful as the laſt? Shall I have Reſolution enough to give you the final Farewell? If you will be guided by my Advice, you will not be ſollicitous to ſee me. Conſult your own Heart on this Occaſion; for, whatever may be the Event, I ſhall comply with all you requeſt. I ſhall be, about Noon, at Lady *** Ah! what Tears will this fatal Day coſt me!

LETTER XV.

WHAT kind of Confeſſion do you requeſt, and in what Inſtance will the Word you ſo much deſire, contribute to your Happineſs? Let me enjoy the Satisfaction of believing you have not entirely penetrated to the Bottom of my Heart; and let me intreat you to leave me the only Secret I wiſh to retain; I ſhall not conceal it from you long, and my Conduct will make you ample Amends for my Silence. What can you require more? I continue in Town, and am no longer ſollicitous for your Departure. Could you maintain ſuch an exact Intelligence with my my Eyes, if you did not underſtand their Language? Ah! would to God you were as doubtful of my Tenderneſs as you are now certain of it! your Love would then be more ardent: But ſhould I diſcloſe to you the true Diſpoſition of my Soul, that Diſcovery would, perhaps, diſpoſſeſs me of your Heart; and the Aſſurance that you were belov'd would deprive you of the Pleaſure you enjoy in wiſhing to be ſo. Without doubt I treat you with Injuſtice, but you may eaſily judge of my Paſſion by my Diffidence. I tremble leſt you ſhould repent of your Choice; I dread the Efforts of my Rivals; I am even apprehenſive of myſelf, and of you moſt of all. My Huſband affects me with Diſquietude, I am agitated by Remorſe, and my Heart is as much diſcompos'd as yours is ſerene. How happy is your Sex, in their Prerogative to purſue their Inclinations without the Checks of Shame and Confuſion! whilſt we, who are under the Tyranny of unjuſt Laws, are compell'd to conquer the Impulſe of Nature, who has implanted, in our Hearts, the ſame Deſires that predominate in yours, and are ſo much the more unfortunate as we are obliged to oppoſe your Sollicitations and our own Frailty. How different are theſe Reflections from thoſe I made two Days ago! At what a vaſt Remove am I placed from my Reaſon! But,

after

after all, was it poſſible for that Reaſon to reſiſt you to any length of Time; and is it not a Weakneſs in me to regret its Loſs? You are my Huſband's intimate Friend; conduct yourſelf with Diſcretion towards him; he is not jealous, but Vanity is his prevailing Frailty; and ſhould he ever ſuſpect he was injured, he would abandon himſelf to all the Extremities that the moſt amorous of Mankind could be capable of purſuing on ſuch an Occaſion. Let us be careful to prevent the Calamities that would infallibly overwhelm us; and we may eaſily ſucceed in that Deſign. His Attachment to other Objects; his Coldneſs to me, and his Application to his Amours, will divert his Attention from the Ardours we indulge; but, if it it be poſſible, let us conceal our mutual Emotions in Publick. I am now preparing, for your Satisfaction and our Security, to withdraw myſelf from the Crowd that I once thought ſo neceſſary to diſſipate my Anxiety. You, my deareſt Lord, ſhall be my All; let us enjoy ourſelves ſequeſter'd from the World; Love ſhall fill up the Spaces of our charming Moments, and let the ſhort Duration of our Days be the only Subject of our Complaints. Your Letter gives me to underſtand that I have been converſant in your Thoughts; I have employed part of the Night in writing to you, and it is thus that I diſpoſe of my my Time in yout Abſence. Can I devote it to a more endearing Purpoſe? My Letter declares that I love you, and I only wait for your Preſence to make you the ſame Confeſſion.

BILLET.

*What is your Opinion of yeſterday's Entertainment? Did not the Duke of *** perform the Honours of it in the moſt inchanting Manner? Is he not the moſt gallant and magnificent of Mankind, and could you reaſonably deſire to be abſent from ſuch a Scene of Pleaſure? Could a Night be paſſed more agreeably than it was in that Place? I can aſſure you, all imaginable Juſtice was paid to your Merit. You was acknowledged to have a noble Air, an eaſy Comportment, a charming Vivacity of Wit, and Eyes ſo irreſiſtible —— In a word, a moſt adorable Form. And who was the Perſon that entertain'd ſo juſt an Idea of your Lordſhip? The moſt amiable Lady in all the Aſſembly; the Dutcheſs her ſelf, to whom I fancy you have promiſed to write, and perhaps you may now be reading a Letter from her. I congratulate you upon your new Conqueſt, and am perſuaded you will greatly advance your Affairs very ſoon; but will you be as expeditious as my ſelf, who have the Duke this Moment at my Bed-ſide?*

LET-

LETTER XVI.

YOU have certainly the moſt ſhining Wit of any Man in the World. How tender is the Style of your Letter; and what a Number of charming Qualities unite to make you amiable! You are undoubtedly the moſt accompliſh'd Perſon of your Sex, and I love you with all the Ardour that ever warm'd a Female Breaſt. You are the delightful Subject of all my Thoughts, and without you, the moſt exquiſite Pleaſures are unaffecting; but there is only one Species of them which I can poſſibly poſſeſs, and to be ſincere with you, I intend to confine myſelf to that alone. I dare ſay you will think this ſomething extraordinary: But whether it be that Romances have miſguided my Mind in this particular, or elſe, that ſuch a Turn of Thought was infuſed into my Soul at my Birth, I can only declare, that I am unable to comprehend in what Inſtance the Affair, you had the Goodneſs to propoſe to me, can be ſo eſſential to my Happineſs as you imagine. I have already anticipated every Circumſtance, which your Wit can recollect to induce me to a Compliance. I have even endeavoured to become a Convert to your Sentiments. I have imaged to myſelf the whole Aſſemblage of your Charms;

the Inquietudes you ſuſtain; your interrupted Slumbers, and all your languid Moments; and yet find your Propoſal as unperſuaſive as ever. Judge then, by the Inefficacy of my Endeavours, what Succeſs you may expect from yours. Perhaps, as you intimate, it may be an unſpeakable Pleaſure to diſpenſe Happineſs to the Perſon we love; but why ſhould not your Felicity be compleated by thoſe Enjoyments that conſtitute mine? Your Heart ſuffices my utmoſt Wiſh, why then cannot you limit your Deſires to the Poſſeſſion of mine? How ridiculous are you Men, with your Train of Inclinations! You have frequently promiſed me, that you would be ſatisfied, if you could obtain from me an Acknowledgment of my Paſſion: Why did I not oblige you to be always making the ſame Requeſt? I am ſenſible that my eaſy Compliance with that Deſire, would naturally diſpoſe you to expect every other Conceſſion from my Weakneſs; but I already know too well, how much it has coſt me to be more indulgent to you than I ought to declare. Do not compel me to change thoſe Sentiments in your Favour that I now entertain. Have you any Inclination to make me believe that I muſt ſoon loſe your Eſteem? That imaginary Happineſs, for which you now ſigh with ſo much Ardour, has none of thoſe inviting Charms which you

are

are willing to aſcribe to it, and perhaps it might extinguiſh the real Satisfactions we now enjoy. Love is apt to grow languid, in ſoft Scenes of Pleaſure, and when our Deſires are no longer intereſted in our Enjoyments, they begin to be very inconſiderable. Our Paſſion has, hitherto, derived all its Sweets from the pleaſing Union of our Souls, and we ought to congratulate ourſelves for the Virtue we have preſerved, when we conſider that we have had the Power to reſign it. But am I not very ridiculous to talk to you of Reaſon? Should I not be ſatisfied with the Oppoſition I have already made to your Deſires; and can I juſtly be offended at a Propoſal, which is authorized by Cuſtom, and very ſeldom rejected? But I have already told you, that my Diſpoſition is very peculiar. The Examples of others contribute very little to my Improvement; and tho' you ſhould reſolve to abandon me, after you had treated me with all imaginable Rigour, I am perſuaded it would be better to loſe a Lover who is diſſatisfied with our Cruelty, than one who is ſatiated with our Favours. I wiſh I could make my Conduct more agreeable to you; but I love you with too much Tenderneſs and Sincerity, to have any Inclination to loſe you ſo ſoon, and my Reſiſtance, in this Particular, ought to convince you of the Solidity of my Affection. Besides, should I prevail upon myself to grant you all the Happiness you desire, I should be deprived of the Satisfaction I receive from your Impatience; and I have not the least Reason to believe that the Joys you represent to be so exquisite, would ever yield me any Recompence for that Loss. 'Tis in vain for you to assure me that Favours are the Food of Love, for I am sensible they are a Sustenance which has always been fatal to that Passion. Reproach me with the severe Names of *Cruel* and *Ingrate*; exhaust all the Displeasure and Indignation of injur'd Heroes; my Resolutions must still flow in their proper Channel. Adieu, my dear angry Count. Any Woman, but myself, would be extremely out of Humour, to be sollicited for such an extraordinary Proof of Love; but I am not Prude enough to assume that Air, and am inclined to think, that Women, in such a Case, are seldom at Variance with a Lover, but with an Intention to make the next Accommodation, between them, responsible for all the Frailty which may ensue. Heavens grant that I may neither be so capricious, nor so weak! We will sup together this Evening in my Apartment; you see I take no Precautions against you; but I know myself, and shall always make my Love correspond

respond with my Virtue. Yes, my Lord, I say *always.*

LETTER XVII.

TO be very plain with you, my Lord, you may think of the Affair as you please, but I am determined to persist in my Resolution. If Love gives you so much Anxiety, resume your Liberty; you find my Chains too weighty, and I can't bear to see my Slave desirous of subjecting me to his Laws. Is your aiming at my Dishonour, any Proof that you sincerely love me? Perfidious Man! How very wretched would you render me, could you derive, from my Weakness, the Satisfactions you desire! Can you imagine then, that if my Virtue made no Opposition to your Wishes, I could yet be so infatuated, as to close my Eyes against the Calamities which would follow such a Proceeding? Amidst the Pangs of Shame, which my own Reflections would create within me, and amidst the Torments I should sustain from you, Ingrate as you are! who would soon compel me to repent that I had sacrificed all my Happiness to your Inclinations; I should see the Master succeed the Lover; and, instead of persisting in your Passion with increasing Ardours, your Love would languiſh into Indifference, and cauſe me to pay dear for the Weakneſs of affording it the fatal Gratifications into which it had betrayed me: I ſhould ſee your Eſteem for me, expiring with that Love; the Aſſiduities I ſhould then receive from you, would only flow from your Generoſity, and my perpetual Apprehenſions of loſing you, would ſoon make that Loſs a Reality. I ſhould, even then, have ſome Remains of Happineſs, were I only to be ſacrificed to one Rival, and could hope that the World would be unconſcious of my Shame. It is in vain for you to call Heaven to Witneſs, that you have no Intentions to treat me with that ungenerous Barbarity. Have not all thoſe unhappy Women, who are the Victims to Man's Perfidy, had Lovers who made the ſame Proteſtations to them, which I receive from you? And yet, have they found thoſe Proteſtations any Security from the Misfortunes I dread; and did the moſt ſolemn Oaths of their Lovers preſerve them from their Infidelity? I tremble at ſo many fatal Examples, and ſhould deſerve to be added to their Number, if I neglected their Admonitions. Perhaps I might not be ſo unfortunate as I imagine; but can you believe the Delicacy of my Paſſion would be ſatisfied with a Conſtancy which proceeded from Conſtraint, and would be equally torment-

tormenting to us both? I'll acknowledge your Discretion to be as perfect as possible; but that's a Quality, which, as yet, I never wanted any Person to exert in my Favour. You might, possibly, screen me from publick-Reproach; but alas! who would have the Power to screen me from the Remorse of my own Heart? Can you believe, that all the Privity with which my Passion for you is conducted, exempts me from that dreadful Pang? I love you, my Lord, and I avow it; but let us not add to this Frailty, those which are still more odious. I had not the Power to oppose the Tenderness I entertain for you; the Emotions of the Heart are not subordinate to the Judgment: But, surely, I have the Ability to be virtuous; and we never cease to be so, against our Inclinations. I begin to think I hate you, since you torment me in this manner: Ought you not, in Justice, to be content with my Love, without solliciting that from me, which I am not in a Capacity to grant? Can you not be certain that you possess my Heart, unless I abandon myself to all your Desires? Ah me! if you did not enjoy that Certainty, you would never have so little Hesitation to offend me! Let me intreat you then, not to abuse my Facility to forgive you: I am sensible that, with all my Resentment, you are dearer to me than I could wish; but rest assured,

ſured, that whatever Tortures a Rupture with you may coſt me, I ſhall ſtill have Reſolution enough to ſacrifice you to my Honour. Where that is not intereſted, I will never refuſe you any thing, to convince you how much I love you. Adieu, my dear Count; I am pretty liberal of my Reproaches; but if I did not love you with a Tenderneſs above Deſcription, I ſhould not be ſo ſenſible of the Injuſtice you offer me. Shall I ſee you to Day? —— I ſhall paſs the greateſt Part of it at Lady *** I know it will coſt me a few Trifles, to make my Peace with you; but then I ſhall regain your Heart upon eaſy Terms, and when you deſire no more than —— Adieu, I hear the Marquis, and am certain he has not good Nature enough to approve what I write to you.

BILLET.

I am perſuaded you have had but a very indifferent Night, and am as much aſſured, that the Converſation of the German *Baron, prov'd as diſagreeable to you, as it was pleaſing to me: I gave you a great deal of Mortification yeſterday; but did you not deſerve it? Why did you put on that gloomy Air, and affect to ſpeak to me with ſo much Coldneſs? You intended to make me jealous, and I chagrin'd you to Deſperation. You aſſured Lady*

*Lady ***, that you loved her; with no other View, than to give me Torment; and I, by a single Glance on a Gentleman, gave you more Disquietude, than, perhaps, you would have created in me, by a real Inconstancy. I had the Pleasure to make you as pensive, as you was at first agreeable. Let me advise you not to play off these little Arts of Love; we Women are much better Proficients in them than your Sex; and I have just Coquettry enough to render you the most wretched of Mankind, whenever you make an unseasonable Attempt to give me any Dissatisfaction.*

LETTER XVIII.

I Can pardon all Injuries from Rivals when they are not beloved; but am unable to forgive you, for suffering your Reason to be disordered, by the Insinuations of a jealous old Lady, when you had not the least Cause to suspect the Reality of my Passion for you. Did I give the least Credit to your Unkle the Governour's Discourse, when he told me, you was indiscreet, an affected little Creature, very fortunate with our Sex, and a hundred thousand Things of the same Nature? Would it not have been very unjust in me, to have form'd an Opinion of you, from

from a Report wherein the Author was ſo much intereſted? Has not the Continuance of my Tenderneſs for you, ſufficiently declared my Diſbelief of thoſe Aſperſions; and did I even ſeem inclinable to credit the Evidence of my own Eyes? Why then do you not imitate my Example? You have been informed that I deceive you, and indulge, with Pleaſure, any Impreſſion to my Diſadvantage. If you really loved me, with the Ardour you profeſs, could you poſſibly be ſo credulous? Do I conceal from you, the leaſt Circumſtance of my Conduct; and are not all my Actions regulated by your Orders? Can you be ſo injurious to me, as to believe I even need your Directions, and that Love cannot ſufficiently inſtruct me how to contribute to your Satisfaction? Would to God you were capable of reading the true State of my Heart! But why ſhould I form that Wiſh! The Diſcovery of ſuch a Profuſion of Love would embarraſs you, and your natural Inſenſibility would be too much diſcompoſed. Ah my Lord! if your Paſſion were but equal to mine, you would never be diffident of my Tenderneſs: Nor do you affect that Diffidence, but to diſengage yourſelf, ungrateful as you are, from a correſponding Return! What can you complain of in my Behaviour? Have you any one Rival, whom I have not ſacrificed to your Repoſe? And did I diſcover any Apprehenſions of thoſe Cenſures I might draw upon myſelf, by ſuch a Proceeding? Have I acted with any Artifice or Reſerve, when I gave you the tender Proofs of my Paſſion? You deſired me not to appear, ſo frequently, in Publick, and I immediately confined myſelf to my Apartment. I never had the leaſt Inclination to examine, whether you had any Right to preſcribe Laws to me, and was content to limit all my Satisfactions to you alone: Your dear Preſence is ſufficient for my Happineſs, and I ſhould have reproached myſelf, had I been conſcious of any Repugnance to that Reſtriction. Perhaps you are diſſatisfied with the Equality of my Conduct; and as you have been converſant with the capricious Inconſiſtencies of Coquets, their little Frauds and unmeaning Language, you now begin to be uneaſy that you have nothing to fear. You are diſguſted at the artleſs Air of my Converſation; I am perpetually repeating to you, that I tenderly love you; I tell it you alone, and my Eyes, which are the faithful Expoſitors of my Thoughts, are directed to none but you. I can perceive that my Ardours grow painful to you, and only contribute to flatter your Vanity. Your Heart is no longer my Property; your Aſſiduities grow languid, and you only viſit me, from Time to Time, to give me a more fatal Senſibi-

Senſibility of the Torments I ſuſtain in your Abſence. In vain do you ſometimes endeavour to conceal your Coldneſs from my Penetration, it pierces thro' the thin Diſguiſe you attempt to caſt around it; which convinces me that your Love is no more than Artifice. I receive the ſame Conviction from the Emotions of my own Heart: You could once perſuade me, with a ſingle Word, that you loved me; but now all your Solicitudes to induce me to that Belief, only ſerve to increaſe my Diſtruſt. Adieu; I have not ſeen you theſe two Days, and I wiſh you had not given yourſelf the Trouble to write to me, ſince you intended to ſay ſo many diſobliging Things. Come to me, however, this Evening, for I ſhall be glad to have ſome Explication with you. Once more Adieu; as much Reaſon as I have to reſent your Suſpicions, it is impoſſible for me to declare how much I love you.

LETTER XIX.

I Was not ſo happy, my dear Count, as to ſee you yeſterday; but it was not in my Power to diſengage myſelf from a Viſit my Huſband propoſed to me; and tho' my Averſion to the Company was as great as poſſible; yet, had I diſcover'd too much Diſ- inclination

inclination to attend him it might have given him ſome diſagreeable Thoughts; and our Happineſs depends upon his Inſuſpicion. I muſt acquaint you then, that we, yeſterday, waited upon his Mother. But, Oh Heavens! what Company did I find there! I needed no ill Humour to make it inſupportable. The whole was a Compoſition of Indecorum and Stupidity, not eaſy to be imagined. The inſipid Marquis of * * *, half ſick and half amorous, with a monſtrous Patch upon his Forehead, and a wither'd Complexion, mutter'd out part of an Opera, and, at the ſame Time, caſt a languiſhing Look at that ſolemn prude Lady* * *, who with a devout and contrite Air, ſigh'd with much Senſuality for the Chevalier *N** * *, whilſt he was uttering abundance of reſpectful Dulneſs to the Daughter of that Bigot. The two Ladies * * * found themſelves Employment in ſaying all the diſagreeable Things of the Men which the Men think of them. My Huſband, with a negligent Loll ſaid the greateſt Indecencies in the World with the modeſteſt Air imaginable, to ſoft Lady * * *. The ſedate prude, Lady * * *, for want of a proper Companion to form a Party of Scandal, amuſed herſelf with the Commendations of our Author, whoſe Merit the dreary Counſellor * * * * conteſted with her learned Ladyſhip. *R* * * * made execrable Verſes with admirable Facility. My Huſband's Mother and mine were invoking the Mercies of God, at the ſame Time that they wounded the Reputation of their Neighbours without the leaſt Remorſe. The reſt of the good Company entertain'd themſelves at Play. For my part, I was the Spectatreſs of this amiable Scene, and can aſſure you that I did not miſimprove my Time, but had the Pleaſure to think, whilſt I was ſurveying the Abſurdities of this Company, that I loved the moſt amiable Man in the World, and was happy in his Paſſion for me. My Vanity was agreeably flatter'd to ſee the worthy Gentlemen in this Aſſembly ſo inferior to yourſelf. How infinitely dear to me, were you at that Moment! But I don't conſider that I am giving myſelf very extraordinary Flights. I intended to write to you, with no other View than to know if you are not diſpleaſed with me, and to intreat you to love me with a perpetual Sincerity; tho' it ſeems I have not writ one Syllable to that purpoſe. But you may eaſily ſupply that Deficiency. I am not in a Diſpoſition to be in Love to-day, and perhaps I ſhould be too cold in telling you thoſe things which you deſerve to have expreſſed to you with all the Warmth of a tender Imagination. This is not the Effect of Caprice; but I think I am not amiable to-day; Vexation

has

has given me a very disagreeable Air, and I cannot persuade myself that you would think my Tenderness any Obligation in my present Condition. My Chagrin is attended with a violent Pain in my Head; and all these Misfortunes coming together, make my Person insupportable even to myself. Surely done may well be melancholy, to be deprived of the Presence of that Person one loves, and to pass a whole Day with a disobliging Husband: And how is it possible to have any Satisfaction, when one sees a Set of reverend Prudes, hears a Marquis uttering soft Absurdities, and especially when one knows, at the same time, that one has a very impatient Lover to deal with, and who will never let one enjoy a little Repose. How can one possibly be in a perpetual Conflict? I see so many Women who yield at last, and perhaps, after all their Resistance, are only chagrin'd that they did not surrender sooner. —— How is it possible for one to have any Tranquillity, at such a Thought! Ah! my Lord, if —— Adieu; I should write to you till to-morrow, if I had not heard that Prude, Lady * * * coming. How disagreeable are these very virtuous Ladies! And would I cease to be one?

LETTER XX.

YOUR Sufpicions give me fome Difquiet; but I think them much preferable to that Security in which you have fo long been funk, and pardon you all the Injuftice with which you treat me. Your Diffatisfaction is the firft Proof you have yet given me of your Paffion, and I am not inclinable to require any more. Your Conjecture was juft, when you imagined that your Friend the Marquis * * * loved me; but you deceived yourfelf when you thought I made him any Return. I confefs, you have fome Reafon to reproach me, for I ought not to have conceal'd his Paffion from you. It was even incumbent on me to have banifhed him from my Prefence, the firft Moment he made me the Declaration of his Sentiments. But you yourfelf prefented him to me; you told me that he was your intimate Friend, and I admitted his Vifits in Conformity to your Inclinations. You are fenfible of my Averfion to new Acquaintance. Could I divine that he would ever entertain a Paffion for me, and when he did, was it proper for me, who am fo well acquainted with your impetuous Difpofition, to impart to you fuch a Secret? I thought it would be better to difcountenance his Paffion,

and

and leave him deſtitute of all Hope, than to expoſe both you and myſelf to a diſagreeable Adventure, which, however it may happen to be conducted, has always an Intermixture of Cruelty. I ſhould never have troubled you wth this Confeſſion, if the Inquietudes I ſuſtain from that Man had not made it unavoidable. I ſhall not give you a particular Account of all the Severities with which I have treated him, to induce him to diſcontinue his Addreſſes; ſuch a Detail would be altogether unneceſſary: I may add too, that you would never prevail upon yourſelf to believe me; and my Senſibility of your Paſſion, inclines you to think me incapable of Indifference to any one, who pleaſes to admire me. But, at preſent, I ſhall not expatiate on your Conceptions of my Conduct, the Idea would awake my Reſentment, and the leaſt Inſtance of that Emotion, would be ſufficient to make you tax me with ſeeking a Pretext to extinguiſh a Paſſion that you imagine no longer delights me. I am ſollicitous to convince you of the Sincerity of my Affection, and every other Care is loſt in this. I have been as vigilant as poſſible to withdraw myſelf from the Viſits I deteſt; and if you will appeal to your own Remembrance, you muſt be ſenſible that I aſſured you I was greatly diſſatisfied with this Perſon, tho' at the ſame time you condemned my Averſion to him; you compelled me to receive his Viſits; and the only Anſwer you vouchſafed to my Complaints was, that I was very capricious in my Diſpoſition. Can you ſuppoſe that I would ſo long have ſuffer'd him to converſe with me in the manner he did, if your Indiſcretion had not compelled me to indulge him in the Liberties he aſſumed. He yeſterday acquainted me with a Circumſtance that made me tremble; he is ſenſible that I love you, and is conſcious of ſeveral Particulars, of which you alone could inform him. I congratulate myſelf, however, that I have given you no Opportunity of making him privy to any other Secret; and that I have not the Mortification of beholding my Honour and Repoſe in the Power of a Villain who has baſely betrayed his Friend. I have ordered my Servants to refuſe him Admittance, and am determined to confine myſelf for ever, to my Apartment, if I can avoid him by no other Precautions. I have ſufficient Reaſon to believe, that this proceeding will drive him to ſome violent Extreams, and muſt expect, when Rage ſucceeds the Paſſion he entertained for me, that he will endeavour to blaſt my Reputation, and will even traduce me to my Huſband. But if you are reſolved to avenge yourſelf, in Oppoſition to all my Intreaties, let me, at leaſt, prevail upon

upon you to wait for a lawful Motive, and do not hasten my Destruction by any unseasonable Resentment. This is the only Condition, on which you will be intitled to the Preservation of my Heart, as well as to my Pardon for your placing me in the most fatal Situation, in which I have ever beheld myself. As yet I have not imparted to you all my Fears and Dissatisfactions. I foresee, that this Affair is not to close in Tranquillity; I am sensible, that I must lose you for ever; but if you had ever loved me, ingrate as you are! your Indiscretion would never have exposed me to the Horror of beholding you risque your Life, and to the Anguish of not daring to see you for the future, without new Confirmations of my Love and Dishonour, should you survive the Danger you are so desirous to confront.

LETTER XXI.

ST. *Far* *** inform'd me that you had engaged in a Duel with *C* *** and I was in the utmost Consternation when I received your Letter. But why did you not come yourself, to acquaint me with the Particulars? Alas! are you wounded? But if you are not, what are the Apprehensions you entertain? Why do you withdraw your-

self

ſelf from me? Have you no Inclination to receive new Diſcoveries of my Paſſion from my Eyes, or have you any particular Reaſons to be afraid to ſee me? You are under no Neceſſity of concealing yourſelf; the Brutality of your Enemy furniſhes you with a ſufficient Vindication; it preſerves my Honour from all Miſconſtructions, and contributes to the Security of your Perſon. But what do I ſay! You ſecret yourſelf on my Account, and I am the only Perſon whom you have not vouchſafed to ſee: Every Circumſtance, which relates to myſelf, throws you into Confuſion; my Tenderneſs grows incommodious to you: Ungrateful Man! you are deſirous of my Averſion, and are indefatigable to deſerve it! But you have habituated my Heart to love you; and, in ſpite of all your Contempt, it will never refuſe you any thing but the Averſion you would compel it to expreſs. If I may believe what I heard from St. *Far* *** you are extremely jealous. You are afraid to behold my Eyes bathed in Tears, becauſe you are reſolved to attribute them to the Misfortune of your Rival. You yourſelf, if I can judge of your Diſpoſition by the Air of your Letter, ſeem deſirous to inſult my Grief, and you would not have informed me of your Succeſs, with ſo much Oſtentation, if you had not been perſuaded that I ſhould be mortified at

ſo

ſo many Particulars in your Favour. Is it poſſible, then, that you can never afford me any Satisfaction, without blending it with the greateſt Diſquietude? Can you imagine, that if I had loved your Adverſary, I would ever have ſacrificed him to your Reſentment? Had I any Intention to change you for another, would not your Indifference furniſh me with as ſpecious a Pretence as I could well deſire? If I had not entertained the moſt tender Paſſion for you, could I ever be apprehenſive of your Diſpleaſure, or ſuffer myſelf to be affected at the Contempt with which you treat me? Ah! my Lord, you are but little acquainted with the Power of Love; and my Heart, tho' it has leſs Experience than yours, could furniſh you with many Inſtructions on that Subject. It could acquaint you, at leaſt, that Conſtraint has no Influence over Love; and that Negligence and a capricious Turn of Mind, inſtead of increaſing that Paſſion, only create Diſſatisfactions and Coldneſs between Lovers, and at laſt render their Diſunion abſolutely neceſſary. Theſe are the Sentiments which I daily derive from your Conduct. I make no Difficulty to acknowledge that I love you; but I find it very diſagreeable to be perpetually finding new Reaſons to oppoſe my Paſſion. It may perhaps grow languid; and ſhould I once diſengage

engage my Heart from your Poſſeſſion, all your Tears and Remorſe will never regain it; and you will then be convinced that you never knew its Value, till you had loſt it for ever. Think of this, my Lord, while it is in your Power to prevent the Increaſe of my Reſentment; I offer you a Pardon, which, as yet, I am in a Condition to beſtow, and which you may poſſibly not be able to obtain to-morrow. When I began this Letter, I did not imagine, that I ſhould finiſh it in a Strain ſo diſagreeable both to you and my ſelf; but if you were as weary of deſerving my Reproaches as I am of making them, we ſhould ſoon ſettle the Affair, either for Love or Indifference.

LETTER XXII.

THE penſive Air which my Husband aſſumed yeſterday, alarm'd me not a little; I was apprehenſive, that you were the Object of his Inquietude, and that he reſented your Aſſiduities, which, I confeſs, have been too apparent to many. His Behaviour, by degrees, eaſed me of my Fears; and, ſince he has made Choice of you for his Confident, I ſuppoſe he has no Suſpicions to your Diſadvantage. I gueſſed by his Diſcompoſure, that he had entertain'd tertain'd ſome new Paſſion; for I am not ſo happy as to be the Subject of his Meditations, in any Form whatever. I conclude, therefore, that he is in Love with your Couſin, and entruſts you with the Care of making his Sighs acceptable. The Timidity he diſcovers, makes it evident, that his Sufferings are very ſevere, and he undoubtedly reſerves for your Couſin, the Pleaſure of making the firſt Overtures. She is not ſo cruel as to intimidate a Gentleman from confeſſing, that he loves her; and his Lordſhip is not of ſuch a Nature as to give her any Uneaſineſs. He deſires nothing more than her Permiſſion to be acceptable; and I would not anſwer for his Paſſion, ſhould he continue three Days in a State of Incertainty. Be ſo good as to inform your Couſin of theſe Particulars, that ſhe may diſpoſe herſelf to give him a Reception accordingly. But what will become of poor little *D***?* How will *R**** behave? and, in ſhort, what will be the Condition of the whole Court? What a Number of unhappy Ladies ſhall we ſoon behold! It will be impoſſible to preſerve every individual! The Marquis is extremely incommodious to his Rivals, and eſpecially for the firſt few Days. Can you think the Lady capable of refuſing him the Satisfaction of being perfidious for one Week?

Week? His Paſſion muſt have no Competitor, during that time at leaſt. However, employ your good Offices for my Husband, whatever may be the Event. Give your Couſin a full Idea of the Flame that conſumes him, and preſent to her View, the melancholy Portrait of a Man, who, for the Space of two Days, has been overwhelmed with ſad Reflections. Tell her, 'tis of great Conſequence not to let him ſigh for any Length of Time, and that the leaſt Chagrin entirely diſconcerts him. Make her ſenſible of the Diſadvantage of loſing time; extol the amiable Qualities of the Marquis, and paſs over the Article of his Conſtancy as lightly as poſſible, leſt the Lady ſhould be terrified. Give her a View of all her Lovers in a deſpairing Condition; ſome of them baniſhing themſelves to their Eſtates; others in a vain Purſuit of Remedies, to mitigate the Pangs they ſuſtain from her Inconſtancy, and reduced, amidſt the Ardours of a new Paſſion, to wiſh for the Re-enjoyment of her Heart with all its Perfidy. On the other hand, be ſure to enforce to her, the grateful Diſpoſition of my Husband, and enhance the Aſſiduities of a new Lover. Count all the Moments, that compoſe the Day; and aſſure her, that the Marquis will not leave her one to regret. In a word, remember every Circumſtance, that may incline

incline her to be favourable to him. You may possibly think it extraordinary in me to charge you with the Transaction of this Affair; but, to deal seriously with you, my Husband's Indolence fills me with Apprehensions: He never deviates into Fondness for me, but when he is at a Loss how to bestow his Time; it is therefore incumbent on you, since you love me, to prevent the Mortifications you will suffer by the Revival of his Passion for me. I don't know whether I ought to make you such a Declaration; and you perhaps may be desirous, that he should relapse into his former Endearments to me: You may wish to see him jealous, because you would not then have such frequent Opportunities of seeing me; or you may hope, perhaps, that the Constraint I should then suffer from him, would incline me to grant you those Favours, which you have never been able to obtain from my Passion. I think I have discovered in you, some Inclination of this Nature; but such Sentiments are very indelicate, and should you not be disappointed in that View, you would owe the Obligation to the Marquis, and not to me. Adieu, my Lord; I cannot imagine, why I am so much in Love with you to-day; I have thought my Severities to you a little unreasonable, and was in the utmost Consternation,

ſternation, leſt your Deſpair ſhould be fatal to you: In a word, I was a little ridiculous; what Pity is it, that ------- Good Morrow.

BILLET.

I cannot poſſibly make you any Promiſe. The Aſſignation you propoſe to me, ſeems to have too dangerous an Aſpect. As yet, I have not been obſerved; but were I to act with leſs Caution for the future, I ſhould infallibly expoſe my ſelf to ſome unpleaſing Diſcovery of my Indiſcretion. Let us not run the Hazard of loſing, by a Moment's Folly, all the Liberty we have acquired by long Circumſpection. Beſides, I can comprehend what it is you would deſire of me; I very well recollect thoſe Inſtances of my Weakneſs, which I gave you Yeſterday, and you may poſſibly be deſirous of improving them to your Advantage. Upon the whole, I find it improper for me to grant your Requeſt; but if you are diſpoſed to pay me a Viſit this Evening, you will find me at Home; but I ſhall not be alone. I love you, and ſhould be afraid of beſtowing more time in convincing yon of my Paſſion than I employ in confeſſing it.

LET-

LETTER XXIII.

NO more Fallings out, my Lord, I intreat you; they coſt me too dear in Reconciliations; and if we have one Diſagreement more, I will not pretend to anſwer for the Effects of my Reſentment. Ungenerous Man! I believe you give me ſo much Inquietude, with no other View but to render me more conformable to your Deſires than I already am. This is an admirable Method of endearing one's ſelf, I muſt confeſs: I can ſee by every Inſtance of your Conduct, that the tender Joys of the Heart, and all its ſoft Overflowings, are not ſo engaging to you as the leſs delicate Satisfactions that flow from Love. I am at a Loſs how to declare my Meaning; but am perſwaded you underſtand me much better than I expreſs myſelf. I am apt to ſmile, when I think on your impatient Deſires, and my ſteady Reſiſtance; which has been ſuch, as ought to convince you that I think it abſolutely neceſſary for us to continue juſt as we are at preſent. I believe many Women, in my Situation, would have yielded to your Importunities, and alledg'd the Fatigue of a long Conflict, to juſtify their Compliance. Without doubt they would be ſo good to themſelves, as to think this a conſtant Vindication againſt the Reproaches of their own Hearts: But I happen to be ſo peculiar in my Way of thinking, as to believe a Woman may have as much Power as ſhe pleaſes, on ſuch an Occaſion; and you may judge of mine, by the Diſpoſition I have diſcover'd. Do you know that *Lucretia* takes up all my Thoughts, at preſent? She, indeed, had one Advantage over me, for ſhe never loved *Tarquin*: But if I can be capable of reſiſting your Prayers, and Tears, and Careſſes, with ſo much Reſolution: If I, who adore you, and am conſcious of your charming Power, can ſtill oppoſe your Paſſion, with ſo much Inſenſibility, it muſt be granted, that all the Efforts of that Lady are infinitely ſurpaſſed by mine. I pardon all your paſt Indiſcretions; but let me intreat you to leave me, for the future, to my Repoſe. Tho' my Virtue is refined from all Frailty, and ſhines in its pureſt Luſtre when it ſuſtains the ſevereſt Aſſaults; yet let me conjure you, not to expoſe it any more, to the Dangers that ſurrounded it at our laſt Interview. Women, alas! are weak and irreſolute: The Moment you parted from me yeſterday, I found myſelf in a moſt deteſtable ill Humour; and as I was endeavouring to compoſe myſelf to ſlumber, the Marquis came, booted and half breathleſs, into my my Apartment: His firſt Expreſſion to me was, that he was horribly fatigued: The next Moment he was pleaſed to think me amiable; and as he never vouchſafes to conſult me in his Inclinations, he was diſpoſed to paſs that Night in my Bed, and acquainted me with his amorous Intentions, more like a Lover than a Huſband. For my part, I don't know what might have been the Conſequence, if I had not, with ſome Abruptneſs, deſired him to retire to his own Apartment. I was ſo fatigued at that Time, and ſo diſguſted at all Mankind, that I believe I ſhould have prevail'd on myſelf to beat him, if he had perſiſted in his Deſign. It would have been a very ſingular Caprice indeed, if I had granted a Huſband the very Favour I denied my Lover. Adieu. I give you an Invitation to dine with us; but remember to be very circumſpect. The Marquis thinks me the moſt inſenſible of all my Sex, and derives from this Idea, all the Repoſe he enjoys. Be very careful then not to undeceive him; and reſt perſwaded, that he himſelf will furniſh us with frequent Opportunities of ſeeing each other, with all the Liberty we can reaſonably deſire: And who can tell, whether I ſhall always be diſpoſed to uſe it as I did yeſterday? I begin to be ſenſible that his Preſence will oblige me to play off ſome ſtrange Piece of Revenge upon him. A Huſband would be too happy, if he could make his Wiſe believe, that he was no longer in the World.

LETTER XXIV.

I Acknowledge myſelf to be jealous; and the Explanation I received from you yeſterday, is ſo far from eaſing me of my Suſpicions, that it has only contributed to increaſe them. You had the Preſumption to introduce my Rival to me.——Barbarous Woman as ſhe is! With what an Inſincerity of Softneſs did ſhe deſire a Share in my Friendſhip! How artfully did ſhe make you the Subject of her Converſation with me! I had not Penetration enough, even to be diffident of her Integrity: I was delighted beyond Expreſſion, to hear her expatiate in your Praiſe; and whilſt I imagined her Language was a ſecret Congratulation of my Choice, ſhe was endeavouring, by my Replies, to confirm herſelf in her own.

How deteſtable is ſo mean an Artifice! and how odious to my Thoughts do you now appear! Perfidious Man! how effectually does my Heart, by its fix'd Averſion to you, avenge itſelf on the fond Paſſion it entertain'd for you with ſo much Credulity!

I might

I might poſſibly have remained in my Error, if your Eyes had not been officious enough to undeceive me; but, it ſeems, I am ſo little in your Eſteem, that you can't vouchſafe to delude me with the leaſt Dexterity. You imagine, I am ſo infatuated by my Paſſion for you, as to be incapable of diſcovering the ungenerous Cruelty that gives me ſuch a mortal Wound: But Love is never deſtitute of Penetration, when it warms the Heart with the Ardours I have experienced. As it has been familiar to me to be belov'd; and as I have accuſtom'd myſelf to reflect, with Pleaſure, on the dear Inſtances of your paſt Tenderneſs; how could you think it poſſible for me to be inſenſible of your Neglect and Averſion? Will you now attempt to diſſipate my Suſpicions, by telling me they are created by Caprice? Can you deny that you have paſs'd thoſe Days with her, which you refuſed to me? When you, yeſterday, replied to my Reproaches, your Eyes were conſtantly fix'd on my Rival; and you ſeem'd to intreat her Pardon, for the Trouble you gave yourſelf in juſtifying your Conduct to me. You would have bluſh'd to have told any one but my ſelf, that you fear'd you was entertaining a Paſſion, which would be, for ever, ineffectual: You introduced, in your Juſtification, a Compariſon between that Lady

and

and my felf; but figh'd at the Neceffity which oblig'd you to reprefent her in a Portrait you imagined to be injurious; and your fecret Thoughts, undoubtedly, reftor'd her all the Charms which your treacherous Lips had denied her. But were fhe, in reality, as much my Inferior, as you would incline me to fuppofe; can you think that Circumftance would ever leffen my Difbelief of your Indifference to her; and would not the Inconftancy of your Difpofition be fufficient to make me apprehenfive of every thing that could be fatal to my Repofe? I have repeated it to you a thoufand times, that my Fears are perpetual. Had I all the Charms you are pleafed to allow me; and were I ordain'd to be the only Companion of your folitary Days, in the moft fequeftred Part of the Univerfe, I fhould not be reliev'd from my Sufpicions of your Inconftancy. You may remember the Time, when I was in no little Danger of lofing you, becaufe the Princefs *** rallied you with a fprightly Severity of Wit, which your Vanity was fo abfurd as to impute to a fond Paffion you fuppofed fhe entertained for you; and can I poffibly forget that I was never favour'd with one Vifit from you, till you had loft all Hopes of being agreeable to her? Happy would it have been for me, had I never known any other In-

ftance

ſtance of your Perfidy! But not to enter upon your paſs'd Conduct, make it your Endeavour to convince me, that the Joy which inſpired you yeſterday, at Play, had me for its Object. Recollect the cold Converſation with which you entertain'd me, and the inanimate Glances of your Eyes, that teſtified the Conſtraint with which you beheld me: Call to your Remembrance the Frequency of thoſe Sighs, which were more owing to your Mortification in being ſo diſtant from my Rival, than to any Satisfaction you enjoyed at my Preſence. Never tell me, that you was obliged to diſſemble a tender Regard for her, that you might the better conceal your real Paſſion for me, from the Obſervation of the Company. Love pierces through all the Diſguiſe of Conſtraint; a tranſient Look, or even the leaſt Geſture, is more perſwaſive on thoſe Occaſions, than all the eloquent Premeditation of Language. Beſides, this would be a ridiculous Excuſe for you to offer. When you really loved me, you acted with leſs Circumſpection; and whatever Pain it gave me, to moderate the Vivacity of your Ardours, I would have pardon'd you a thouſand Indiſcretions, much ſooner than I can forgive ſo much Inſenſibility: Yet I have ſeen you—Ingrate! I cannot think on the Particulars without Indignation. Adieu.

I bluſh

I bluſh to conſider I have loſt ſo much Time in lamenting my Fate. Be ſure to abſent yourſelf from me, for ever: Return me my Picture, and all my Letters; for it would not be decent in you, to detain from me thoſe Teſtimonies of my Weakneſs; and you can have no Reaſon, at preſent, to heſitate in your Compliance with my Requeſt. Let me fortify my Heart againſt you, and even againſt myſelf; you ſhall no more triumph over my unhappy Frailty; and, if I muſt needs devote ſome Tears to your Loſs, I will at leaſt preſerve myſelf from the Mortification of weeping in your Preſence.

LETTER XXV.

NO, my Lord, my Reſolution is fix'd, and I am determin'd to ſee you no more. All your Expoſtulations will be unavailing, and you are too indifferent to me, at preſent, to create, in me, the leaſt Deſire of any Juſtification you can offer. Your Apprehenſions of my Hatred are ill founded: You are not the Object of that uneaſy Paſſion in me; but I muſt acquaint you, at the ſame time, that all my Tenderneſs is entirely extinguiſhed. You may reſt aſſured, that our Hatred, on theſe Occaſions,

casions, is proportionable to our Love; and, that you may be satisfied of my Sincerity in this Particular, I only promise you the whole Stock of my Indifference. You may make what Remarks you please upon this Declaration; I am but too well avenged, if you really continue to love me. It certainly must be very disagreeable to sigh, without the least grateful Return; but as you are so extremely amiable, I may suppose this to be a Misfortune you have never experienced. I take no Notice of your Change, because I consider it as the Effect of your Caprice; and since you were passionately fond of Lady * * * a few Days ago, you may possibly be as much in Love with me to-day. As to my Heart, which you are pleased to demand, I must give you to understand, that it is no longer at my Disposal; at least you may be very certain, it will never be your Property again. It will therefore be most for your Interest, to let all Affairs rest between us, as they are at present. Should I consent to a new Intercourse with you, it would only be with a View to deceive you, in my Turn But this is a Satisfaction altogether unworthy of my Attention; and, to be plain with you, I am determined never to love you more. Your Vanity must be extremely mortified, when you cast your Eyes on these melancholy

choly Characters, form'd by the same Hand that has frequently writ to you in so contrary a Strain: But you have no Reason to be surprized at my Imitation of your own Example; and I should certainly have died with Grief, if my Inconstancy had not made it impossible for me to be sensible of yours. Let me advise you, then, to relieve me from your Sollicitations, which, instead of inspiring me with any Sentiments in your favour, will only degrade you in my Thoughts. You challenge me, in your Letter, to prove that you ever loved Lady * * but I am so little interested in your Conduct, that I shall never charge myself with that Province. You have my Consent to make her the happy Object of your Passion; treat her with all the Tenderness she merits, and be careful to preserve her from the Torments you have caused me to sustain. Make it evident, if possible, that you are worthy to possess so amiable a Conquest; and if you are no longer apprehensive of her Rigours, endeavour to secure yourself the Continuance of such uncommon Favours. You tell me, you will prepare for your Departure, if I intend to be inflexible; I can only say, that if you have formed such a Resolution, I wish you Abundance of Happiness and Satisfaction in your Travels.

LETTER

LETTER XXVI.

HOW irreſiſtible is the Power of Love! I am convinced of your Guilt, and yet find myſelf compelled to pardon you! How difficult is it to form an Averſion to the Perſon we adore; and with what Pleaſure are we inclined to believe him faithful, even when we have ſo many Reaſons to be apprehenſive of loſing him for ever! Take back my Heart I reſtore you; and may the Poſſeſſion of it be ſo inſtrumental to your Happineſs, as to ſecure you from the Poſſibility of changing! May the Warmth and Conſtancy of your Paſſion, prevent me from hating you for the future! I am willing to ſuppoſe I was deceived, when I imagined you had devoted your Inclinations to another Object; and it will not be my Fault, if I do not ſoon preſent you with a more pleaſing Confeſſion of my Miſtake. I am not deſirous to torment myſelf; but tho' my Heart is incapable of the leaſt Tincture of Caprice, it is not entirely exempted from Suſpicions. Every Circumſtance of your Conduct allarms the Delicacy of my Love, and a ſingle Glance directed to another Object, calls up a thouſand extravagant Imaginations in my Soul. The fatal Loſs of your Heart ſeems to me inevitable,

ble, in the Agony of that Moment, and the Idea of your Indifference condemns me to Inquietudes I am incapable of sustaining. Can you believe, that the Ardours of my Paſſion are abated; and, if I did not love you, even to Madneſs it ſelf, could I poſſibly be affected with your Behaviour? Alas! there are ſome Inſtances of it, which, as innocent as they may appear to you, never fail to overwhelm me with Deſpair! How can your Manner of thinking be different from mine! And ſince I am always ſedulous to pleaſe you, why do you deny me a ſuitable Return! Did you intend, by your affected Cruelty, to kill me with inconſolable Sorrow! Have you any Cauſe to ridicule thoſe Sentiments in my Soul, which your Indifference, your Inconſtancy, and even your Averſion it ſelf, had no Power to extinguiſh? Was there any Neceſſity for your deluding me with the Apprehenſions of a Rival? and if your Paſſion had the leaſt Similitude to mine, could you poſſibly conſtrain your Eyes to afford her one favourable Regard? Are you then ſuch an abſolute Maſter of your Heart, as to be capable of acting ſuch a Part as this? Ah! never give me Cauſe to entertain ſuch an Opinion; your Inconſtancy would be leſs tormenting to me, than your Perjury in pretending a Paſſion for me which you never experienced.

perienced. But how ſhall I be ſatisfied that you have no Inclination to change? You, indeed, are pleas'd to give me ſuch an Aſſurance; but is that ſufficient to convince me of your Sincerity? The Agitations of my Soul, at the Remembrance of the Dangers I have ſuſtain'd, and my perpetual Fears of repeating them, compel me to entertain a ſecret Diſtruſt of all your Proteſtations; and cauſe me to reproach my own inconſiderate Credulity. I am even ſenſible, tho' I acknowledge it with Reluctance, that my Diffidence of your Integrity, has oblig'd me to conſider you with a Coldneſs to which I was formerly a Stranger; and I find it very difficult for me to believe you as innocent as you repreſent yourſelf. I ſhould rejoice to be perſwaded that your Penitence and Remorſe were ſincere; but the Remembrance of your paſt Conduct, and my Apprehenſions of the Pangs I may yet be fated to endure, entirely chill me for the preſent; and I ſtand in need of very good Reaſons, to revive a Paſſion for you, as ardent as that which I have formerly experienced. I even force my Imagination to repreſent you in an amiable Idea, and ſigh to find myſelf ſo different from what I have lately been. I am ſenſible that I have loſt thoſe tender Sollicitudes and ſoft Deſires, which were once my delightful Entertainment, and needed not the Aid of ſedate Reflections, to form the Happineſs I then enjoy'd. Had you deferr'd your Vindication a little longer, I ſhould certainly have loved you no more. How well does the Sincerity of this Confeſſion repreſent to you, the Importance of ſuch a Reſolution to my Repoſe! Do not imagine, however, that I ſhall be incapable of Satisfaction, when you ſhall think fit to reviſit me: For tho' my Paſſion may have ſome Abatement, I am ſtill convinced that I love you infinitely more than you are able to conceive. How happy would you render me, were your inſenſible Soul but warm'd with part of the Flames that are kindled in mine! I ſuppoſe I need not enjoin you to ſee Lady * * * no more; however, let your Heart inform you, whether ſuch a Deprivation will coſt you dear, and give me no Occaſion to believe, that you are making a Sacrifice in my favour, with Reluctance, when you ceaſe to behold her. Adieu.

The Moment I concluded my Letter, the Marquis came into my Cloſet, upon a very ſingular Occaſion; for, after he had told me that he was going to *Verſailles*, he aſked me, why I did not ſee you as uſual; and obſerving me in ſome Confuſion at that Queſtion; Madam, ſays he, with a very ſerious Air, you grow more capricious every Day,

Day, and it ſhould ſeem as if you delighted to play off your fanciful Airs upon my Friends; the Count is one, for whom I have a particular Eſteem, and you will oblige me, by granting him the Pardon he deſires to obtain: Not that he is guilty in any Inſtance, but he is too polite to remind you of your Incivilities. I muſt deſire you, therefore, to conduct yourſelf in ſuch a manner, that I may ſee him here, at my Return, with his uſual Air of Satisfaction, or elſe you muſt permit me to think you accountable for any Diſcontent he may happen to diſcover. But who, ſaid I, has acquainted your Lordſhip that we have had any Variance? He himſelf, replied the Marquis; but I deſire you not to treat him ill, for I had all the Difficulty in the World to extort this Myſtery from him. But whatever the Affair may be, I muſt inſiſt upon your granting him a favourable Reception, or elſe I aſſure you, that I myſelf will introduce him to you, every Day, for your Puniſhment. Theſe Women, continued he, as he was retiring, can never live in Peace with People. I am much obliged to you, my Lord, for providing yourſelf with ſuch an Interceſſor; your Proceeding is very ſingular, I muſt confeſs: But if I had not a natural Diſpoſition to love you, I can aſſure you that you would have derived very little Advantage from his Recommendation. I am ready to die with laughing, at his Zeal for his Friend; but must you not confess, that it would be pity to deceive him?

LETTER XXVII.

YOU complain of my Indifference, and are at a loss to comprehend how it is possible for me, amidst the Flow of your softest Transports, to be insensible of that Emotion which they naturally ought to create in my Soul. I have been affected with this Emotion for some time, and am not a little concerned that I should begin to lose the Conception of it now. You infer, from my pretended Insensibility, that the Ardours of your Passion are superior to mine: You are very liberal of your Reproaches; and having no Idea of any Pleasures in Love, but such as are imparted by the Senses, you consider those refin'd Impressions, which inspire the Soul with Joys, much more exquisite and delicate than the Delights which are the sole Objects of your Desires; I say, you consider them as so many Chimeras and Illusions. Ah! how is it possible for you to be unacquainted with them; and why am I, with all my Penetration, so incapable of describing them? Were

Were I lefs fenfible of their Power, I fhould certainly explain them with more Perfpicuity. You charge me with Indifference; alas! why can I not comply with the Importunity of your Defires, without a Crime! The warmeft Glow of your tender Tranfports would be cold and languifhing, if compared to mine, and I fhould foon caufe you to blufh, for believing my Paffion lefs violent than yours. Am I, then, without Defires? Can you imagine me exempted from their tormenting Impreffions; and is not my Soul agitated with Diforders that have no Intermiffion? As my Happinefs is much inferior to yours, am I not neceffitated to conceal my Sentiments from you; and can I poffibly refign myfelf to their Impulfe, without offending the Severity of that Virtue, whofe Aid, weak as it is, has hitherto preferved me from the Lofs of your Efteem, and the infupportable Forfeiture of your Heart? Were it not for this fatal Certainty —— Ah me! into what Extreams would my Emotions betray me, had I no Subject for my Letter but this! How many Expreffions have efcaped me, which are injurious to my Virtue, and unfatisfactory to you, who perhaps may confider my Deviation from Reafon as a Circumftance that ought to be difregarded? Why have I not the Power to erafe thefe Confeffions,

for

for which I ſo juſtly reproach myſelf! But you will ſurely be too generous to improve them to my Diſadvantages. Had it not been for *Dupré*, who waits with Impatience in my Chamber, and would be unwilling to allow me ſufficient Time to write another Letter, I ſhould have preſerved myſelf from the Mortification of ſo many Follies. Lay no Streſs upon them, I intreat you. Will you believe me, when I aſſure you, that I ſhall be more ready to diſown them than I was to commit them to Writing? Adieu.

I am almoſt tortur'd to Diſtraction: My Mother commands me to accompany her, I know not where; and I muſt be baniſh'd, the whole Day, from your Sight! It was to no purpoſe for me to tell her I was indiſpoſed; ſhe is poſitive that Health itſelf ſmiles in my Countenance. It will be impoſſible for me to ſee you. Ah me! what Mortifications am I now to endure!

BILLET.

I know not whether I do well to acquaint you that I am at this time alone: But I find myſelf diſcompoſed, and have an Inclination to ſee you. Perhaps I ought not to be deſirous of a Viſit from you, after the fine Deſcriptions of myſelf, which you have received from

from the Marquis. I am obliged to him, for commending me with so much Zeal; and if he is pleased with the Merit he allows me, you may judge how agreeable it ought to be to the Man I love, and who alone is the Object of all my Transports. A Husband can only behold a breathing Statue; 'tis the Lover alone for whom the Soul is form'd. I am not at all doubtful of the Pleasure you will receive, in verifying his Discourse. But however that may be, I shall not be favour'd with his Company at Dinner; and should you be disposed to fill the Place he is pleased to leave vacant, I am not sensible that your Civility will expose you to any Censure. I could have engaged some of my own Sex, had not I believed your Presence would be more entertaining to me; for I am a mortal Enemy to all insipid Indolence. Be so obliging then, as to indulge me with your Company; and I promise you to do all I can, to render mine as agreeable to you as possible. Heaven grant, that the Sight of me may be all the Satisfaction you desire me to grant you.

LETTER XXVIII.

YES, my Lord, I confeſs that if my Huſband's Arrival yeſterday was very ſeaſonable for himſelf, it happened to be perfectly inconſiſtent with your Intentions: My irreſolute Virtue made but a weak Defence, and your impatient Ardours had almoſt ſurprized me into an abſolute Inſenſibility of my Duty. The enſnaring Opportunity, the Promptitude of your Paſſion, and the Conformity of mine; in ſhort, every Circumſtance conſpired againſt me, and I was ſenſible, in that Moment, of Impreſſions I had never experienced till then. My Eyes, when they were even fixed upon you, were incapable of beholding you: I was reduc'd to that State of Stupidity, in which we reſign ourſelves to every Freedom your Sex is pleaſed to attempt; and my Thoughts were diſorder'd by an Intoxication, more eaſy to be conceived than expreſs'd: What then would have been my Condition, had not the Marquis arrived at that Inſtant! I have protracted the Loſs of you one Day longer, by not gratifying your Deſires: But, ſhall I always have that Reſolution? Yes ſurely; for the Situation in which I then beheld myſelf, as infatuating as it appear'd to my Senſes, and as inchanting as it can poſſibly prove, is too dange-

rous

rous ever to leave me the leaſt Inclination to repeat it. I am ſenſible you never expected ſuch a Concluſion as then happen'd; and perhaps you may imagine, that my Impatience to accompliſh what Chance interrupted, is equal to yours; but you injure me by that Suſpicion. Is it poſſible that in thoſe cruel Moments, when Nature reſigns us to ourſelves; when all the Scenes, wrought into Enthuſiaſm, conſpire to ſeduce us; when our Tranſports are kindled, without Intermiſſion, by thoſe which riſe in the Lover, and inſinuate the Idea of thrilling Joys into the Imagination; is it poſſible, I ſay, that we can deſire ſuch a delicious Frenzy to be defeated? It is, my Lord, and I can dare to avow it: A Reſignation to the warm Deſires of a Lover, after we have been awaken'd from that fatal Diſpoſition I have experienc'd, and a ſoft Indulgence to his Happineſs, becauſe our Frailty was once inclinable to grant it; is a Weakneſs, of which I have no Conception. In conſequence of theſe Reflections, I ſhall never conſent to another Interview; for I am no longer miſguided by my former Indiſcretions. You will be diſpleas'd at this Reſolution; and perhaps I may not find all the Satisfaction in it that I could wiſh: But I ſhall never act in any other manner. Could I be certain, indeed, that we ſhould be again interrupted by my Huſ-

Huſband, I mgiht diſpoſe myſelf to receive you; for, without him, my Virtue is very imperfect. This dear Marquis! With what Gratitude have I embrac'd him! He was at a loſs to account for my Careſſes; and as all his Fondneſs is devoted to your fair Relation, he received my obliging Tenderneſs with ſuch an Air of Diſſatisfacton and Conſtraint, as would have diverted you extremely. I yeſterday imagined, when he firſt made his Appearance, that Huſbands have ſome particular Preſages which inform them of what is tranſacted in their Abſence: But they are daily giving us ſo many Proofs to the contrary, that, it was impoſſible for me to continue long in that Perſuaſion.

Surely yeſterday was very fortunate to Huſbands. The Satisfaction my Eſcape from you afforded me, animated my Features with ſo much Vivacity, and diffuſed ſuch engaging Graces over all my Perſon, that you would have died with mere Love, had you beheld me in that amiable State. I ſhall certainly indulge a little Cruelty for the future; and does not your Lordſhip diſcover a very formidable Aſpect in ſo much Virtue? What will you ſay then, when I aſſure you, that it is preparing to be more untractable than ever? But I am conſtrained to be imperious, ſince my Compliances

pliances are inconſiſtent with my Honour. You had an Inclination to improve my Frailty to your Advantage, and I ought not to pardon that ungenerous Intention. Ah this Virtue, Count! Have theſe who practiſe it, any Senſibility of Love? I begin to be fortified by that Thought: There are, poſſibly, ſome Caſes that may be excepted, but it would be diſhonourable to derive any improper Advantage from them. You ſee the Perplexity in which I am involved; your Lordſhip in one Scale, and Virtue in the other: How difficult is it to adjuſt the Ballance! But that I may be able to keep it even, I muſt intreat you never to ſee me for the future, unleſs it be at a diſtance, or in publick; and if you are diſſatisfied at this Requeſt, you muſt amuſe yourſelf with your own Deſires. I grant you this Permiſſion, till you receive new Orders from me. Adieu.

BILLET.

Ah! my poor Count! ſleep in the Name of Heaven! Sleep, I ſay, that you may, at leaſt, have the Enjoyment of pleaſing Dreams. Let theſe agreeable Illuſions recompenſe you for all the Mortifications you have ſuffered by my Rigours. Alas! you are in ſuch a Condition at preſent, that I am fearful of granting you the most inconsiderable Favour, lest I should be obliged to repeat it. Don Quixot, *when he left the* Black Mountain, *was not half so emaciated as yourself. What would you have one do with so dejected a Lover? Resume your florid Complexion: I permitted you to be indisposed, when you was desirous of my Compassion; but why should you now recur to that unnecessary Expedient? I intend to be at the Opera, this Evening, where you may enjoy the Pleasure of beholding me. You may think an Assignation, at such a Place, something extraordinary, if you were not very sensible that we are never to have any in private. However, be there betimes.*

BILLET.

I happen'd to sigh at the Opera, at one Word you utter'd, and my Eyes corresponded with that Sigh: I imagined you understood me, since you were pleased to tender me your Acknowledgments with so much Civility; and yet you have desired me, this Morning, to favour you with an Explanation. All that I can say to you, at present, will not convey to you the Sense of what I said then. The Language of the Lips does not always imitate the Sentiments of the Heart; and perhaps

perhaps mine no longer preserves the Disposition in which you found it yesterday; or at least I would flatter myself to that effect. You desire to know if I am disposed to see Company; I have almost an Inclination to say, No: But you have too much Merit to suffer me to impose upon you. You would willingly be informed, if I shall be alone; I can easily tell you that I shall: But, will you draw no Conclusions from that Confession?

[Some Letters are here suppress'd.]

LETTER XXIX.

AS much Love as you please, but a little more Discretion, or I am undone. You threw me into so much Perplexity, yesterday, with your Impatience; and such an Air of Emotion was visible in your Eyes, that it was impossible the Company should not discover what is so much our Interest to conceal. Am I then so indifferent to you, that you can be content to lose me, for the sake of a Gratification, which would afford you so little Pleasure? At what a fatal Time were we in danger of being ſurprized! Is it poſſible that in the midſt of publick Hurry——Ah! how I tremble at the Remembrance! Let me intreat you, if you really love me, never to expoſe me to ſo much Danger for the future. Have we not ſufficient Time in the Day? How inconſiderate are you grown! Your Deſires are never ſo ardent, as when their Accompliſhment is impracticable. When I reſign myſelf to your Tenderneſs, in thoſe Places where we can ſuſtain no Hazard, I always find you extremely calm and moderate. This is an Obſervation which has been forced upon me by your Follies; and I believe you are ſo juſt to me, as not to charge me with any yielding Frailties. At the ſame time I declare, that I am not inſenſible, but my Heart is more favourable to me than yours; and that which conſtitutes my Happineſs, would be an inſupportable Coldneſs, in your Opinion. You have no Comprehenſion of any thing beyond your Deſires, and are unacquainted with thoſe delicate Anxieties that affect a Heart capable of Senſibility; nor have you any Idea of Love itſelf, but what I wiſh to be ignorant of for ever. I, without doubt, addreſs myſelf to you in a Strain to which you have been little accuſtomed. Your Heart torments you with no Reproaches, and you diſcover to me, with-

out

out the leaſt Diſguiſe, every Emotion that is capable of affecting it. All the Advantage I ſhould derive from my Complaints, would be, to find myſelf deceived with more Dexterity for the future: But my Expoſtulations would not be ſo frequent, if you could impoſe upon others with more Succeſs. Can you imagine, that you have conducted yourſelf with all the Diſcretion that is juſtly my due, tho' you had never acquainted any one with the Nature of our Intercourſe? Can you be ignorant, that our Actions are the moſt expreſſive Declarations of our Thoughts? Would you have all the World ſuſpect your Paſſion for me; and are you deſirous they ſhould believe you want nothing to render your Happineſs compleat; or is this ſo immoderate, that you cannot poſſibly ſuſtain it; and would it loſe its Eſtimation by being unknown? Why do you affect to be perpetually converſing with me in Whiſpers, at the ſame time that you are committing a thouſand Indiſcretions? Why is my Reputation the leaſt Part of your Care? If you would allow yourſelf, however, but a ſhort Space for Reflection, you would be ſenſible that I deſerve to be treated with more Decency; and that ſuch a Conduct is abſolutely neceſſary to my Repoſe. Let me adviſe you not to depend on my Huſband's Indolence;

you have all imaginable Reaſon to be apprehenſive of his Reſentment, ſhould he once entertain any Suſpicion of my Weakneſs. Let us be ſeen together, in publick, as little as poſſible. I am extremely apprehenſive of your Imprudence, and all your Probity is incapable of reconciling me to your Tranſports. I even dread my own, and am conſcious that my Eyes diſtinguiſh you from other Men, by a very viſible Preference. How ſhall I conceal thoſe Emotions that agitate my Soul, the Moment I behold you! Let us habituate ourſelves to a little Conſtraint, for our own Security; a ſingle Word that we imagine to be of no Conſequence; a tranſient Glance; a mere Preference; in ſhort, every Circumſtance of this Nature, is always explained by the World, in a very diſadvantageous manner. What a Number of People are there, who make Detraction their conſtant Employment; and if Calumny is levell'd at ſo many Perſons, ought we not to be apprehenſive of its malignant Effects? Let me intreat you to think the greateſt Proof you can give me of your Paſſion, will be your Sollicitude to conceal it. Can you perſuade yourſelf that ſoft Deſires are eſſential to no Heart but yours; and do you think I offer no Violence to my own Inclinations? But ſince I am capable

of

of oppoſing them, why cannot you exert yourſelf with the ſame Succeſs? You ought to bluſh, when you conſider that you have leſs Preſence of Mind than myſelf. Adieu. You deſire to ſee me; and I am unwilling to grant you that Requeſt: But, however, you may come, if you are ſo diſpoſed; I ſhall not be under the Inſpection either of Friends or Enemies; and as Vanity is to be the Motive of my Conteſt with you, your Valour may prove very inconſiderable for want of Spectators. Let me enjoy your Company at Dinner; I never was ſo amiable and unthinking as I am at preſent. How ſincerily do I pity you!

LETTER XXX.

YOU have diſguſted me a little, but I am very glad you writ to me, becauſe the Formality of an Anſwer gives me a favourable Opportunity of acquainting you with what I had to ſay. To make a regular Beginning, then, I muſt inform you, in the firſt place, that your Apprehenſions are altogether extravagant; and, to convince you that I think ſo, I have reſolved not to favour you with one Syllable of Love, or the leaſt Aſſurance of Fidelity, either for the Time preſent, or that which is to come.

I am

I am not diſſatisfied that I have created you a few Suſpicions; but all that I can do for you, is to proceed in my uſual Track, and, if after this you are diſpoſed to be incommodious, all the Detriment will be your own. We will now proceed to other Particulars.

You are ſenſible that my Huſband fancied himſelf indiſpoſed yeſterday; and, as the Care of his Health is the moſt important Pleaſure he enjoys, I had ſome Reaſon to imagine he would confine himſelf to his Apartment, for the Remainder of the Week. This Circumſtance would have ſubjected us to ſome Conſtraint; but he has been pleaſed to change his Opinion. He awaked this Morning with a very promiſing Complexion, and ſome Vivacity in his Eyes; after which he came into my Apartment, with a moſt deplorable Air, to have my Sentiments of his Countenance. It appear'd to me juſt as it was; by which I mean, that it was ſomething better than mine. He received my Congratulations for his Recovery, and I aſſured him, that what he miſtook for an Indiſpoſition, was only the Effect of a Diſcompoſure which had diffuſed itſelf over all his Charms, and ſhaded part of their Luſtre. He diſputed my Opinion, which obliged me to conduct him to my Glaſs, in my own Vindication. He ſmiled when

when he ſurveyed himſelf, and immediately gave me to underſtand, that he was ſenſible he grew better. This Diſcovery brightned his Melancholy into ſo much good Humour, that he continued a conſiderable time at my Toilet, and became the moſt amiable and gallant Man in the World. I was almoſt tempted to be a Supplicant for the Continuance of his tender Regards for me; but I am inclined to think my Petition would have been rejected: For he left my Chamber, and I accompanied him to his own Apartment, where he dreſs'd himſelf with all the Coquettry of a Woman who expects a favour'd Lover. I did not fail to expatiate on the Graces of his Perſon, and even aſſiſted him in the Adjuſtment of his Habit: In ſhort, I ſo frequently aſſured him that he was perfectly charming, that he was determined to viſit your Couſin, with whom he paſs'd the Remainder of the Day. For my part, I found myſelf in a Diſpoſition to employ the Time he left upon my Hands, to the beſt Advantage, in ſpite of your ill Humour; and at laſt perſuaded myſelf, that I ſhould have ſome Occaſion for you, if I intended to enjoy a few agreeable Hours. But, with your Permiſſion, we will have a little more Company to enliven us. I am apprehenſive, that you will be diſpleaſed with ſo much Soli-

tude,

tude, eſpecially ſince you are ſo very little in love with me to-day: But whatever you may think of my Proceeding, I have not ſo much Complaiſance for your Caprice, as to give myſelf any Uneaſineſs, when I can act much better. You may come, then, aſſoon as you pleaſe, for I was never more deſirous of your Company.

LETTER XXXI.

THE Affairs which detain you at *Paris*, make you loſe the moſt charming Month of the Year, in Perplexity and Diſcontent; and your Abſence deprives me of all the Pleaſures I ſhould enjoy in a Place which would ſeem delightful to me, could it poſſibly be graced with your Preſence. Have your Thoughts any Similitude to mine? Do you diſcover any Charms in *Paris*, when I am no longer there; or do you look with Indifference on every Object around you? Have you any Inclination to ſee me in that City? Do you recollect that I ſincerily love you; and is that Remembrance capable of contributing to your Happineſs, in the ſame Proportion as my Paſſion for you is the only Source of mine? How exquiſite would my Felicity prove, if amidſt the Pleaſures that preſent themſelves

to

to your View, your Heart would confeſs that it was ſtill deſtitute of ſome dear Enjoyment! Do you derive any Satisfaction from your Fidelity to me, and can you ſtill love me with all the Extaſies I experience for you? The Reality of Joy is only to be taſted in a Paſſion as ardent as mine. Moderation in Love, is a cold Diſcompoſure of the Mind; but if your Letter tranſmits to me the Language of your Heart, I have no Cauſe to be diſcontented. In what a charming Warmth of Expreſſion does it flow! I almoſt imagin'd, when I read it, that your Paſſion was paramount to mine; but is it poſſible for you to write with ſo much delicate Wit, amidſt the Troubles that perplex you; and are you ſincerely ſenſible of the Impreſſions you deſcribe? You tell me, you are a Stranger to every Satisfaction; and I can aſſure you, that I have no happy Moments but thoſe wherein you are the delightful Subject of my Meditations. How do I regret that Part of my Time, which I am under a Neceſſity of devoting to other Attentions! Will this cruel Abſence admit of no Mitigation, but that which your Picture affords me! Dear to me as it is, the Solace I receive from it is very imperfect, when I think on the Original! Did you but know the incoherent Follies I utter to thoſe lovely Traces of the

Pencil!

Pencil! But, is my Portrait capable of finding you any Employment? Do you really need its Aſſiſtance to direct your Thoughts to me; and can you indeed be ſatisfied with its little Miniſtration in that Particular? Ah! how languid is the Paſſion you entertain for me! Is it juſt in you, to leave me in the melancholy Solitude to which I am abandoned; and ought you not to be ſenſible of all the Horrors of your own ſequeſtred State? You may poſſibly make your Law-ſuit furniſh you with a Pretext for not ſeeing me ſo frequently as you ought. The Aſpect of your Proctor may be more agreeable to you than mine: But, have all the Suits in the World, any Competition with that which I can cauſe you to loſe? I would reſign all my other Expectations, for the Pleaſure of beholding you in this Place. Shall I not be deluded in the Hopes you give me, of ſeeing you in four Days? Will the Court, and your own particular Affairs, permit you to be punctual to your Promiſe? I am now in a real State of Widowhood: My Huſband is engaged in the ſame Place that detains you; and as his Return will not be ſpeedy, ought you not to improve the Liberty you derive from his Abſence. The perpetual Flutter of the City is diſagreeable to Lovers; the Heart is always fetter'd by unpleaſing Decorums,

corums, and the perfect Enjoyment of one's self is only to be attained in the soft Calm of Solitude. Haste then, if it be only to experience whether my Cruelty be abated, or not: Let your Curiosity incline you to try, whether my Tenderness for you can be increased by the Efficacy of your Presence. I will at least acknowledge, that the verdant Beauties of Nature, and the silent Gloom of the Woods, lull me into a Train of Meditations, which have no other Object but yourself. Your charming Image rises before me in all my Slumbers: I then think you the most amiable Swain in the World; and sometimes the happiest of all your Sex. But alas! these Delights are but unsubstantial Dreams: Prepare then to bless me, by your dear Return, with Joys that are real. Adieu, my Lord. You indulge yourself in Complaints; but, can you tell me why? Once more Adieu: Be sure to remember that I love you, and am doom'd to die with Anguish in your Absence.

LETTER XXXII.

EIGHT Days are now elapsed, since your Departure; eight fatal Days have I pass'd in unspeakable Inquietudes; whilst you, perhaps, have been unwilling to devote one Moment of this tedious Period to my Remembrance. You have writ me a Letter, I confeſs; and any one, but myſelf, would have thought it exquiſitely tender: But, had you the Power to tell me, with any Tranquillity, that your Return will be retarded eight Days? Is it poſſible that ſo long an Abſence ſhould not ſeem as cruel to you, as it really is to me? Has my Heart, then, loſt its Eſtimation in your Thoughts, becauſe I have permitted it to be totally yours? The Vivacity of my Paſſion enables me to diſcover the languid Calm of yours. Ah! how unkind was it to leave me to the Anguiſh of my forlorn Solitude! The Moderation of your Deſires diſcompoſes me without ceaſing, and I am ſometimes tempted to wiſh you would ſacrifice all other Obligations and Affairs to your Sollicitude to reviſit me: I even forget that I have injoin'd you to the contrary; but the Moment I recollect that Injunction, I am offended at the Punctuality of your Obedience. Why do you expoſe me to the Inconſiſtency of ſuch extravagant Thoughts? Do you find it ſo difficult to allot one Moment to my Satisfaction; and ſhall Sleep ingroſs that precious Time which is the Property of Love? You fill up all the Hours of my Life; and have I no Pretenſions then to any of yours? Were you once ſenſible of the

the Diſquietude I ſuſtain; did you but know how I am perſecuted by rural Coxcombs, and tawdry Officers of the Revenue, I am ſure you would pity my Condition. Your Abſence is no way neceſſary, to give me a Diſreliſh for their Converſation; no Circumſtance in Nature can recommend their inſipid Liveline ſs. Unhappily for me, they have already begun to torment me with ſo much Reſpect, that I am at a loſs how to diſengage myſelf from the Profuſion of their Civilities. *P* *** has his Houſe entirely filled with theſe amiable Gentlemen; and it is ſo near mine, that I am beſieged the whole Day, and eſpecially by the young Triflers. They have ſuch bewitching Airs, ſo ſmooth a Flow of Wit, and diſburden themſelves of their teeming Conceits with ſuch a military Freedom of Thought, that were I not ſo much prepoſſeſs'd in your Favour as I am, I ſhould certainly be undone, in ſpite of all my Virtue. What Infatuation and Impertinence am I expoſed to! 'Tis ſaid, however, that theſe good People are very fortunate in their Amours: What a Reproach is this to my Sex! I believe, their frequent Reſorts to our provincial Courts of Law, have infected them with an Air of Stupidity that diſcovers itſelf, even in the beſt Strain of Livelineſs they are capable of affecting. I have already received from theſe flimry

Teazers, no lefs than thirty Declarations of Love, each rifing above the laft in tender Expreffions. You would be too much diverted were you to fee them, in their Emulations to pay their Court to me at my Toilet. With what an amiable Set of little Creatures am I furrounded! Virtue, in their Company, would be a ridiculous Superfluity, fince a moderate Share of Tafte fuffices to guard one againft all their Seducements. Had not *St. Far**** relieved me yefterday with a very feafonable Vifit, I fhould certainly have been fick with mere Chagrin: But his agreeable Gaiety requites me for all the fleepy Civilities I am compelled to hear from my Lovers; and I now think myfelf happy, fince I have an Opportunity of making you the Subject of my Converfation with him. *P**** entertain'd me, laft Night, with a Supper that compleated my ill Humour. My little Clufter of Fops were extremely facetious, and darted their Glances at me, in a moft unmerciful manner: They even exhaufted all their Invention to divert me; and yet, you may reafonably believe, I pafs'd the Time without a Moment's Satisfaction; and indeed I muft confefs, that if my Thoughts of you had not fupported me amidft thefe cold Amufements, I fhould have died with Vexation. Adieu; but remember to return as foon as poffible, poſſible, and diſſipate, with your ſuperiour Air, this fluttering Legion of Inſignificants that beſiège me. Believe me, it is your Intereſt to be very expeditious; and to induce you to that, is it neceſſary for me to tell you that I, this Moment, hear your Uncle's Cough? But however, I ſhall go and divert myſelf with making him ſeal my Letter. Once more Adieu, my deareſt Count! I have no Time to acquaint you with any thing more; but you may repreſent me to your Imagination, entertaining you with the ſofteſt Language that Love can utter; and perhaps, even then, you will have but an imperfect Idea of the exquiſite Impreſſions with which you have inſpired me.

LETTER XXXIII.

WHO can poſſibly have told you that I want any of your Excuſes? You have been pleaſed to favour me with a ſmall Inſtance of your Inconſtancy, which gives me no manner of Diſcontent: The Example is of your own propoſing, and you are ſenſible how apt our Sex is to imitate yours in that Particular. You are afraid I ſhall act agreeably to the Precedent you have ſhewn me: It would have been Wiſdom in you to have made that Reflection before;

but you firſt inſult me, and are afterwards apprehenſive of my Revenge. You and *St. Far**** were pleaſed, yeſterday, to bring into the Country, a Party of Nymphs who ſing in the Opera; and truly I can ſee nothing extraordinary in ſuch a Proceeding, eſpecially as I am certain you ſelected thoſe of the moſt unblemiſh'd Virtue in the whole Band: And tho' it may be ſomething difficult to make ſuch a Choice, I yet refer myſelf, in that particular, to your delicate Taſte and Penetration. Beſides, no Law has ever made it a Crime to love Muſic; and, I believe, Harmony muſt needs be more affecting in the Calm of a Wood, than it can poſſibly be in the Confuſion of a Theatre, amidſt a troubleſome Crowd of Spectators. But what if the whole Affair be quite otherwiſe, and that my Imagination, which was always ſollicitous to juſtify your Conduct, ſhould, for once, give Things their worſt Conſtruction; what would be the Conſequence? I ſhould bluſh, could I poſſibly be jealous on ſuch an Occaſion: No, I can but make ſome Abatements of my former Conſtancy; but this, perhaps, is what you never ſuſpected, and you might flatter yourſelf that your Indiſcretion would never provoke me to form ſuch a Reſolution: But you may, poſſibly, be much deceived. There are Times when I find myſelf expoſed

poſed to the prettieſt Temptations in the World, and I am not diſpleaſed to have my Senſibility of their Power juſtified by your Example. I once prided myſelf in a Conſtancy, which could not fail to be incommodious to us both; but I have intirely changed my Plan. When we are indulging the full Career of our Inclinations, if we ſhould hereafter happen to relapſe into a mutual Tenderneſs for each other; we may then repeat our Interviews, without being ſeized with the Tranſports of a Paſſion in its infant Flame. Abſence, perhaps, may give us ſome little Regrets; but we ſhall have no Jealouſies, no Expoſtulations or Caprice to experience. It will then be our happy Fate to be unacquainted with thoſe Delicacies that create ſuch an Inequality in Love. We may be mutual Confidents to each other; and ſo amiable a Gentleman as yourſelf, muſt needs be capable of entertaining me with a Number of pleaſing Adventures. We may aſſiſt each other with our beſt Counſels, if it be poſſible for ſo inconſiderate a Perſon as yourſelf, to offer any that are material. Should you then happen to have been in any Adventure like that of yeſterday, I ſhall have the Friendſhip to tell you, that little Gaieties of that nature, degrade a Gentleman; and that when he conſorts himſelf with Perſons of ſuch a

Claſs,

Clafs, he is in fome Danger of acting an ungraceful Part: That amidft a thoufand Inconveniencies which attend fuch little Diverfions, it muft be very mortifying to his Vanity, when he fees himfelf on a Level with thofe good People whom fuch Ladies affociate into their Pleafures. You may judge, by this Sketch of Morality, what improving Lectures I am preparing for your next Indifcretions. Heavens grant, that thofe you committed yefterday, may be your laft! Adieu. You imagine I fhall not be vifible to-day; but you are really miftaken.

LETTER XXXIV.

I Am at a lofs to know where all thefe Follies will end; but am perfuaded, that from the Moment People firft began to fay tender Things to one another, there never was a more ridiculous Pair of Lovers than ourfelves. Eight Days ago I was jealous; and were I to credit all I hear, I fhould have Reafon to continue fo ftill. To-day you are feized with the fame Diftemper; doubtlefs becaufe you intend to copy after my Example; but I can affure you, I am not fo compleat a Model as you may imagine. You are pleafed to tell me that I am a Coquet, and it may poffibly be

true.

true. You ſay I love to pleaſe; but can you give me any Reaſon why I ought to renounce all Mankind? You will certainly be much ſurprized, when I declare that I act with Diſcretion, in the very Inſtances for which you reproach me; and yet nothing can be more certain. I have obſerved; for tho' I love you, I can obſerve ſometimes; and indeed I obſerve, becauſe I love you: I ſay, I have obſerved that it is good to awaken your Paſſion. Alas! when it is once ſatisfied, it grows ſo languid, that it becomes neceſſary to animate it with a little Jealouſy. When you are in any Apprehenſions of a Rival, you ſay the pretrieſt Things to me in the World: You then forget that you are happy, and repreſent yourſelf in the Condition of one who wiſhes to be ſo: But when we happen to be well together, you can place yourſelf, with all the Negligence imaginable, in an eaſy Chair, over-againſt me, without uttering one Word; and I am ſometimes tempted to believe you think as little as you ſpeak. You lately entertain'd me with a few Endearments that ſeemed to be extremely tender, when, in reality, your Thoughts had no ſuch Employment. Let me have your beſt Reaſons for this Abſence of Mind. You are certainly a moſt ſingular Lover, and I confeſs there is ſomething very agreeable to me, even in that Singularity.

larity. At present, indeed, I have but very little Share in your good Graces: You left me, yesterday, in a very abrupt Manner, and, without doubt, made a gallant Resolution never to see me more; tho' I could venture a considerable Wager, that you can't give me one Reason for that Air. You have taken it into your Head to be jealous of *R* * * *, and will not so much as suffer him to write Sonnets in my Favour; but you don't consider how touching it is to see one's Fame diffused through the World, under the tender Name of *Sylvia*. Permit me then to enjoy the Pleasure of Immortality: His Verses promise me that Blessing, whilst you only bestow upon me those Moments for which you can find no other Employment. Is this any Compensation to me for losing the Benefit of his Muse? I likewise acknowledge, that he entertains me in my Chamber, when you are pleased to absent yourself from it; and is very diligent in teaching me to make Verses. How delighted will you be, when in some future Glow of Passion, my inspired Imagination shall address to you the softest soothing Elegies; when it shall call you the resistless *Corydon*, and trace out those inchanting Moments, when you triumphed over my defenceless Liberty, for ever! As to any other Particulars, it is not, as yet, the proper Season

son

ſon for your Jealouſy to make its Appearance. You ſee there are ſome People in the World, who complain of my Rigours; but it would not be proper for you to deſpair, before I have favour'd them with my Compaſſion. You are certainly imprudent to have any Difference with me at preſent: What an odd Time have you choſen for your Reſentment! The Marquis is in the Country, and in what Manner would you have me diſpoſe of myſelf? I am reſolved, for your Puniſhment, that you ſhall dine with me this very Day, and I don't intend to part with you till Night. You may reaſonably imagine that I could employ my Time better; but if you had really loved me, I had not given you this Invitation. I cannot mortify you more ſucceſsfully, than by allowing you ſo much Time to aſk my Pardon. Be ſure not to diſappoint me, unleſs you intend to make it a very ſerious Affair.

LETTER XXXV.

YOU have ſucceeded in your Law-ſuit, and at the ſame time have gain'd a Rival: Can there be ſo happy a Man in the World as yourſelf? I omit the Gallantries of your Advocate, as well as your Obliga-

tions

tions to me: But I have perform'd Wonders with your Judges. Could yon ever have imagined, that the old, consumptive, asthmatic, and Palsy-shaking Marquis of * * * should ever take it into his Head to be my Lover, and catch the Opportunity of your Absence, to make me a formal Declaration of his Passion. He began his Suit with an extraordinary Present of Sweetmeats, which are the usual Lure of these venerable Seducers. This engaging Present was accompanied with a Letter, a thousand times more insipid, if possible, than all his Confectionary. Yesterday he favour'd us with his Company at Dinner, and, when that was over, found Means to disengage himself from my Husband, and came directly to my Apartment, where he knew I was alone; with a full Persuasion that I should prove an easy Conquest to so amiable a Person as himself. He approached me with a trembling Pace, that was more the Effect of his Age, than of any Timidity; and, clasping my Hand in his, was pleased to compliment it with a Kiss. I began to be offended at this Politeness; but as his Lordship took it for granted, that a particular Account of his former Conquests would dispose me to be more favourable to him, he named at least twenty Ladies of the old Court, who had been sensible of his Merit: He

He gave me as many ancient Receipts, very proper to warm the Imagination, and breath'd out, at leaſt, the ſame Number of Sighs. But, finding that he derived no Advantage from all the Pains he took, he threw himſelf at my Feet, proteſting that I had baniſhed every other Beauty from his Heart; that Conqueſt was inſeparable from my charming Eyes, whoſe Beams had rekindled thoſe Flames in his Soul which Decorum diſſuaded him from cheriſhing, much more than Nature. He added, that he had ſighed for three Months paſt, without daring to diſcloſe to me the Cauſe of his Anguiſh; that he was apprehenſive of the Ridicule an amorous Man draws upon himſelf, when he has ſurvived that youthful Part of Life, which makes ſuch Impreſſions pardonable; but that I had made him incapable of receiving any Benefit from that Conſideration: He concluded with intreating me to pity his Sufferings; and, to induce my Compliance, aſſured me that he was the diſcreeteſt Perſon of his whole Sex. As yet, I had not utter'd one Word, and he already preſumed, from my Silence, that I had no Intention to be inſenſible; when upon the Cloſe of his Harangue I happened to caſt my Eyes upon him, and immediately burſt into the moſt hearty Fit of Laughter that ever eſcaped me. Nothing could be ſo diverting, as to ſee this trembling old Gentleman on his Knees, gently graſping one of my Hands, while his hook'd Stick lay at my Feet, as a Tribute paid to me by his Paſſion; his twinkling Eyes half overſhadow'd with the Growth of his Brows, and his Lips embarraſs'd with the abſurdeſt Stammer that ever afflicted a Lover. The more he enlarged upon his Paſſion, the leſs was I able to contain my Mirth. He then began to be diſpleaſed, and I was encreaſing my Diverſion at his Expence; when my Huſband unexpectedly came into the Apartment. The Moment the old Marquis beheld him, he made very ſurprizing Endeavours to riſe, but was not able to recover himſelf from his unlucky Situation. Ha! my perfidious Friend, cried the Marquis my Huſband, I can gueſs at the Converſation you have had with my Spouſe: Aſſiſt him with your Hand, Madam, continued he, addreſſing himſelf to me, don't you ſee that his Rheumatiſm will confine him at your Feet till to-morrow Morning! Let me adviſe you, my Lord, ſaid he to my reverend Lover, not to make any more Addreſſes to that Lady; ſhe is more perverſe, if poſſible, than yourſelf; and you may not always happen to find me in the gay Diſpoſition I diſcover at preſent; for which Reaſon it will be proper to ſeparate

for

for this time. The old Marquis paid his Reſpects to me in the utmoſt Confuſion, and retired. For my part, I am very ſorry he is not worth my playing you a ſmall piece of Inconſtancy; but I comfort myſelf with the Hopes that a more inviting Opportunity may happen to offer; for I am certain I have it in my Power to avenge myſelf on your Coldneſs, and even your Inconſtancy. The Perfidy of Lovers only furniſhes fine Women with a Pretext for new Paſſions.

LETTER XXXVI.

WITH how much Coldneſs do you complain of my Abſence! When your Heart can only ſupply you with inanimate Expreſſions, why don't you borrow Life from your Imagination? Could you but be ſenſible of the Manner in which you promiſe me an eternal Paſſion, you would bluſh at your calm Deſcription of thoſe Impreſſions that ought to inſpire you with all the Warmth of Rapture. You entertain me with nothing but Wit, and have ſent me the moſt agreeable Letter in the World: You relate to me a Variety of pleaſing Paſſages; but of what Conſequence to me, are the Adventures that occur at *Paris!* I ſay, to me, who am ſollicitous to know nothing but the true State of your Heart! You acquaint me that you are well, which to me was the only pleafing Particular in all your Letter: But you have not once difcovered the leaft Inquietude for my Welfare. Do you even complain of your tedious Abfence from me; and can you poffibly be fo gay, when you no longer behold me? Is it to infult me then, that you write with fo much fhining Wit? Is it thus that you requite my melancholy mufing Hours; and have you no other Confolation to offer me in my afflicted Solitude? You tell me, indeed, that you love me; but ah! 'tis in fuch a languid Strain —— You have no Senfibility of the Paffion you would exprefs! Shall I never, then, be certain that I poffefs your Heart; and can Abfence contribute to your Repofe, when to real Lovers it proves fo infupportable a Pang? How juftly may I reproach you for loving me with fo much Moderation! What exquifite Joys do you lofe by your Infenfibility! Even now, when I am confcious of all your Indifference, I enjoy a Felicity to which you will be an eternal Stranger. I am fenfible, at leaft, that I live, and have the Satisfaction, Ingrate as you are, to live for you alone. I recollect all our paft Delights; and that dear Remembrance infpires me with Joys, infinitely fuperior to any you can poffibly experience in in the moſt tender Moments. My Slumbers are more animated than your Heart has ever been in the full Vivacity of its Tranſports; and when even your Coldneſs drives me to Deſperation, I have a ſecret Pleaſure to conſider that your Love has no Competition with the Warmth of mine; but my Anguiſh would ſoon be fatal to me, ſhould you entirely ceaſe to love me. Why do I incommode you with theſe Reproaches, does not your Indifference render you ſufficiently miſerable? I have an Inclination to believe, that were you capable of loving more, all your Tranſports would be devoted to me; and it is impoſſible for me to ſuppreſs the Satisfaction I enjoy, when I would perſuade myſelf that I am the only Object of your Paſſion.——I the only Object of your Paſſion! How could I entertain that ſeducing Hope! If you lov'd none but me, you would, long before now, have abandon'd a Place, where I am no more preſented to your View, and where every Object around you ought to awaken in your Soul, the cruel Idea of the Felicity you no longer enjoy: You would fly with Deteſtation from every Snare that ſeduces you to be unfaithful to me. But alas! I already know you too well! Gay Scenes of Pleaſure are your only Purſuit; and whenever they riſe before you, you forget that you are beloved beyond Expreſſion; and that there is an unfortunate Perſon in the World, who only lives for you, and has no Happineſs but what flows from the Tenderneſs with which you once have treated her. But ah! how killing is that Reflection! and how vainly do I endeavour to fix my Tranquillity on the Proteſtations you have made me! I am in perpetual Dread of your Inconſtancy: I am rack'd with Jealouſy, without beholding the fatal Object; and my Heart is as much tormented as if ſhe was placed in my full View. The Paſſion with which you have inflamed my Soul, is for ever preſenting you to my Imagination; but amidſt the Delight I derive from your Remembrance, I am unable to perſuade myſelf that you continue to be conſtant. O! tell me, am I then ſo happy as to deceive myſelf? Be ſo generous as to eaſe me of the Agonies I now feel, and preſerve me from thoſe I yet dread. I am ſufficiently tortured by this cruel Separation from you; and for the Completion of my Misfortunes, I know not when I ſhall be ſo happy as to leave this Place. My Mother's Indiſpoſition detains me from you, and my Huſband orders me to continue here, though I know not why. Can you count, like me, the diſmal Days of our Abſence? Do you remember, that 'tis now a Month ſince I laſt

laſt beheld you? Do you conſider, that I muſt ſtill live fifteen Days, without ſeeing you (would to Heaven I had no other Calamity to fear!) and that I may poſſibly not hear from you in all that tedious Space? Adieu, my charming Count! In what manner ſoever you may be diſpoſed to treat me, I am ſenſible that I ſhall love you while I live. But will this Aſſurance be ſo ſatiſfactory to you, as to make you undeſirous of kindling a Paſſion in any other Breaſt? Why am I not permitted to write to you any longer! Were it not for the Impatience of the Poſt, I believe I ſhould never finiſh this Letter: But my Letters are diſagreeable, and I fear you will hardly prevail on yourſelf to read them to the End. Did I love as languidly as you, they would, if poſſible, be ſhorter than yours, tho' even theſe in your preſent Strain of Indifference are much too long. Adieu.

LETTER XXXVII.

WHO could have thought that ſuch a ſolemn Prude as Lady *** ſhould prevail upon her rigid Virtue, to make you the warmeſt Declaration that was ever known? What a Scene of Diverſion has ſhe created me, and how much am I oblig'd

to

to you, for affording me ſuch an uncommon Pleaſure! What a formal Collection of Languors, Anxieties and Impertinence is her Letter! The Infantas of former Days expreſſed themſelves, in ſuch a Strain, to their impatient Knights: And ſince you can ſacrifice ſuch a fine Adventure to me, I ought to return you my ſincere Acknowledgments; but will you permit me to make my own Reflections on the Motives that inclin'd you to ſuch a Sacrifice? You are an Enemy to all Uneaſineſs; and the refined Sentiments ſhe was preparing for your conſtant Entertainment, would not have amuſed you ſo much as my Indiſcretions. You grew perſuaded that you ſhould hear long Diſſertations on the Merit of Conſtancy, and that ſhe would be eternally repreſenting to you the Pleaſure that a Paſſion, purified from Vice, diffuſes into a delicate Soul: You expected to be told, that a Lover ſhould never preſume to entertain the leaſt Hope; and muſt even think it criminal to improve the happy Moment. Theſe were all the Pleaſures you imagin'd would ariſe to you, from a Commerce with her: But let me adviſe you to undeceive yourſelf; thoſe Women who appear ſo extremely rigid, are not more incapable of Deſires than the reſt of their Sex; and this Lady, by reading Romances, is but too well inſtructed in the Neceſ-

Neceſſity of abridging them. You would not have ſuffer'd under her Empire ſo much as you imagin'd; and her Impatience, by its Prevention of yours, would not have permitted you to continue one Day in the leaſt Doubt of a perfect Felicity. How meritorious is your Goodneſs on this Occaſion! You might have diſguiſed your Infidelity to me, in ſuch an Amour, with ſo much Eaſe, that I ſhould never have ſuſpected your Proceeding. How could you poſſibly reſiſt the Charm of ranking this Lady in the Number of your Conqueſts? Each Day produces Events which ſurprize me; but, without diminiſhing the Merit of your Sacrifice, I muſt confeſs I never entertain'd the leaſt Apprehenſions of ſuch a Rival; and if you had really loved her, I ſhould have been ſufficiently avenged on your Perfidy, by the inglorious Shame you would ſoon have been fated to ſuſtain. Congratulate yourſelf, then, for your Inſenſibility of her Endeavours to pleaſe you, and reſt perſuaded that I have received ſo much Satisfaction from this Inſtance of your Fidelity, that, were it poſſible for me, I would love you more than I do at preſent. But I have the Misfortune, amidſt ſo many delightful Circumſtances, to be affected with a mortal Inquietude; tho' I believe it will receive ſome Mitigation, when I acquaint

you

you with the Cauſe. I think I have lately obſerved, that my Huſband no longer entertains a Paſſion for your Couſin. The Diſcontinuance of his frequent Viſits to her; the Abatement of his Impatience; the Increaſe of his Endearments to me; his artful Detractions, whenever ſhe is the Subject of his Diſcourſe; his new Diſlike of ſquare Arms and ſhort Noſes; his long Continuance at home; his Sollicitude to pleaſe me; his Converſations on the Hurry of the World, and the Inconſtancy of Women; the Careſſes I receive from him, and his Confuſion whenever he beholds me, are Circumſtances that make me fear he has an Inclination to renew a favourable Intercourſe with me. I may poſſibly be alarm'd without any juſt Reaſon; but I am perfectly acquainted with his Caprice: It muſt always be indulged; and perhaps I am now ſo unfortunate as to be made its Object. Adieu: I will ſee you to-day, at the Place you already know. Love me, my dear Count; love me, I intreat you, for ever! Your Tenderneſs will enable me to ſuſtain the ſharpeſt Calamities; and, when I am in your Preſence, I am no longer ſenſible of their Severity.

BILLET.

*Lady***, in compliance with your Desires, makes you an Offer of her House, and you have her Permission to perform the Honours of it to-morrow, since that happens to be your Resolution.* St. Far*** *will accompany you; and would to Heaven, my Conduct were to be survey'd by Spectators more rigid than those who are then to be present; and that they would prove as incommodious to me, as I fear they will be otherwise! I am preparing to revisit those Places where I gave you the first Instances of my Weakness; and I am but too sensible of those which you still intend to require from me. Your Letter glows with inchanting Love; I am conscious of your Transports, and entirely diffident of myself. Why do you remind me of those Moments which I would consign to eternal Oblivion! Can you entertain your Imagination with no other Ideas? What a Number of Reproaches have I in reserve for you; and how delighted should I be to come to a Disagreement with you, were I not apprehensive of the Reconciliation that would ensue.*

LET-

LETTER XXXVIII.

I Am preparing to quarrel with you in the moſt improbable and ridiculous manner that can poſſibly be imagined; but I am in a very ill Humour to-day, and you muſt ſubmit to ſuffer the Effects of my Caprice. You ſee that I anticipate you in your own Deſigns; and, as I begin with an Acknowledgment of my Folly, I ſuppoſe I ſhall diſcover as little Diſcretion thro' the whole Courſe of this Letter. I was not with the Dutcheſs yeſterday; but Lady *** made her Grace a Viſit. This Lady, as you muſt needs be ſenſible, is ſo extremely fond of Love, that when ſhe has not Time to ingage in it herſelf, ſhe is ſure to make it the Subject of her Converſation. She deſired to know your Sentiments of Conſtancy, and you very frankly anſwer'd her, that nothing in Nature could be more diſagreeable. This Opinion of yours was conteſted by the Company; but that they might not ſuppoſe you defended your Notion out of mere Obſtinacy, you was pleaſed to aſſure them, that you yourſelf had experienced Conſtancy to be a very incommodious and unpleaſing Quality; and, to remove all manner of Doubt, you related ſeveral Adventures wherein you had formerly been engaged.

It

It ſeems, you could hardly contain the Satisfaction you enjoy'd, in deſcribing the Pleaſure of acting a perfidious Part; and you thanked Heaven, that your Inconſtancy had never been anticipated by the Falſhood of any Woman you ever convers'd with. You may ſuppoſe me to be piqued at this Confeſſion of yours; and indeed I began to imagine I ſhould find it very pleaſant to practiſe a little Inconſtancy myſelf; but at laſt I grew ſo ridiculous, as to believe it would be more agreeable to experience it from you. This, indeed, is taking a Part upon one's ſelf that ſeems a little melancholy; but then, one has the Pleaſure of being pitied in ſuch a Condition, and of hearing one's ſelf recommended, as a rare Example to a degenerate Age; which indeed may ſeem to be ſome Compenſation for what one loſes in other Particulars. But though I am perſuaded you had then an Inclination to indulge your Wit, at the Expence of your Sincerity; yet I am not at all ſatisfied to hear you urge ſuch little Pieces of Hiſtory (and which perhaps may be very true) in Vindication of an Opinion that diſpleaſes me; and, I think, in your preſent Situation, you ought not to ſuppoſe there was ever any ſuch thing as Inconſtancy in the World. That you love me, I am infallibly ſure; nay, I am convinced you adore me, in ſpight of all your Indolence: But if that Adoration had not been mutual, what would have been your Condition? I may improve this Pretext, and tell you, in my Juſtification, that ſince you derive ſo much Pleaſure from Inconſtancy, you muſt certainly have an Inclination to practiſe it: But I find, to my Misfortune, that the Idea of loving you with the ſofteſt Sincerity, is ſtill predominant in my Soul; for which reaſon I flatter myſelf, that while I am under the Influence of ſuch a Thought, you will have the Generoſity to be conſtant to my Paſſion. This is ſuch a cruel Expectation, that I begin to tremble for you: But I am diſpoſed to be malicious; and, to compleat your Mortification, I lay my Commands upon you, to paſs the Day with me; for I have a Curioſity to know if you have Preſumption enough to juſtify, in my Preſence, the Opinion you maintained yeſterday. Adieu: This is all I have to offer to you at preſent, and, I muſt confeſs, it was not ſo material, as to make it neceſſary for me to write ſuch a long Letter: But I found myſelf chagrin'd; and took up my Pen before I had fully determined myſelf as to my laſt Command. I thought it would not be decent to expoſe you too ſuddenly; and though I am piqued againſt you, it is not worth my giving myſelf the Trouble to morti-

mortify you in a ſerious manner; and yet, I muſt confeſs, I have ſome Inclination to it. My whole Letter is a Collection of incoherent Thoughts; and you now ſee the Reaſon of my writing ſo many inſignificant Particulars, which I ſhould never have ſent to you, if I had been guided by Diſcretion: But you have ſo much Time upon your Hands, that I have no occaſion to reproach myſelf, for ſupplying you with a little Employment, and you will find ſome, in reading this Letter, whether it be to the purpoſe or not. I ought, and indeed intended to quarrel with you; but, have I put that Deſign in Execution? What, in the Name of Heaven, can I never conclude! Adieu; I am determin'd to love you for ever.

LETTER XXXIX.

MAKE no Scruple to confeſs that I am very amiable, and that, in ſpight of your frequent Inclinations to change, my Charms ſtill detain you in their captivating Chains. You may take it for granted that your Liberty is irrecoverable; one Glance from me, is ſufficient to deſtroy all the Reſolutions you can form in my Diſfavour; and the Moment you behold me, you blush to think you could ever have the least Intention to be inconstant. Have you not Reason, my dear Count, to be confused at such a Thought? Do we know with whom we engage, when we are in pursuit of new Conquests? Can the tormenting Uncertainty of our Ability to please, and the painful Endeavours to penetrate into the Disposition of an unknown Heart, be productive of any Joys like those we experience, when we read the soft Sentiments of a Heart we know to be our entire Property? Can you make any Discovery in mine, which does not contribute to your Felicity? Your dear Image resides there without a Competitor, and every Thought it forms, has you for its charming Object. How sedulous is it, to exclude all other Ideas; but, with what a Heaven of Joy is it always elated, when it presents you with its unblemished Tenderness, and deludes itself into a Belief of mutual Returns! What Proofs of undissembled Love have I not already afforded you; and how mortifying is my Incapacity, to oblige you with any which you have not experienced before! Believe me, my dearest Count, my Passion has no Bounds: Ah! why then should my Manner of disclosing it be confin'd to any limitations! Can you possibly

poſſibly reſolve to change? What Pleaſure can you promiſe yourſelf from ſuch an Intention, unleſs it be the untimely Death of one who loves you to Adoration?

You had, yeſterday, the Cruelty to aſſure me, that it might be poſſible to extinguiſh your Paſſion; and can you really entertain ſuch an Inclination? Have I ever given you a juſt Cauſe to treat me with ſo much Barbarity? You tell me, I yield to your Tranſports with Reluctance; but alas! you turn your Eyes from mine, when you injure me with that unkind Accuſation. Ah me! my Heart can teſtify that I have been affected with too much Senſibility! Can Love only conſiſt in the Gratification of warm Deſires: Are there no Moments, wherein the Virtue of a Lady may interpoſe between the Softneſs of her Soul, and the Ardours of her Lover; and is all her Conduct to be one continued Scene of Compliance? But I diſcover the Sentiments by which you are influenced; you have an Inclination to wear out your Paſſion; and, can I be ſuch a fatal Enemy to my Happineſs, as to aid you in that Intention? Shall I conſent to loſe you for ever, when I am ſenſible that each Day endears you to me, more than the laſt? I am not ignorant of the Effects produced in Love, by a Flow of conſtant Pleaſures: The Novelty of their first Appearance disposes us to taste them with Transport; and the Desires, inflamed by a long Resistance, furnish them with Charms, that alas! are soon sated to lose their Attractions. Habit, perhaps, and the Sallies of Fancy, may keep alive a faint Inclination to them, when they no longer touch the Heart; but what would become of me, were I once to behold you in such a Disposition; and from whom could I expect Relief, should I be reduced to lament your Indifference, even in those Moments of Love which you are now so perpetually impatient to claim! But, I believe, my best Expedient to escape that Calamity, will be to awaken your Complaints of my Coldness. I have some Inclination to make you renew your first Ardours, and to have the Pleasure of seeing you repeat all the Assiduities that should be previous to your Conquest of my Heart. I begin to think those are the only Means left me, to rekindle your Passion; but do you still continue to esteem me worthy to be lov'd? I had determin'd not to entertain one soft Desire all this Day; but I happen'd accidentally to cast my Eyes on my Glass, and found myself so very amiable, that I had no Power to persist in my Resolution. Adieu: I return you my Acknowledgments for your Letter; you never writ so many tender Things to me before;

fore; and you may come whenever you please, to gather their Fruits. I have a thousand Satisfactions to impart to you, with relation to the Passages of yesterday, and the Impertinencies that escaped me, at the Conclusion of this Letter; but I never know what I write, when I am confessing that I love you.

LETTER XL.

I Am at a loss to know when your Follies will end, or when I shall cease to indulge them. I begin to be weary of the one, and don't find myself disposed to be much longer a Dupe to the other. From the first Moment we began to love, or rather, from the first Moment I began to love you, I never experienced so much Torment as you have given me for these four Days past; nor did you ever entertain such irrational Thoughts till now. Of what Consequence is it to you, to know whether I have been sensible of a Passion for any one, before I lov'd you? What Prerogative had you over my Heart, before I knew there was such a Person in the World as yourself? Did I imagine, when I first prevail'd upon myself to love you, that you had disregarded all my Sex to the very Moment you

you conceived a Paſſion for me? But, taking it for granted that you have formerly been devoted to another Object, why ſhould I be diſquieted at your Conduct in that particular, if the Ardours you now profeſs for me, be really ſincere? I confeſs, it would have been not a little pleaſing to me, to have kindled the firſt Deſires in your Breaſt: But, tho' I was very young when I became acquainted with you, it was then a conſiderable time ſince your firſt Paſſion had been extinguiſhed; and could I, with any Juſtice, conſider your Indulgence of it as a Crime? But had I been indiſcreet enough to have given you any Intimations of ſo peculiar a Jealouſy, would not your Anſwer have been, Could I poſſibly divine, Madam, that you was reſerved for me; and ſhould I decline the Conqueſts that preſented themſelves all around me, to render myſelf more deſerving of a Lady, to whom I was then an abſolute Stranger? And now, my dear fanciful Count, I ſhall offer you the very Reply you ought to receive from me. Had I been in the Situation wherein you are pleaſed to ſuppoſe me, it was impoſſible for me to preſage that I ſhould, one day, be ſo happy as to receive the Homage of Count * * *, and be delighted with it at the ſame time: But, if any Gentleman before him had tender'd his Addreſſes to me, in a Manner that

I then

I then thought agreeable, I ſhould have been guilty of no Infidelity to Count * * *, had I approv'd of the Perſon who ſighed for me at that time. Be ſo ingenuous then as to acknowledge, that you are only ſtudious for a Pretext to juſtify the Inconſtancy with which you are preparing to treat me, tho' I muſt aſſure you, I am too malicious to afford you that Advantage againſt me. You can no longer ſupport the Diſſatisfaction that is ſo incommodious to you; and this is the only Source of all the Ruptures you attempt with me. You demand from me, the ſincere Particulars of my Life, and the exact State of my Heart, before and ſince I had any Knowledge of you; and you expect to be acquainted with all the Impreſſions you have created in my Soul. Your Intention, in this Proceeding, is only to furniſh yourſelf with Reaſons to deſpiſe me, or at leaſt to have an Opportunity of paying a Compliment to your own Vanity. I ought therefore to deny you the Gratification you deſire, were I not perſuaded that I ſhould thereby confirm you in your Error: And though you may poſſibly be not diſpoſed to credit the Circumſtances I ſhall relate, yet I have the Satisfaction to conſider that they will not be falſified by your Incredulity. I am obliged to you for the Hiſtory you offer me of your own Life; but

but I am not a Perſon of much Curioſity. Beſides, it may be ſuch another Fiction as that which I am now preparing to give you, for the Puniſhment of your Extravagancies; and there are a thouſand Particulars in ſuch a delicate Subject, that had better be concealed than diſcloſed. However, I begin thus:

Repreſent to yourſelf that State of Life, in which young Perſons of my Sex begin to be ſenſible they ought to pleaſe, and are deſirous of ſucceeding; and then be ſo good as to aſſure yourſelf, that I had no ſuch Perception, and that I was an equal Stranger to thoſe Inclinations. The Advantage of an Education in the polite World, with the Aid of ſome Reaſon, a conſiderable Share of neceſſary Pride, and a Series of good Inſtructions, ſufficiently diſcloſed to me the Abſurdities of Mankind. I beheld them without the leaſt Satisfaction, and found myſelf diſguſted at their Converſation. The youthful Part of the Sex ſeem'd to me, a Set of Impertinents, and the Men in Years were vicious and incommoding. I conſider'd their Commerce with the Women, and generally made ſuch Diſcoveries as render'd them the Objects of my Diffidence, or Averſion.

here was one Gentleman, indeed, and I ſhall immediately name him, leſt my Silence ſhould infect you with a new Vein of Jea-

Jealousy. This one Gentleman, then, was the Marquis ***, who, as you are sensible, is now dead; and he, I confess, had acquired the Art to please me. The exact and easy Politeness which graced every Part of his Behaviour; an unaffected Turn of Wit, altogether uncommon in such an early Bloom of Youth; his Assiduities to me, and his sincere and artless Manner of acquainting me with his Passion, inspir'd me with pleasing Inclinations in his favour: But the Restrictions to which my State of Life obliged me to conform, and the Counsels I derived from my Reason, prevented me from disclosing to him, the Progress he had made in my Heart. While I was under the Influence of these Dispositions, I was married, contrary to my Inclinations; and yet I never opposed the Will of those who were pleased to make that Choice for me. The Marquis was inconsolable upon this Occasion, and my Inquietudes were no-way inferior to his: But, as I suffer'd myself to be guided by Virtue, I began to surmount them by degrees. My Husband treated me in a very tender Manner; but, as I was prepossess'd with another Passion, which, by its Calamities, was endeared to me the more, I received the Testimonies of his Affection with a cold Indifference. The Marquis took a Resolution to travel, and his Absence gave me an Opportunity

portunity to be more attentive to the Merit of my Husband. I endeavoured to suppress every criminal Sigh, and at last began to render my Duty a Pleasure. The Change which was then wrought in my Soul, delighted me beyond Expression: I was sensible that I loved, and my Joy was the greater, as I was conscious that I entertain'd a Passion for which I had no Reason to reproach myself.

I passed two Years in this State of Tranquillity: I lov'd the Marquis my Husband, and was mutually belov'd by him: I enjoy'd all the Liberty I could possibly desire, and those Moments which were not filled up by my Love, I devoted to Reading and Music, as well as to all other Attentions which amuse, at the same time that they instruct. But this happy State was of no long Continuance; my Husband gave a Loose to his Inconstancy, and his Indifference would have disclos'd it to me, tho' the World had been entirely silent on that Subject. This Discovery overwhelmed me with Despair; my Tears flowed without Intermission; I sigh'd, and utter'd my Anguish to him, in gentle Expostulations, for the Torments he caused me to sustain; but all those Sighs and Expostulations were unavailing. In vain did I employ the most obliging Endeavours to reclaim him: His

Indif-

Indifference to me grew daily more conſpicuous; from Coldneſs he proceeded to Contempt, and he heightened that Contempt into Barbarity. I have a Spirit capable of Reſentment, and never ſuffer any one to injure me with Impunity. I was ſo indefatigable to extinguiſh my Paſſion, and his Conduct ſupplied me with ſuch unanſwerable Reaſons for that Proceeding, that I at laſt, ſucceeded in my Attempt. This fatal Proof of the perfidious Diſpoſition of Mankind, confirm'd me more than ever, in the Horror I had entertain'd for the Sex. You may eaſily ſuppoſe, that I was not ſollicitous to acquire a Lover; on the contrary, I had ſo habituated myſelf to Inſenſibility, that all the ſeducing Language of thoſe who were pleaſed to think me amiable, contributed but the more to my Diſquiet. I had too little Conſideration for my Huſband, even to condeſcend to avenge myſelf on his Baſeneſs; and indeed, the Vengeance that was then offer'd me, was altogether as diſagreeable to me as the Avengers themſelves; and ſuch was then my Inſenſibility, that I needed not the Dictates of Duty, to reſtrain my Inclinations. I now began to be charmed with the Tranquillity that was reinſtated in my Soul: I was ſo happy as not to hate my Huſband; I amuſed myſelf with his repeated Inconſtancies, and lived in perfect

Felicity, when at laſt, the Marquis himſelf introduced you into my Apartment. The Moment I beheld you, I found myſelf affected with unuſual Impreſſions; your Converſation was extremely pleaſing to me, and I was ſoon ſenſible that you lov'd me. It was then indeed, that all my Virtue was neceſſary to make me reſolve to be offended at your Paſſion: But alas! I was unable to accompliſh that Reſolution, and you yourſelf are conſcious that I had no ſuch Power. At firſt, I was ſo unhappy as to flatter myſelf, that the Change I experienced in my Diſpoſition, was no more than a weak and tranſient Impreſſion you had created in my Soul; I reſigned myſelf too much to that Imagination: I even raillied you for your Paſſion, and you derived ſufficient Advantages from that Proceeding. You afterwards writ to me, and I imagined that the Severity of my Anſwer would diſcourage you from tormenting me any more. But I might poſſibly expreſs my Intentions very imperfectly; you continued to write to me, and I, to inſpire you with too good an Opinion of myſelf, aſſured you ſo often by my Letters that I did not love you, that I at laſt grew weary of thoſe Repetitions, and writ to you that I really lov'd you. This you have experienced, Ingrate as you are! This I am daily confirming to you by new Proofs; but, as as you treat my Paſſion with Contempt, I begin to repent of thoſe Indiſcretions, which your Indifference to me, repreſents in ſuch a criminal Light, that I wiſh they had always been as viſible to me as they are now. My Repentance increaſes every Day, and I hope it will prove ſo effectual at laſt, that I ſhall entirely ceaſe to love you. Adieu, my Lord; theſe are all the Particulars I had to relate, and perhaps they may be more than you had any Inclination to know.

BILLET.

You could not have invited me to a Party of Pleaſure, in the Country, at a more unſeaſonable Time; I am ſo much indiſpoſed, that I have not cloſed my Eyes laſt Night; and what convinces me that I am extremely ill is, that my Thoughts have not been too much employed on you: In ſhort, I find myſelf ſo very weak and indolent, that I am ſurprized I have any Spirits left; and my Indiſpoſition is the more afflictive to me, becauſe I am perſuaded it will create ſome Variance between us. I can only ſay, in my own Defence, that I had no Inclination to be out of order. You are ſenſible that I was extremely chearful yeſterday, and perhaps that may have occaſioned the Melancholy which has ſeized me to-day. You may ſuppoſe then, that I am in *an excellent Disposition for the Country. I think the Weather perfectly dismal; my Horses are all sick, and my Coachman is already drunk. I am determin'd not to accompany Lady*** in her Coach.* St. Far*** *is always with her, and I have Reason to fear the World will say I have an Affection for him. It would be still worse to accept of your Coach, and therefore you may conclude that it is impossible for me to be one of the Party. However, you may favour me with a Visit, if that will amuse you. Perhaps I may have Company; but if we should happen to be alone, we will converse on some agreeable Subject or other: We will talk of Love, I mean in a* Platonic *Strain; or, if you please, we will divert ourselves at Cards; and this is all I can do for you, with any manner of Conscience.*

LETTER XLI.

AH my dearest Count! I am now fated to sustain the greatest of all Calamities, and we shall soon be the most unfortunate Persons in the World! My Presages, alas! were but too well founded; but, not to keep you in Suspense, my Husband no longer loves your Cousin. He has thrown himself at my Feet, and intreated me me to pardon his Indiſcretions; he even burſt into Tears, and utter'd the moſt ſolemn Proteſtations that I ſhould, for ever, be the only Object of his Paſſion: He then acquainted me, that he intended to paſs the whole Summer with me in *Britany*. Ah! how ſhall I evade this fatal Departure! Can I poſſibly abandon all Regard to my Reputation? What will my Family think, ſhould I refuſe to accompany him; and, what Conſtructions will he paſs on my Diſinclination to obey him! How inſupportable will be my Misfortune, ſhould he diſcover the Cauſe of my Indifference! Ah! my dear Count, we muſt now be ſeparated for ever! You have no Conception of thoſe violent Emotions with which he is agitated in his Reſentment: An eternal Exile will be the leaſt of my Sufferings. To what a Scene of Miſery am I reſerved; and where ſhall I fly to a Reſource that can protect me from his cruel Reſolution! My Mother, who has been a Witneſs to my Tears, and is acquainted with all his Infidelities; that dear Parent, whoſe Conſolation I formerly ſhar'd, is now diſpos'd to conſider this Reconciliation as the moſt fortunate Event that could happen in my Favour, and will join her Perſecutions to thoſe I ſhall ſuſtain from my Huſband, ſhould I refuſe to comply with his Intentions. I ſhall be cenſured and forſaken, if I ſeem averſe to our Departure; and I ſhall die with Deſpair, if I am compelled to be ſeparated from the only Perſon who can reconcile me to Life. I ſhall be tormented, without ceaſing, by my Huſband's Paſſion, and at the ſame time, muſt prove a fatal Prey to my own. I ſhall either be betray'd by my inconſolable Sorrows, or tortur'd to Diſtraction, by my vain Endeavours to ſuppreſs them. I ſhall be urged each Moment, to unfold the Cauſe of my Afflictions, and riſing Sighs will be my only Reply; till at laſt, I ſhall be expoſed to all the fatal Effects that Jealouſy is capable of producing. But, I ſhould, even then, be happy, amidſt all the Calamities I foreſee, could I perſuade myſelf that I ſhall be for ever dear to your Remembrance. If you can be ſo generous as not to abandon an unfortunate Creature, whoſe Paſſion for you; renders her ſo wretched, there are no Torments, which my Certainty of being lov'd by you, will not enable me to ſupport with Joy! I ſhall receive too delightful a Recompence for my Woes, if you condeſcend to ſhare them. Adieu. Viſit the Dutcheſs, this Evening, that I may ſee you, and once more enjoy the only Felicity my Misfortunes have left me.

The End of the Firſt Part.

LETTERS FROM The Marchioneſs de *M****, TO Count de *R****.

LETTER XLII.

LET us no more, my dear Count, be rack'd with the Fears of a Separation; the ſame Caprice which prompted my Huſband to a Reconciliation with me, has once more conſign'd him to his ancient Chains, and your Couſin is ſtill triumphant. Do you believe this Event is as pleaſing to her as it proves to me? I am now convinced that his Jealouſy of that Lady, created us all our Alarms; and he pretended to be enamour'd of me, with no other View than that ſhe might imagine he was cured of his Paſſion for her. My Mother

ther is ſo aſtoniſhed at this ſudden Change, and reſents the Indignity with which he treats me, to ſuch a Degree, that, without conſidering the Tendency of her Expreſſions, ſhe has read me ſuch Lectures, as would not appear to her very amiable in Practice. As to the Marquis, he hardly remembers any of his late Proteſtations and penitent Speeches, but proceeds in his uſual Track, tho' with a little more Circumſpection than formerly. 'Tis true, he is relapſed into ſome Part of that Behaviour which I uſed to repreſent by the Name of Coldneſs: But, what Reaſon have I to regard the Manner in which he lives with me, provided he ceaſes to torment me. Let it be our Care, my dear Count, to perſiſt in our mutual Paſſion; and ſince our Fears of an eternal Separation are over, let our Ardours awaken into a new Vivacity. The Alarms I have lately ſuſtained, were altogether ſuperfluous to me; my Heart would have perſiſted in its fond Attachment to you, without their officious Aid, but yours would have ſoon been languid, in the continued Serenity of Repoſe. I am obliged to the Marquis, for thoſe inchanting Inſtances of your Paſſion, which you have lately afforded me. I have ſeen you in thoſe Emotions of which I never, till now, could believe you capable. I have beheld your Eyes moiſten'd with the

firſt

firſt Tears they ever ſhed for me, and indeed they were an Offering which I little expected from you. I am ſenſible that Love alone could excite ſuch a tender Flow: How precious to me are thoſe endearing Drops! With what Raptures of Gratitude ſhall I treaſure them in my Remembrance! Surely we were form'd for each other, and one Moment's Diſunion would be inconſiſtent with the Texture of our Souls. We ſhould grow inanimate in the leaſt Intermiſſion of our Love. Ah! what would become of me, ſhould I be fated to loſe you! Is it poſſible for me to live a Moment without you; and, may I not add, that even your Condition would be very wretched, if you no longer had me to love you? One Day, perhaps—— But, I dare not indulge that Thought; it ſhoots a chilling Tremor through my Soul, and thoſe Preſages which elude all my Endeavours to ſuppreſs them, are perpetually filling me with Terror and Confuſion. They certainly ſpring from the Circumſtances that at preſent attend me; and tho' I have been relieved from the Calamity that threaten'd me, I am unable to conquer my Apprehenſion of others. Alas! I may have many to experience ſtill! How can I be ſure, that at the very Time, when I imagine you love me with all the Warmth of a raptur'd Imagination, I ſhall have no Cauſe to dread

that

that ſudden Diſtaſte which is the uſual Effect of a long and tranquil Paſſion? Who can convince me that my Huſband, in the Courſe of his natural Inconſtancy, will not render me as unhappy hereafter, as I have lately been? Perhaps Death —— Ah! would it pleaſe Heaven that we may be ſeparated by that alone! Adieu. Be very certain that I adore you, and that nothing ſhall ever prevent me from being totally yours; no not even your Indifference.

LETTER XLIII.

ST. *Far**** had Reaſon to acquaint you in his Letter, that I was learning Philoſophy; but he ought not to have inform'd you, that I applied myſelf to that Science, to be taught the Method of extinguiſhing my Paſſion for you. As your Abſence perpetually diſquiets me, I imagin'd, the beſt Expedient to render it more ſupportable, would be to find ſome Employment for my Thoughts; and you ought to think yourſelf obliged to me, for chuſing an Amuſement of this Nature. Few Women would have had Recourſe to Logic for Conſolation, in the Abſence of a Lover; and I believe that you yourſelf would not have been guided by ſuch an Inclination, in the ſame Caſe.

Caſe. But it ſeems you are afraid that Philoſophy will furniſh me with Reſolution enough to moderate the unfortunate Paſſion I entertain for you. How admirable would it be, could it accompliſh ſuch a Miracle! But you may reſt ſatisfied, that all the Benefit I have hitherto gain'd from it, has conſiſted in a grave Attention to long and tedious Reaſonings, in which I have ſometimes been ſo abſurd as to engage; and indeed I have made ſuch a Progreſs, that if Heaven does not aſſiſt me very ſoon, I ſhall not be able to underſtand myſelf. My Maſter is the prettieſt Pedant in the World, moſt inchantingly powder'd and curl'd; and, if I am rightly inform'd, he has the Happineſs to ſpeak *Hebrew*, with all the Politeneſs imaginable. I believe, I have a little diſconcerted his Syſtem of Morality. His Ideas are all confuſed, when his Eyes are fixed on me, and he expreſſes them with more Obſcurity than he conceives them. He ſtammers out a ſet of barbarous Words, which are render'd ſtill leſs intelligible by his Glances; and, I ſhould have diſmiſſed this charming Tutor before now, if I had not expected from him a Declaration of Love, in the *Hebrew* Language, which, without doubt, muſt be extremely pathetic: I may venture to ſay, upon the whole, that my Diſlike of this Science is all the Ad-

vantage

vantage I have received from it. The Inquietude I sustain from your Absence, is far from being abated, by my Endeavours to amuse my Thoughts; and I don't find my Heart one jot the more philosophic, for all the learned Lessons I have attended to. In vain does my Reason counsel me to forget you, and all my sad Reflections have as little Effect, as salutary as they may seem. My Soul is wounded with Remorse, and I sink under the Weight of my guilty Conduct. I pursue my Passion in its fatal Career, and blush to think I ever attempted to oppose it. I know that you will one day cease to love me, and am sensible that the Bands form'd by Frailty and Caprice, are easy to be broken. This Conviction increases my Torment, instead of contributing to my Relief. I am overwhelmed with the Apprehensions of your Inconstancy; and the Idea of that Calamity I shall sustain by losing you, makes me incapable of discovering those Advantages I might possibly derive from your Infidelity. Could I recover myself from the fatal Infatuation that has seized me, my Conduct would be no longer obnoxious to my own Reproaches: But alas! I should then lose the exquisite Bliss of loving you to Idolatry; and, where could the World furnish me with a Compensation for that Loss?

Yes,

Yes, my dear Count, I love you with all the Tenderneſs that ever ſoften'd a gentle Breaſt; but I incommode you with this Declaration. You write to me with an unuſual Coldneſs; you believe that I ſhall ceaſe to be yours, and intimate to me that my Reflexions make you apprehenſive of that Event. Ah me! have you any Reaſon to impute thoſe Reflections to me as a Crime? Have they ever triumphed over my indulgent Frailty? And, if I have not been ſupplied with Virtue enough to reſiſt your Paſſion, can you believe that the remainder of it will have any Power to tear you from my Heart. You are offended at my Remorſe; but, am I capable, at all times, to prevent it from rending my Soul? From the firſt moment I lov'd you, every Inſtance of my Conduct has been a Deviation from my Duty. I ought to reproach myſelf for every Word I have written, and for every Thought I have conceived. You have no rigid Duty to combat, no ſtrict Principles to violate, in devoting yourſelf to me. You may impart to me all your Thoughts, and reſign yourſelf, without Reſerve, to the Irregularity of your Deſires. Theſe are the happy Prerogatives you claim a Right to enjoy. But can I, who have ſacrificed to your Inclinations, all I had to beſtow; can I, who live for you alone, be bleſs'd blesſ'd with any Composure of Soul, when the least Sigh that escapes me is a Crime, and when the Effects of my fatal Passion perpetually threaten me with the Loss of the only Person capable of reconciling me to my Frailty? Adieu: You will not be much amused with this Letter; my Design, however, was not to create you any Disquiet; but, at present, I can only form afflictive Ideas. Think of your Return, and revive me with your charming Presence. I would urge you to hasten your Departure, but that I know you have Orders to continue where you are: But, as painful as they prove to me, I should not be insensible of Satisfaction, were I certain that you sometimes wish to see me. Adieu: Be careful of your Welfare, I conjure you, if it be only for my sake.

LETTER XLIV

HOW much is a Woman to be pitied when she loves, and how ridiculous is a Man when he is the Object of that Passion! You may think this moral Reflection entirely misapplied, because you imagine it intended for yourself; but I am willing to undeceive you: And tho' I might, without any Injustice, repeat this Observation, with respect

respect to you and myself; yet I must own, you have no Concern in it at present. Lady *** and *St. Far* *** have lately disagreed to such an extreme, that whether it be that *St. Far* *** has no longer an Inclination to be constant, or that Lady *** has, by her ill Treatment, obliged him to turn his Attention to another Object; she seems to be persuaded that he has thrown himself into the Arms of Lady *L* ***, who, in order to favour him with a more decent Reception, has withdrawn herself from *D* *** This Piece of Inconstancy has exceedingly displeased our Friend, who may possibly have been made sensible, by this Change in *St. Far* ***, that she still has a tender Regard for him; or perhaps her offended Vanity may disguise itself with an Emotion of Love. Whatever the Case may be, she is extremely dejected at her Loss, and can't be easily persuaded that *St. Far**** enjoys much Comfort under his. She likewise finds it as difficult to conceive, how that Gentleman, who always seem'd to embrace her Sentiments, could possibly attach himself to a Woman who has made herself so remarkable, by thinking in a different Strain. The most disconsolate of these two forsaken Lovers, is *D****, who, as he has but just made his Appearance in the World, and finding it necessary to establish a Reputation, determin'd his Choice in favour of Lady ***, as the moſt proper Perſon in all *Paris*, to make a young Gentleman known. He has paid his Addreſſes to her, received a favourable Treatment, and been diſmiſſed, in the ſhort ſpace of one Month; ſo that the poor Gentleman has entirely loſt his Reputation. Lady *L**** may now think ſhe has ſome Pretenſions to paſs for a Judge of Merit, and indeed Women of her Claſs always conduct themſelves by her Taſte. *D**** might have expected very ſhining Advantages, but I doubt he will now find it difficult to attain them, ſince he has been rejected, before the firſt Month of his Services was expired. What Reflections muſt ſuch an Adventure as this, produce! All Eyes are, at preſent, fixed upon *St. Far****; a Number of curious Obſervers examine the Turn of his Shape, the Air of his Perſon, and are very induſtrious to diſcover the particular Graces that have had ſuch an Effect on Lady *L****; but all agree in general, that his Mien is extremely martial, and in complaiſance to the Lady's Taſte, they ſuppoſe him to have a great deal of Merit. For my part, I think *St. Far**** ſeems a little chagrin'd, amidſt all his Applauſe; and, indeed, Lady *** is a Miſtreſs not to be loſt without Regret. No one can be ſo well acquainted with her Value as himſelf: He ſighs

ſighs when he mentions her Name to me, and I believe would be deſirous of a Reconciliation, if he could imagine ſhe would ſtill be favourable to him, after the Rupture between them has been made ſo publick. On the other hand, Lady *** would be very willing to regain him; but how? What a Mortification would her lofty Spirit ſuſtain, were ſhe to diſcloſe her Sorrows and ſoft Paſſion to a Man who has other Engagements, and would be confirm'd in his new Choice, by ſuch a Confeſſion! And, ſhould ſhe only treat him with Indifference (which I think would be her diſcreteſt Proceeding) he may happen to forget her in Reality. How ſhall the Honour of her Sex be render'd conſiſtent with the Paſſion that torments her? It has been judged neceſſary to have Recourſe to you, in a Tranſaction of this Importance. Take an Opportunity then, to diſcourſe with your Friend, and if his Paſſion for Lady *L* *** be only a Flight of Caprice, or the Effect of Deſpair, give him Hopes of obtaining her Pardon: But, if it ſhould appear to you that he is actually in Love, let me caution you not to expoſe my Friend, nor give that Inconſtant the Pleaſure of knowing he is regretted. For if he reſolves to be ſo ungenerous as to forſake her in this manner, ſhe muſt endeavour to pique his Vanity by feigning a Paſſion for another. We have five or ſix Gallants, who are exceedingly well qualified to mortify him; and ſhe ſhall either love one of them, or give him Reaſon to believe ſo, by her Conduct. And don't you think now, that I have diſcloſed to you a Number of extraordinary Secrets? But I lay my Commands on you, not to abuſe the Confidence I repoſe in you; and I expect an immediate Anſwer. Adieu, my dear amiable Count: I ſhould be very unwilling to give Lady *** the ſame Trouble I charge myſelf with for her.

BILLET.

*My Huſband has this moment acquainted me, that I am to be favour'd with the Company of that diſagreeable Creature Lady***, who intends to paſs the reſt of the Day with me. This, you ſee, breaks all our Meaſures; but I am reſolved to diſconcert his in Revenge. He is now preparing to viſit your Couſin, with whom, I know, he has an Aſſignation. Be there at Dinner, and engage her Huſband in ſome Party of Pleaſure, which ſhe cannot poſſibly decline; and, to prevent any Excuſe ſhe may form, let him aſſume that poſitive Air which he ſo well knows how to improve. Be ſure not to give her any Opportunity of writing to her Lover; and, to compleat my Revenge,*

Revenge, I would have that Neglect seem to be an Air of Infidelity. I know you will exasperate your Cousin by this Proceeding; but you must plead your usual Inconsideration for your Excuse. As to any other Particulars, she will not be more unhappy than myself, who am not to see you all this Day. Conduct her home in the Evening, in the politest manner you can; but forbear to inquire the Cause of that ill Humour she will certainly discover: This would take up too much Time, and I shall be impatient to return you my Acknowledgments.

LETTER XLV.

HOW can you possibly imagine, that I am your Enemy? You are pleased to think I yesterday assumed an Air of Coldness and Constraint; but can you impute that to me as a Crime; and was it not incumbent on you to dissipate those Clouds that darken my Soul? Your Coldness, I am certain, was very evident all the Day. You was incapable of entertaining me with any tolerable Conversation; and whenever your Eyes were fixed upon me, they expressed a Dissatisfaction and Contempt which you had no Power to conceal. Have I offended you in any criminal Instance? There

There was a Time, when I believed a new Paſſion would render me leſs amiable in your Eyes; but I know you too well at preſent, to treat you with that Injuſtice. Your Heart is ſometimes ſo unkind, as to appear to you in its natural Diſpoſition: It is utterly incapable of any endearing Sentiments; what then would you have it expreſs? Nature has imparted to you an Inſenſibility, which Politeneſs may perhaps correct, but will never be able to extinguiſh. You were not form'd for Love; and as you are always Maſter of yourſelf, you are only the Spectator of thoſe Tranſports you create in others. I always behold you penſive, in thoſe Moments which ought to baniſh Reaſon, and which you never fail to employ in ſuch a manner as juſtly awakens mine. You diſcover an Impatience for ſuch Pleaſures as you are incapable of reliſhing; and if you ſometimes feign the Warmth of Deſires, your Intention is only to flatter your Vanity, or give Diſquiet. You can often entertain me with the moſt amiable Language, while the diſpirited Calm in your Eyes perpetually contradicts your Expreſſions. You have no Idea either of Love or its Object, but you give yourſelf the Trouble of feigning the one, that you may appear polite; and you never ſee the other, but with an Intention to divert yourſelf with a credulous unfortunate

fortunate Creature, who has resign'd herself to your Power, and whom you sacrifice with a cruel Pleasure, to your Coldness and Caprice. You are ever industrious to torment me, and practise all the Barbarities of Absence, Disdain, and groundless Jealousy. You are always insensible of gentle Impressions; and when you might render me compleatly happy, by the least Inclination to please me; when my Resignation to your Desires merits your softest Returns; and when I languish in the Expectation of that delightful Moment, which ought to bless me with your charming Presence, your Eyes disclose to me the most cruel Iudifference; and if you are attentive to any thing, 'tis to give me some new Cause for Tears. Were I to view a Rival, and could attribute your Coldness to the Passion you entertain'd for her, I believe my Tortures would not be equal to those I now sustain, in beholding your Conduct to me, so different from what it ought to be, when I have no Competitor in your Heart. Why is not my Husband disposed to be jealous? The Necessity you would then be under of eluding his Precautions, might possibly awaken you from your Indolence. Your Desires would be inflamed by the Difficulties of affording them their Gratification; and your Passion would acquire a more ingenious Vivacity, to surmount

mount the Obſtacles he might interpoſe in your Way: Your Viſits would then be more frequent; your Tenderneſs would increaſe, and I ſhould have the Happineſs of beholding you more attentive to pleaſe me. But, O Heavens! How do I diſcover my Folly, in wiſhing to experience ſo many Calamities! I muſt love you to a ſtrange Extreme indeed, to be willing to ſecure your Heart at ſuch a Price. Could all your fondeſt Affection afford me any Compenſation for the Torments I ſhould ſuſtain from my Huſband; and would it not be more advantageous for me to make ſuch an Improvement of your Indifference, as would diſengage me from a Paſſion that gives you ſo much Inquietude, and begins to be odious to myſelf? Adieu: I am offended at my Frailty, in loving you ſo tenderly, and for having ſo much Reaſon to complain of your Conduct; and ſo little Power to baniſh you from my Heart. Alas! I ſhall have but too much Time to torment myſelf with this Reproach!

LETTER XLVI.

AH my Lord! the War is now kindled in reality; but what diverts me most is, that I shall be no longer the Victim to a disobliging Temper. That lively Passion, whose Constancy was so surprizing to all who knew the Parties interested in it, is now extinguish'd. The Adventure is very agreeable, and I will entertain you with the Particulars.

The Marquis came, this Morning, into my Apartment, with a negligent and languishing Air: His Eyes discovered the Chagrin that affected him, and I could not resist my Inclination to enquire the Cause. Madam, said he, with a very mysterious Aspect, there are some Things one would wish to conceal from one's self. This dark Expression increased my Curiosity, and I intreated him to acquaint me with the Cause of his Disquietude. What would you desire me to acknowledge, replied he? the Particulars I could impart to you, are not proper for your Attention. I have already too much Reason to reproach myself for my Conduct towards you, and I should seem inclined to insult you, were I to inform you of the Affair that disquiets me. I assured him he might proceed, without any such Appre-

Apprehensions. I shall dispose myself to obey you, continued he, since you expect this Instance of my Complaisance.

You are sensible how sincerily I once loved you; and I was really persuaded, when I married you, that my Passion would be for ever incapable of Abatement. But tho' you presented me with every Attraction that could engage a Heart, I have not been able to guard mine against the Influence of an irregular Imagination, misled by the false Maxims of the World, and the perpetual Ensnarements of your Sex. Curiosity first inclin'd me to converse with them, in the Manner I did; and my Indolence was flatter'd, when I found them such easy Conquests. My Intercourse with them became habitual, and by degrees appeared extremely pleasing. My Reason, indeed, would frequently direct my Thoughts to you; I was sensible you was perfectly amiable, without making you that Confession; for I found myself intimidated by the Severity of your Dispósition; and especially, as I was conscious I had given you the justest Cause for Complaint. The Apprehension of sustaining your Reproaches, prevented me from offering you the Satisfaction I ought to have afforded you; and the Difficulty of obtaining my Pardon, sunk me into new Irregularities. You, at last, expressed your Inquietude

quietude at my Proceeding; but as I was then misguided by a violent Passion, the Returns you received from me, were unworthy of the Goodness with which you treated me. I thought at last, that you began to consider me with Indifference, and you have since confirm'd me in that Opinion. I am so impartial as to be sensible I deserve it; for which Reason I can never prevail upon myself to reproach you. But, I keep you all this while in Suspence. You are acquainted with the Passion I entertain'd for Lady * * *, and the Returns she has afforded me: I will even confess, that the Report which prevailed of her Disinclination to Cruelty, and the Catalogue of her Admirers, which I received from a particular Friend, were my strongest Inducements to make her a Declaration of Love. I fancied I should be able to fix her Heart, and must own that her Insensibility to all but myself, would have given me an exquisite Pleasure. I likewise foresaw, that her Rigours would be of no long Continuance; or if I should happen to be repulsed, I knew she would furnish me with those Consolations that were not to be expected from a Lady more amiable than herself. In short, I was preparing for an Affair of Fancy, rather than any real Passion. I made her my first Overtures, with the Air of a Man who did not expect much Severity from her, and whose Flames were only his Amusement. I inform'd her of my Intentions, and it hardly cost me two Days to gain a favourable Compliance. As much acquainted with the World as I thought myself, I was insensible of the Risque a Man sustains, when he engages with Coquets; and she is certainly the most dangerous Person of all that Class; artful, beyond Expression, in the very Moments she seems to be most unguarded. Her Transports are as much studied as her Conversation; her Air, her Glances, her Sighs, and all her Motions, are the Effect of an Art which proves the more dangerous, as it is conceal'd in the Appearances of an unaffected Simplicity of Manners. I imagin'd all Commerce between us would have concluded, the Moment she left me nothing to desire; but this was the very Circumstance that inspired me with a real Passion. I then began to experience those Emotions that Love alone can create: The Gratification of my Desires awaken'd new Transports in my Soul, which I in vain endeavoured to extinguish, by my Attention to different Pleasures. These but added new Fewel to my Flames, and contributed the more to my Intoxication. I was no longer Master of myself, but was agitated by the Passion that consum'd me, to

such

ſuch a degree as render'd me inſenſible to the reſt of the Sex. I withdrew from all other Enjoyments, to devote myſelf to her alone, and my Soul was incapable of any Idea but what ſhe inſpired : I was even ſo inconſiderate, as to diſbelieve the Relations I had heard of her Diſpoſition; and the Moment I cheriſhed a Paſſion for her, I imagined it impoſſible for me to have any Competitor in her Heart. All the Cenſures the World caſt upon her Conduct, were conſidered, by me, as ſo many Aſperſions that ſprung from the Jealouſy of Women, or the impertinent Remarks of young Coxcombs, who had not Merit enough to give her any Impreſſions in their favour. That Jealouſy with which Lovers are uſually affected, was unknown to me; and I was fearful of offending her, by any Intimations of Diſtruſt. I beheld, with a perfect Indiſturbance, all the Gallants of every Claſs, preſenting her with their Addreſſes; and Things would always have proceeded in this Train, if her Coldneſs, which at laſt became too evident, had not given me juſt Reaſon to be apprehenſive of her Inconſtancy. I then began to be convinced that I had Rivals, but flatter'd myſelf that their Aſſiduities would be ineffectual; and when I even perceived they were not indifferent to her, I endeavoured to perſuade myſelf ſhe was only aiming at a new Proof of my Paſſion. I was likewiſe ſenſible there were ſeveral Converſations between the Sexes, from whence nothing of moment could be inferr'd; and that an amiable Woman is daily obliged to hear a thouſand inſipid Speeches that diſpleaſe her, even when they flatter her Vanity; that our Sex eſteem it a neceſſary Part of Politeneſs, to ſay a number of gallant Things that never flow from the Heart; from whence I concluded, that thoſe Perſons who were ſo eloquent in her Praiſe, were either not enamoured of her Perſon, or at leaſt, were unſucceſsful in their Paſſion. When I likewiſe conſider'd the Number of thoſe who beſieged her, it was impoſſible for me to imagine they could all be happy. When I obſerved her Conduct, I found it perfectly uniform to all the reſt of my Sex; ſhe aſſumed the ſame Air, and repeated the ſame turn of Converſation, and every one of her Admirers ſeemed entirely ſatisfied with her Proceeding; which made me conclude, that if they were all equally touched, the Indiſtinction of her Conduct, would naturally create Jealouſy among them. As to mine, I was obliged to ſuſpend it among ſuch a Crowd of Adorers, for want of a proper Object to employ it upon. But how ſollicitous was I to deceive myſelf! There was not one of theſe Perſons, who had the leaſt

Reaſon

Reaſon to be diſcontented with her Treat ment, and they all made a gradual Advance to her Favours. Thoſe, who had firſt diſcloſed their Paſſion, received the ſofteſt Teſtimonies of her Tenderneſs; and the moſt unfortunate among them, enjoyed ſuch a Share of Favours, as made it evident that the laſt would be granted, when a commodious Opportunity appeared. How was it poſſible for me, to form any Suſpicion of ſuch a Conduct! Can we believe the Perſon we love, capable of ſuch a contemptible Proceeding! With what Dexterity did this perfidious Woman delude me! How often, to diſengage herſelf from my Ardours, and to gratify thoſe of my Rivals, has ſhe endeavour'd to perſuade me that her Huſband, who is the moſt tractable Perſon in the World, was jealous at my Viſits; and, to eaſe him of his Suſpicions, how frequently has ſhe obliged me to accompany him to all Parts of the Town, that by this manner of abſenting myſelf from his Wife, I might convince him that I had no Inclination to pleaſe her! But, it ſeems, ſhe improved his Abſence and mine, to the Advantage of a happy Rival, whoſe Pleaſures I had the Goodneſs to facilitate. How often have I denied myſelf the Satisfaction of ſeeing her, for fear my frequent Viſits ſhould render me ſuſpected! and when we have, at any time, been accidentally ſeen together, in ſome retired Place, with how much Caution have I endeavour'd to ſecure her Reputation from Cenſure, when ſhe could be capable of admitting a new Lover into her Apartment, and indulging Pleaſures, which the Remembrance of her Treachery to me enhanced in her Eſtimation! I muſt confeſs, I was not abſolutely jealous; but when I obſerved at laſt, that my Paſſion was not ſo pleaſing to her as formerly, I began to be no longer certain of hers. But I was ſtill weak enough to believe, that I had given her ſome Cauſe for the Indifference ſhe diſcovered, and imagined that my treating her with an Increaſe of Tenderneſs, would awaken her Paſſion into its firſt Vivacity. I repeated my Viſits, Night and Morning, and my Aſſiduities had no Bounds; I was no longer reſtrain'd by the Conſideration of a jealous Huſband, and conſequently, her Opportunities to deceive me, were not ſo frequent as before. But, as I did not penetrate into her Deſigns, any more than ſhe could be deſirous that I ſhould ſuſpect them, ſhe diſengaged herſelf from me, by meer Careſſes; ſhe recovered her former Liberty, and reſtored me to my firſt Hopes. I was, for ſome time, as much enamour'd as ever, till, at laſt, her peculiar Conduct to the Chevalier *St. Far* *** rekindled my Jealouſy. I was weary of living

in

in ſo much Uncertainty; and to ſucceed in my Intentions to diſcover the true State of her Heart, I concealed my Suſpicions and Chagrin, in an Air of Satisfaction and Unconſtraint, and had the Art to deceive her effectually.

The Chevalier had enjoyed all that can be obtained from a Woman incapable of a Refuſal. They were perfectly conformable to each other, and caſt about to ſecure a Day, when no Mortal ſhould interrupt them. She told me the preceding Evening, that ſhe was obliged the next Day to accompany her Huſband into the Country, and was afflicted beyond Expreſſion to be thus ſeparated from me; but that it was neceſſary for her to comply with his Deſires. I ſeem'd to credit her Diſcourſe; but happening to caſt my Eyes upon her, a few Moments after, I ſaw her Hand claſp'd in *St. Far* ***'s. I roſe and took my Leave, with a Reſolution to unfold this Myſtery. The Day, which ſhe imagined would be ſo fortunate, arrived, and a Perſon, in whom I placed a particular Confidence, came early in the Morning, to acquaint me that the Huſband was gone out, and that he had ſeen the Chevalier admitted into the Houſe, a Moment after. My Affliction, at this Account, was not ſo great as I expected, and I calmed it with the Hopes of avenging myſelf on her Per-

Perfidy. I even conceived a malignant Joy, at the Idea of that Confusion she would discover at my Appearance, and went immediately to her House. She was so confident of my Credulity, that she had not given any Orders to her *Swiss*, relating to me. I went in, without the least Noise, in order to surprize her the more effectually. She had retired to a Pavilion, built for Pleasure, in the Garden; all the Windows, except that which fronted the House, were shut; and it happened very fortunately, that she did not observe me, when I came into the Garden. I approached the Place of her Retreat, and judged by the Silence which reigned there, that I must refer myself to their Actions, for the Discovery their Silence denied me. I employed my Eyes as well as I was able, and could not have chosen a more favourable Moment, for the Satisfaction of my Curiosity; and when you consider the Disposition with which I enter'd the Garden, you will be surprized that I should be such a calm Spectator of what pass'd between them, as I really proved. I had not the least Inclination to interrupt them, and retired from the Window, when I thought they would be in a proper Situation to see me. I quitted the Garden, in full Satisfaction at the Discovery I had made; when, to render my Joy compleat, I was

stopp'd

ſtopp'd by one of her Women, whom I had gained to my Intereſt, and who, as ſhe aſſured me, was extremely ſhock'd, to ſee her Lady's inſincere and barbarous Conduct to ſuch a Gentleman as myſelf. She detain'd me, till ſhe had put into my Hands, a large Collection of Letters, which ſhe had found Means to ſteal from my perfidious Fair

Are you not ſurprized at my Patience, or, more properly, my Weakneſs, in writing you this long and deplorable Hiſtory of my Huſband's Adventures? But you will pardon me, my dear Count, for I interrupted him, to have an Opportunity of aſſuring you, that I love you with infinite Tenderneſs, and ſhould have employed my Time to more Advantage, if I had choſen this for the Subject of my Letter. I ſhall know, to-morrow, which of us two receives moſt Pleaſure from this Aſſurance. A happy Night attend you: I am not able to write to you any longer; you may judge then how much I am fatigued,

LETTER XLVII.

I Can't poſſibly prevail on myſelf to pardon you: I am now alone, as you are very ſenſible, and yet you neglect to viſit me. How weak are all the Reaſons you alledge in your Excuſe! Can they poſſibly ballance the Inquietude I ſuſtain by your Abſence? Decorum, Buſineſs, and, were I inclined to be unreaſonable, I would ſay, Duty itſelf, and every other Conſideration, ſhould be incapable of detaining you from me. Am I then unworthy of ſuch a Sacrifice in my favour? But, as much Reaſon as I have to accuſe you, Ingrate as you are, you ſhall ſtill derive ſome Advantage from my Solitude. Yes, I will write to you; but, for your Puniſhment, you ſhall only receive from me, the Sequel of the Hiſtory I left unfiniſh'd yeſterday. Imagine then, that the Marquis continues his Relation in this manner.

I hurried away to my Coach, as quietly as I could; and, to prevent Interruption in the agreeable Lecture I was preparing for my falſe one, I intended to paſs a few Hours in the Wood of *Vincennes*. But you will never be able to gueſs what Object was firſt preſented to my View, in that Solitude. It was no leſs than the Huſband of my perfidious

dious Fair, walking very myſteriouſly with a Lady, who, the Moment ſhe ſaw me, conceal'd her Face in the Flow of a Lawn Hood. This Sight ſurprized me the more, becauſe I never ſuſpected my good Friend to be a very fortunate Man with the Sex. He came up to me, as I was preparing to ſtrike into another Walk. I have no Intention to diſſemble with you, ſaid he; you obſerve the Affair that engages me at preſent, be ſo good to me, as to conceal it from my Wife; her Jealouſy drives me to Diſtraction, and I ſhall be the moſt unfortunate Man in the World, ſhould ſhe diſcover my Proceeding in this Place. You muſt likewiſe grant me another Favour; the Lady you ſee there, happens to know you, and finds herſelf embarraſſed in your Preſence. I promis'd him all the Secrecy he requeſted, and then retired. I was a little chagrin'd, at firſt, to find him ſo engaged, becauſe I had an Inclination to convince him, that he had no Reaſon to be ſo apprehenſive of his Spouſe; and ſhould have ſet him right in the Affair of her pretended Jealouſy, by ſhewing him the Letters I had in my Poſſeſſion, ſeveral of which were written to me. But I began to think it more adviſable to let him continue in his Error; and, as I had been deceived ſo egregiouſly, I was willing he ſhould ſuſtain the ſame Fate. When I came

came to examine the Letters I had received, I found a ſtrange Diverſity of Style: Some were filled with warm Declarations and Acknowledgments, from little Fops; others amuſed me with the Languors and proffer'd Services of an Officer in the Revenue; and a third Parcel expreſſed the fluttering Fondneſs of a Courtier. The Variety, in ſhort, was infinite, and I could have diverted myſelf extremely, if ſome of my Letters, which made part of the Collection, had not render'd the others leſs ridiculous. When I had finiſh'd my Reading, I found my charming Miſtreſs neither inſpired me with Love or Reſentment; and, if I except a ſlight Emotion of Self-Regard, which mortified me a few Moments, I may venture to ſay, that I behaved like a Man of Philoſophy upon this Occaſion, and was ſurprized to find myſelf ſo little affected at her Levity; for I had not then conſider'd, that Tenderneſs is naturally extinguiſhed by Contempt. I recollected the Diſpoſition I was in, when I made her the firſt Declaration, and reſolved to aſſume an Air of Tranquillity, that I might not ſeem to be her Dupe, in ſuch an Adventure as this. I was willing, however, to have the Satisfaction of caſting her into ſome Confuſion; and, as I imagined a Letter would not be ſufficient to accompliſh my Deſign, I determin'd to arm myſelf

ſelf with a moſt inſulting Air of Coldneſs, and preſent her with my Congratulations on her new Conqueſts. I thought this Proceeding the beſt of any, as I was ſenſible I no longer loved her, and was certain, that, inſtead of diſcloſing to her any Inſtance of Weakneſs in our Interview, I ſhould enjoy the utmoſt Satisfaction in the Confuſion ſhe would diſcover. With this Diſpoſition I paid her a Viſit the next Morning: She was then at her Toilet, in that amiable Negligence, which is ſo advantageous to a Lady's Charms. I found the Chevalier in her Apartment, and the Preſence of her Lover had ſoften'd her Eyes into ſuch a melting Languiſh as was almoſt irreſiſtible, though devoted to a Rival. She bluſhed a little when ſhe beheld me, and I approached her in my uſual manner. She had been inform'd of the Viſit I intended her the Evening before, and imagined I now came to make her ſome little Reproaches. The Compoſure in which I appeared, recovered her from her firſt Confuſion; and, as ſhe had not ſeen me in the Garden, ſhe took it for granted that ſhe had likewiſe eſcaped my Obſervation. She then began to excuſe herſelf, for not acquainting me with her being at home. The Chevalier, upon this, thought fit to withdraw. I was very much indiſpoſed yeſterday, ſaid ſhe, and could not accompany my Husband into the Country, and I should have been offended with you for not staying, when you came here, if the Disorder in my Head had not stupified me into a Sleep the whole Day! Sleep, replied I very gravely, is not to be found fault with, provided one enjoys agreeable Dreams. I have no Cause to complain in that Particular, said she, since you was the only Subject of my Dreams. I then retorted with a Smile, I am told Madam, by some Persons who take an Account of your Dreams, that the Chevalier contributed to their Agreeableness, much more than myself: But I can't complain of that Circumstance, because I am sensible we have not the Command of our Ideas when we sleep. Let me intreat you not to blush, continued I, but is it possible you should sleep the whole Day? Extremely possible, replied she, with an easy Air. I have likewise had my Dreams, said I, and you really had a large Share in them. I will acquaint you with the Particulars, for they are extremely entertaining.

I dreamt, that when you was seized with the Sleep you mention, you fancied yourself to be in the Pavilion, in the Garden; and that in those Moments when you was infinitely delighted with dreaming of me, the Chevalier accidentally came in, and made it his first Employment to shut all the Windows,

dows, except one that was neceſſary to give a View of thoſe Perſons who ſhould happen to come into the Garden; and that when you aſked him the Reaſon of theſe Precautions, he fell upon his Knees before you, and diſcompoſed you to that degree, that my Idea vaniſhed from your Remembrance; and, what was very extraordinary, as you continued to caſt your Eyes on the Chevalier, you imagined him to be myſelf, tho' he was really the ſame Chevalier as ever: That amidſt this Diſpoſition of your Thoughts, you entertain'd him with all the Tenderneſs you uſed to reſerve for me; and obſerving that he diſcovered ſome Timidity, you condeſcended to recall him from his Confuſion by the ſofteſt Careſſes, and animated him to enjoy the Felicity of your Ardours, till at laſt he yielded to his Tranſports, with which you kindly intermixed your own, not comprehending, as yet, by what Miracle I had been able to aſſume the Perſon of the Chevalier, in that tender Moment. To what Purpoſe, ſaid you to yourſelf, does he appear to me in that Form? I never lov'd the Chevalier; and this is a very improper Expedient to engage my Conformity to his Deſires; and yet by a ſurprizing Impulſe of my Tenderneſs to him, I afford him my Favours, even while he aſſumes a Form that I always diſliked. You then made ſeveral judicious Reflections on the peculiar Oddneſs of Dreams, and the ridiculous Ideas they infuſe into the Imagination. I likewiſe dreamt, that when you at laſt awaked from your Slumber, you was not a little alarmed at the imaginary Injuſtice with which you had treated me in your Sleep, and you declared your Abhorrence of that Irregularity of Fancy, by which you was influenced in thoſe Moments. After which you ſunk down in a ſecond Slumber, and dreamt over the ſame Scene five or ſix times, till at laſt you ſtarted up in a very abrupt manner, to ſhake off the impertinent Perceptions which had ſo long diſcompoſed you: But, even then you conceived ſuch Impreſſions from your Dream, that you ſtill continued to ſee me in the Form of the Chevalier. I awaked too at the ſame time, in the utmoſt Vexation, that I had dreamt of ſo many extravagant Particulars.

I ſhall not pretend to repreſent the Emotions I raiſed in my perfidious Miſtreſs, by this fine Relation, ſince the utmoſt Power of Language is incapable of expreſſing 'em. Rage, Shame, and Averſion ſpread themſelves, in their ſtrongeſt Complexion, over her Features. Artifice was no longer availing, and I beheld her with an Air ſo expreſſive of my Contempt, that it was impoſ-

ſible

ſible for her to be deceived in my Meaning. She found it in vain to deny the Charge, ſince ſhe had ſo much Reaſon to believe I had been the Spectator of her Conduct. What ſhould a Lady do in ſuch a Situation? Were ſhe to intreat my Pardon, that would be a Condeſcenſion too mortifying; and any Denial of the Fact would be entirely ineffectual. Have you Time enough upon your Hands, to hear my Anſwer? ſaid ſhe. I aſſured her I had. You have then ſeen all that paſſed, replied the Lady; and nothing can be leſs a Dream than the Particulars you have related. I might have denied them, had I been ſo diſpoſed; but I have no Intention to give myſelf that Trouble. I acknowledge my Paſſion for the Chevalier, and am charmed that your Curioſity has furniſhed you with a Diſcovery, which you would otherwiſe have ſoon received from me. You would have compelled me to that Confeſſion, as much Inclination as I might have to preſerve a Decorum with you; for you are really become ſo inſupportable to me, that it is impoſſible for me to conſtrain my Thoughts any longer. Another, perhaps, would endeavour to form ſome Excuſe; but all that I can, at preſent, ſay to you is, that I love the Chevalier, and that you will for ever be my Averſion. You might have been ſenſible of this before; for

I have given you ſufficient Proofs of my perfect Indifference, in hopes that you would reſerve for ſome other Object, the diſagreeable Aſſiduities with which you are deſirous to honour me. But, ſince I have now made you ſuch a ſincere Confeſſion, I flatter myſelf that I ſhall have the Happineſs never to ſee you hereafter; and indeed I think that Happineſs ſo great, that I am only concerned I did not ſecure it much ſooner. Adieu, my Lord; I once more aſſure you that I love the Chevalier. And is he the only Perſon you love, Madam? replied I. I will love a hundred more, retorted ſhe, if that will afford you any Satisfaction; but you will never be one of that Number; and therefore let us break off here, and part for ever. I muſt confeſs, this uncommon Effrontery ſtruck me dumb with Aſtoniſhment. I imagined I ſhould mortify her, by making her ſenſible I had beheld the Scene of her Perfidy: But ſhe anſwer'd me in ſuch a Tone, as threw me into as much Confuſion as ſhe herſelf ought to have experienced. I thought it would be to no purpoſe to ſhew her the Letters I had brought, with an Intention to confound her the more, and contented myſelf with taking my final Leave of her, in the moſt contemptible Air I could aſſume. I muſt confeſs, I was a little piqued at her Inſenſibility of my Scorn, and reſolved to inform the Perſons who had writ the Letters to her which were in my Poſſeſſion, that ſhe had ſacrific'd them all to me. That Proceeding, indeed, would not have been agreeable to the Rules of ſtrict Sincerity; but I thought myſelf priviledg'd, at that Time, to give a Looſe to my Reſentment: Not that her perfidious Conduct created me any real Chagrin, but I was willing to avenge myſelf for the Contempt with which ſhe had treated me in our laſt Converſation. The firſt Perſon I happen'd to meet, was *St. Far* ***. I was ſenſible he had profeſſed a violent Paſſion for your Friend Lady ***; and as I did not then know, that all Commerce between them was broke off, I was ſurprized he ſhould chooſe ſuch a Time, to diſcover his Inconſtancy to her. I had obſerved indeed, that he had been lately very much attached to the celebrated Lady *L* ***; but it ſeems he had quitted her for my falſe Fair one; tho' when I firſt ſaw him at her Houſe, I had no Suſpicion that he had plac'd himſelf in the Train of her Admirers. I imagined ſome little Flights of Caprice had paſſed between your Friend and him, which had diſcontinued their Interviews for ſome ſhort Time: And, as I was acquainted with their mutal Paſſion, I concluded that his Thoughts were rather turn'd to an Accommodation with her, than to any new Paſſion. Inſtead of ſuſpecting him to be my Rival, I conſidered him as a Man affected with that Chagrin, which is commonly experienced in the Suſpenſion of an agreeable Intercourſe; and that he had an Inclination to amuſe himſelf by viſiting his Friends. You are ſenſible how much I was deceived in my Opinion. I have already told you, that I had an Intention to do my Fair one a malicious Office with my Rivals. *St. Far* *** was the firſt who came in my Way, and I thought he appeared very melancholy for a Man of his good Fortune. May I aſk you, ſaid I, why you retired ſo abruptly from the Lady's Apartment? I imagined, when I ſaw you enter, replied he with a negligent Air, that you might have ſome Affairs to ſettle with her, and I withdrew, to give you an Opportunity of accompliſhing your Deſign. Such a Proceeding, return'd I, might be natural in a Friend; but it appears very extraordinary in a Rival. I your Rival? cry'd he with ſome Vehemence, is it poſſible then that you ſhould be in Love with Lady ***? Yes certainly, ſaid I; and if you had not known it, I ſhould not have received ſuch an Anſwer from you. Hear me then, replied he: There are different manners of being in love, and only one that is agreeable to her Taſte. I concluded your Attachment to her was the Effect of the eaſy Reception ſhe afforded you, as well as of your natural Indolence, which prevents

your

your Attention to other Amuſements; and I had no Reaſon to believe, when I ſaw you ſo well with her, that you were engaged in any Circumſtances of much Delicacy, becauſe I am very ſenſible they are her Averſion.

I ſhould, however, have paid a Deference to your Pleaſures, if ſhe had not been deſirous of engaging me in ſuch an Intercourſe, as I could not be unpolite enough to decline. I came into it, however, with Inclinations very different from Love, and ſhould certainly have made ſome Progreſs in the Affair, if the Intimation you have now given me, did not oblige me to reſign my Pretenſions. She has not granted you any Favours then, as yet? ſaid I, with an ironical Smile. She has given me Reaſon to entertain ſufficient Hopes, replied he; but they are the leaſt of my Concern. I have not, as yet, found my Paſſion for her ſtrong enough to render me impatient: The World is ſo full of theſe Coquets; they are ſo little engaging; we come after ſo many Predeceſſors in their Affection, and are ſucceeded by ſuch a Number of Gallants, as happy in their Favours as ourſelves, that when a Woman of this Character invites one to an Amour, it is impoſſible to make one's ſelf the leaſt Compliment upon one's good Fortune, and we are obliged to conſider ourſelves as the Inſtruments

ſtruments of a contemptible Woman's Caprice. I may infer, then, from theſe judicious Obſervations, anſwer'd I, that you entirely reſign Lady *** to me, without having made the leaſt Improvement of her Inclinations in your favour. This indeed is a Circumſtance that ennobles the Sacrifice you make me: For had ſhe yeſterday gratified your utmoſt Deſires, I might ſuppoſe you only reſigned her to me now, becauſe ſhe had no more Charms to engage you any longer. Why do you make ſuch a Suppoſition? cry'd he in ſome Surprize; I have only received from Lady *** ſome Aſſurances of an approaching Happineſs; which, as yet, I have not been very ſollicitous to obtain. As I am entirely prepoſſeſſed with another Paſſion, and devote all my Attention to a Heart, whoſe Loſs I exceedingly regret, I have complied with the Overtures tender'd me by this Lady, with no other View than to create an Impreſſion of Jealouſy, in the Object I have loſt. But I am very unfortunate in my Experiments; I have left Lady *L**** for Lady ***, without creating the leaſt Mortification where I intended, and find myſelf of ſo little Conſequence, as neither to give Pain, nor receive Pity. Theſe indeed are dreadful Misfortunes, ſaid I, and I can never ſufficiently applaud Lady ***, for endeavouring,

ing, yesterday, to afford you some Consolation. The happy Pavilion, where you received so many Instances of her obliging Disposition —— has been the Scene of the same Complaisance to many others, interrupted he very smartly. You have detain'd me here two full Hours, to let me know that she had an Inclination to pass the Day with me; and I shall tell you, in two Moments, that she will never receive another Visit from me. I had some Curiosity, and have gratified it effectually. I shall contribute, not a little, to your Satisfaction, by resolving to see her no more; and, believe me, I will oblige you, in that Particular, with all my Heart. I would advise you, however, to conduct yourself by my Example; for I really think her unworthy the Pursuit of any Gentleman. This is what I intend, replied I; but I am piqued, and have been betray'd, which is not your Case. I can't be satisfied without some Vengeance; and I think I have the Means to accomplish it. I have here all sorts of Letters, which inform me of the Names and Quality of my present Rivals. I have an Inclination to send them back to the Gentlemen who writ 'em, or at least to circulate them thro' the Town. And, to carry on some Part of my Project, I here return you all yours, and shall forbear all Aggravations of Ridicule, in Gratitude

titude to your Sincerity. And, what can you propose from a Revenge of this nature? said he. To see her reduced to the Necessity of loving her Husband for some time, answer'd I, and to have no Opportunity of deceiving any Man for the future. What need have I to entertain you with any more Particulars, Madam, continued the Marquis; my Project has succeeded beyond my Expectation: I have embroiled her with all the World, and she is sensible she owes this good Office to my Industry. I can now declare to you, that I am as much delighted with her Aversion, as ever I was with her imaginary Tenderness. But nothing has so much incensed her, as the Conduct of *St. Far* ***, who has effected a Reconciliation with your Friend, and abandoned my fair Deceiver, the very Day that succeeded the Happiness she afforded him.

What can she now think of her Charms! What a mortifying Event is this for her imperious Vanity! and how well do her present Sufferings compensate the Pangs she once caused me to sustain! Heavens, how I hate her! Don't be so certain of that, reply'd I, you are exasperated at present, and this mighty Emotion of Hatred, may be only a strong Indication of Love. You despise her, and I think you are to be commended; but Contempt alone does not always

ways extinguiſh a violent Paſſion: We may regret our Choice, and be ſenſible of it, in all its Horrors; but when we are acted upon, by a ſtronger Impulſe than we receive from Reaſon, we adore our Chains in the very Moments we deteſt them. You ſtill ſeem to be in a very incommodicus Situation; and to what Cenſures will you expoſe yourſelf, ſhould you reſolve to ſee her again? Perhaps ſhe herſelf would be delighted to bring you to a new Engagement, in order to enſlave you more ſeverely than ever. You have acquainted me with your Thoughts, without Reſerve, and I ought to expreſs myſelf to you, with the ſame Sincerity; for which Reaſon, I tender you thoſe Counſels that are altogether diſintereſted. As you have brought the Affair to ſuch an Extremity, it would be very indecent, in you, to viſit her any more; for thoſe Perſons who have been Witneſſes to the Rupture between you, will think your Reconciliation unpardonable. Should you renew your Commerce with her, you will infallibly be the Jeſt of the whole Town. You have habituated yourſelf to Love; and I have nothing to ſay upon that Subject; but I wiſh you would preſerve yourſelf from Ridicule. I acknowledge the Force of your Reaſons, replied the Marquis; I am ſatiated with Love, and will never expoſe myſelf to the Neceſſity of making you my Confident, in ſuch odious Affairs as this. They coſt me too dear, and I can't conceive how you could be able to extort this Confeſſion from me. I would not depreciate the Confidence you repoſe in me, ſaid I; but you may take it for granted, that the Publick is never ſilent at ſuch Adventures as theſe. I have been already inform'd of all you have now told me, with a ſmall Variation of Circumſtances. We had ſome other Diſcourſe together, and he retired, after eating a very moderate Supper; having firſt intreated me, when I found my Heart more diſpoſed in his favour, to honour him with the Tidings; for he aſſured me he would endeavour to deſerve them, and added all that could be ſaid by a Man who thinks himſelf compleatly happy in the Tenderneſs of his Wife.—— Gracious Heavens! would you imagine that I have employed five Hours, in writing to you? To what a Length have I drawn out this Letter, without one ſoft Expreſſion in your favour! But this is a ſmall Omiſſion, ſince you already know how paſſionately I love you. Adieu; be ſure to viſit me this Evening, if you poſſibly can. As diverting as a Huſband may be, he is infinitely exceeded by a Lover. Does not this convince you, that I have forgot all my Reſentment?

LET-

LETTER XLVIII.

I Was ſenſible, that if I had an Inclination to make a new Conqueſt, I ſhould cauſe ſome Captive of your Sex to ſigh. My Charms have had their Effect, and I am adored beyond Expreſſion. The Ardours I now receive, are very different from yours. You military Gentlemen, who imagine your Pretenſions to the Fair, are not to be conteſted, treat us with the ſame Barbarity you practiſe in a Town you take by Storm, and refuſe our languiſhing Virtue the Glory of a ſhort Reſiſtance. You have no Reliſh for any little Anxiteies, and expect that your Merit, and our Frailty, ſhould ſecure you all the Gratifications you deſire. But for once, you muſt let Arms pay their Homage to the Gown. Prepare for a Retreat, good Colonel, for I have made ſuch Impreſſions on a little Magiſtrate, who is ſo gentle and obſequious, that upon a proper Occaſion, he will be able to eraſe the late *Celadon* from my Remembrance: He has even aſſured me, that if he had but the happy Power to pleaſe me, he would for ever devote himſelf to my Service, in ſpite of the Flame that conſumes him. He has not, as yet, preſumed to fix his Eyes directly upon me, and no Mortal, but ſo dangerous a Rival as himſelf, could have banifh'd you from my Heart. You think yourfelf too amiable, ever to lofe your Afcendant over it; and yet you fee, that all your Security depends upon the Heart of a Woman. Mine yielded at the firft Menace; and, how could I refufe it to a Man who promifed me an eternal Refpect? Can there be any thing more feducing than fuch an Offer? He figh'd, and cry'd I love you, with fuch an Air of Modefty, and blufhed fo innocently when he utter'd this Confeffion, that if any one had feen my imperious Mien, and the Timidity of my Magiftrate, I fhould really have been taken for the Aggreffor. I can likewife affure you, that this Youth is Mafter of many amiable Qualities. Do you imagine that he fits at my Toilet, with his Arms a-crofs, like yourfelf, and can only exercife his Criticifms on my Ribbons, or difconcert, by his Follies, the Care that is taken to adjuft my Hair? I can affure you that he vifits me, with other Views. Believe me, a Senator can employ his Time to a better Purpofe. There is not a Prefident of any Court of Juftice, who can plait ones Hair, to more Advantage than himfelf. He can form a Lock into a flowing Curl, at the fame time that he makes one a Declaration of Love; and this is certainly a fufficient Accomplifhment. He is my Council, in all my intricate Affairs; his Tafte is wonder-

ful,

ful, and, were he disposed to derive any Advantage from his Talents, he might value himself for his Capacity to furnish admirable Designs, for the Improvement of our Silks: Our Courts of Justice are excellent Schools, to form a Man for the polite World; and you may justly conclude, that the Qualifications he has acquired, will infatuate all the Ladies, and exinguish the severest Virtues of our Sex: He will certainly supplant every Gentleman, who resolves to be successful in his Sighs; he will dissolve the most intimate Union of Hearts, and can never fail to create Jealousy in those Lovers who are most confident of their Merit, unless he limits his Ambition to the Pleasure of saying, your Ladyship was never dressed to more Advantage! How exquisite is his Taste! But, I am so generous as to acquaint you with all the Qualifications of your Rival, to make you the more sensible that the Wound he has given me, is incurable; and that you may cease to indulge an unfortunate Passion, which I can no longer approve. Let us forbear then to carry Things to any farther Extreams; it would be imprudent in us, to exhaust the Fondness of our Hearts; we shall meet with more Satisfaction for the future, when we have left ourselves some remaining Desires to gratify. Our Union has, more than once, been in Danger of Extinction,

 from

from Satiety; and our Endeavours to renew it, have almoſt proved ineffectual. The Impreſſions we have retained, have render'd us more unhappy than thoſe Perſons who have no Senſibility of Love. I am convinced of this Truth, and we never ought to ſee each other, till we are perfectly indolent. A little Perfidy is a Refinement of Love, and that Paſſion grows languid, when we ceaſe to be apprehenſive of its Succeſs.

BILLET.

Any Anſwer to your Letter would be unneceſſary: You have not requeſted any thing from me, and declare yourſelf to be perfectly ſatisfied. I would willingly congratulate you, on the Pleaſures you enjoy; but Compliments are a little perplexing. A Letter would be too long; and I can hardly think you will believe this Billet too ſhort. Your Attention is too much engaged, to give me an Opportunity of declaring that I love you; and you are too amiable, to make it poſſible for me to ſay, you are indifferent to me. I have not Reſolution enough to reproach you, and am equally incapable of preſenting you with my Thanks. You may ſuppoſe, from all theſe Circumſtances, that I now write to you, without knowing what I do. You tell me, that were it not for my Idea, which is inſeparable from your Imagination, your Inquietudes would overwhelm

whelm you. I tender you my Acknowledgments for that Honour; but, I believe, my Generosity will equal yours, when I declare, that my Thoughts of you, discompose me not a little. You inform me, that you converse with amiable Ladies; but, would you have that Opinion of them, if your Thoughts were only devoted to me? The Men I daily see, are so exceedingly disagreeable! But the Women you pass your Time with, are perfectly charming: You desire no other Satisfaction, and I happen to be absent. I had some Inclination to reproach you; but you are not worthy of my Jealousy. You tell me, that you shall continue where you are, long enough to write me three Letters; but I shall never pardon you for any of 'em, except that which informs me of your Return.

LETTER XLIX.

WE are to take a Tour into the Country to-morrow: The judicious Marquis has an Inclination to make you one of the Party, and is now preparing to engage you. I shall then have the Pleasure of seeing you, and may converse with you, every Moment of that delightful Time. Does your Impatience correspond with mine? Do you wait for those Days, with the Impressions I experience? Do you really desire them; and can you, without any Disgust, behold yourself

ſelf in the Preſence of a Woman who adores you? Does your Ability to impart ſuch thrilling Tranſports, affect you with the Joy you ought to derive from that Power? I love you, beyond the Poſſibility of the warmeſt Paſſion: But, you may imagine I am loſt in extravagant Thoughts, while I am perſuading myſelf, that I am unable to preſent you with all the Endearments you merit. The Offer of my very Soul, is too inconſiderable to ſatisfy my Sollicitude to pleaſe you: You are the abſolute Lord of all its Powers; and yet I ſtill imagine my Flame too languid. To what Unhappineſs am I fated! Amidſt a Paſſion, that ought to be ſerene, I am forming Deſires that are never to be compleated! My Paſſion glows into Madneſs; no Conſideration has Power to calm it, and every Circumſtance contributes to its Increaſe. You appear equally amiable to me, in your Tranſports and Indifference; and, as if the Conflict I ſuſtain in the Day were inſufficient, I am even ſeduced by bliſsful Slumbers. What ſoft Illuſions! What charming Nights! What unutterable Raptures do I experience! And if your mere Idea can diffuſe ſuch Diſorder, through all my Senſes, what Joys ſhould I not derive from your Preſence! You could not poſſibly accuſe me of Inſenſibility, in thoſe happy Moments: But you muſt not expect to be conſcious of

any

any Delights that equal mine. These transporting Pleasures flow from the Excess of my Passion: You languish in a Profusion of the softest Felicity, and I burn, when only your Idea is presented to my Imagination. Why are not your Raptures as intense as mine! But, let me rather say, Why do I reproach you in this manner? Into what Extreams do I suffer myself to be hurried by my Emotions? What a Number of Words have I employed, in telling you we are to make a Party of Pleasure; and how can I fill so much Paper, when I have so little to write? How loquacious are we made by Love! I am resolved to think no more of it. My Thoughts begin to grow distracted; would to Heaven they were not too much so already —— Good Morrow. —— Ah! I forgot to acquaint you, that the Marquis, who is this moment paying his Assiduities to Lady *T* * * *, has desired me to engage her to be one of our Company; and there is Reason to believe she will engross his Thoughts so effectually, that he will not be very attentive to our Conduct; but you must not think this Circumstance will discharge you from all Caution in your Behaviour, Lady *T** * * will be accompanied by a Number of Women, who call themselves my best Friends; but who, for all that, would not be displeased, were I to furnish them with

any

any little Opportunities of making me the Subject of their Detractions. Adieu, and remember to be prudent, in the Presence of these good People; I should rather say, endeavour to prevent me from being indiscreet: I may possibly be more so, than you desire, in our Moments of Unconstraint. Adieu, my dear Count.

BILLET.

*No more Extravagancies, or we shall infallibly come to a Rupture: I can no longer avoid it, for your Conduct grows insupportable. What, in the Name of Heaven, is a Lover? I am resolved to define the Character, though I should happen to displease you. A Lover, then, is one who acts a very ridiculous Part. I could not prevail on myself to be angry, yesterday, merely for the sake of asking pardon to-day. Count *** whispered in my Ear; can you guess what Business he had there? He acquainted me with an impertinent Affair; would you know the Particulars? He inform'd me —— but you shan't have it in a Letter, for I will tell it you at our next Meeting. Are you not desirous of a Reconciliation with me? I am sensible you are ashamed of your impatient Temper, and you have reason to be so; but I am not certain whether I shall have Time to see*

see you. You may come, however; for I have nothing to do, and perhaps your Company may amuse me. How ridiculous am I to be so good! This is something incredible; but a Reconciliation is a very agreeable Affair.

LETTER L.

I Would advise you to change your Opinion; for, if I am not very much deceiv'd, *St.Far****'s Repentance is ineffectual. You fancy his Pardon must needs flow from the Tenderness Lady *** formerly entertain'd in his favour; but the Cruelty, with which that Tenderness has been treated, has extinguish'd it for ever. The Patience of Lovers has its Limits: Little Frailties may be disregarded, but a delicate Soul suffers by dispensing frequent Forgiveness. A Moment's Resentment draws on a Train of Reflections; and though they are usually erased by Love, a new Injury revives them in all their Severity: The Heart grows languid; Reason begins to resume her Empire; and, when she has once regain'd it, Love can no longer banish her from her Throne. Consider how a Passion is created in the Hearts of our Sex, and how different you must appear from yourselves, to induce our Compliance with your Desires. What a Strain of Tenderness and

obse-

obſequious Reſpect do you diſcover, to arrive at that Moment which gives you a Prerogative to diſcloſe your natural Diſpoſition! With what Rigours do you overwhelm us, when you have no longer any to apprehend from our Conduct! And, to what an abject Slavery do you reduce us, when the Proofs you have received of our Tenderneſs, ſhould render you more amiable and aſſiduous, than you appear'd when we were inflexible to your Deſires! How can you imagine that a Lady, who has been accuſtomed to your Addreſſes, and all the engaging Arts which your Sollicitude, to ſoften her Inſenſibility, ſuggeſts to your Imagination, can pardon your capricious Treatment; your imperious Airs; your falſe and diſhonourable Jealouſies, which you only affect, with a View to conceal your Coldneſs, when your Paſſion is once ſatiated? Why would you have her perſiſt in her Affection, for one who no longer has an Inclination to be amiable, and compell her to a Conſtancy you ceaſe to merit, and which you would only create, to render her the Object of your Contempt? You, undoubtedly, will not agree to theſe Truths; and, would to Heaven that, in order to diſclaim them, you did not reſemble the Men I have been deſcribing! You will aſſure me of your Fidelity, and you may poſſibly be Maſter of that Accompliſhment; but you reſemble

thoſe

those Prudes, who are perpetually boasting their Virtue, but are not the more approv'd for that Declaration. You are not anxious to please others; but, at the same time, you discover no Inclination to be agreeable to me. You are incommoded with your Constancy; I am perpetually sensible of the ill Humour it creates you, and you make me pay dear for the Pleasure of beholding myself without a Rival. But I must return to *St. Far* * * * (for I can't conceive, how you came to be the Subject of all these Expostulations) I fancy you deceive yourself, when you suppose Lady * * * has any Inclination to renew a Correspondence with him. You and I have been privy to their Passion, and have almost been constantly employed in excusing the Extravagancies of *St. Far* * * *, and have frequently been reduced to condemn the indiscreet Affection of the Lady our Friend. *St. Far* * * * has been guilty of an Injustice in this Rupture, which he can only repair, by an immediate Acknowledgment: But, instead of condescending so far, he has added the most injurious Inconstancy to his other Crime. But, as her new Conquests have now made him sensible of her Merit, he is impatient to regain her Favour. This is a Circumstance very much to her Honour, and should teach her to set a just Estimation on herself. Perhaps this very Conviction has given *St. Far**** a Disgust to his Inconstancy. He knows, there are some Women disposed to love him; but is sensible, at the same time, that they are undeserving of any Return, and that there are Hearts whose Conquest affords but little Satisfaction. In a word, Lady *** may hope to regain a Lover more tender, and better persuaded of her Merit, than he was before his Change. All these Reflections are just; but she continues inexorable. She has not only refused to receive his Letters, but has been entirely unaffected with his languishing Air. You amorous Men are surely the most diverting Creatures in the World. A continued Affectation reigns through your whole Persons, even to the Tone of your Voices. Your Eyes are overcast with Languors, and are ever directing their melancholy Glances to the beloved Object. Your spiritless Steps seem, at every pace, to reproach her with some new Rigour: Your long and frequent Sighs, your broken Slumbers, your Disorder and Distractions (and oh! these are an essential Article) tend to prove, that you are no longer Masters of yourselves. These were the Allurements by which you seduced me; for the more I reflect on your Distractions, they appear so extremely powerful, that I forget each Particular I ought to remember. I was once so absurd

abſurd, as to believe you exceedingly amorous, becauſe you ſeem'd to have loſt your Reaſon; but I have ſince been ſenſible, that this is only a Vice which ſprings from Habit or Conſtitution. Dejection affords you a fine Reſource; you appear diſconſolate to all the World; and 'tis now the general Report, that a certain Gentleman, whoſe Gaiety was once ſo applauded, is ſeized with a mortal Melancholy. Theſe Tidings have even been conveyed to the Lady he loves, and ſhe began to conſider his Condition as a ſerious Affair. She was ſenſible that Affliction was a natural Advance to Deſpair, and was apprehenſive leſt his inconſiderate Behaviour ſhould grow too remarkable; till at laſt ſhe thought it better to preſerve a poor Gentleman, than be acceſſary to his Death. What unfortunate Creatures are our Sex, to ſuffer ourſelves to be ſeduced by ridiculous Appearances that ought to create our Contempt!

*St. Far**** appears to Lady ***, like a Man abandon'd to Deſpair; and, in my Opinion, ſhe ſeems to be entirely unaffected with his Condition. Perhaps her Heart may deceive her; but, however that may be, I can't diſcover in it any Symptom of Tenderneſs in his favour. She ſpeaks of him with Indifference; but I ſhould be better pleaſed to ſee her moved with Reſentment. I will intercede for him once more, ſince you deſire it; but it is not eaſy for you to conceive how much an Inconſtant, who would reſume his former Chains, is deſpiſed by a Woman of Underſtanding: Beſides, his manner of anſwering you, when you offer'd to introduce him to her, is a Circumſtance that is ſeldom forgotten. I am now preparing to viſit her, and you will find me in her Apartment, where we will join our Endeavours to obtain his Pardon. As to your Particular, I would adviſe you always to love me in ſuch a manner, as to have no Cauſe to deſire my Forgiveneſs.

LETTER LI.

A Certain Lady is retiring to Solitude, diſguſted with the Flutter of the Town: But, how can ſhe forſake it with Satisfaction, when ſhe leaves the deareſt Object of her Soul! To prevent this Mortification, you are deſired to be at home at five, with Monſieur *St. Far****; and you will have an Opportunity of being conducted to a Place you are unacquainted with at preſent; and the Name of it is not to be diſcloſed to you. It may be proper, however, to inform you, that you are to engage in ſome terrible Adventures; but you are a Knight, and

and profeſs to be amorous, and conſequently can never be deſtitute of Courage. After you have paſs'd thro' an immenſe Country, you will be conveyed to a Caſtle, which a ſingle Giant, of the Canton of *Bern*, renders inacceſſible to all ſplenetic Perſons. A ſtately Portico will firſt preſent itſelf to your View; but when you have admired the Architecture, in compliance with the eſtabliſhed Cuſtom on ſuch Occaſions, you may make a farther Advance; for neither Monſters nor Griffons will oppoſe your Paſſage, and you are not to begin your Feats of Arms in the Court of the Caſtle. A Number of courteous Knights will conduct you, in Ceremony, to a Range of ſplendid Apartments, where a Set of young Damſels will perfume you, and direct your Steps to a myſterious Cabinet, where you will be received by two Princeſſes, more radiant than the Stars in the Firmament, and repoſing themſelves, with a negligent Air, on Sofas glittering with Gold and Purple. At the ſight of you, a ſoft Confuſion will tinge their Cheeks with the fineſt Vermilion in the World, and diffuſe new Charms over all their Features. After a few Sighs, which their enraptur'd Hearts will breathe with ſome Reluctance, a Lilly Hand will be tender'd to you, with a languiſhing Air, and you muſt not fail to kiſs it with Tranſport. In the mean time, a

Flow of Joy will ſuſpend all the Faculties of your Soul, and you will be permitted, in a very obliging manner, to utter all the incoherent Expreſſions that occur to you, till you have recovered yourſelf from your firſt Emotions. When this painful Preliminary is over, you will be conducted into delightful Gardens, which Art and Nature have conſpired to embelliſh. An eternal Spring reigns in that ſoft Retreat; there the Zephyrs perpetually breathe a delicious Air, while the Nightingales chant their melodious Loves, and, in conjunction with the Warbling of the other Inhabitants of blooming Forreſts, render this charming Scene a ſecond Iſle of *Venus*. Amidſt a thick Wood, that deepens into a pleaſing Gloom, you will diſcover a Grotto, more lovely than all the other Beauties of that amiable Solitude, and cover'd with twining Myrtle. There the *Fauns* reſort, to enjoy the uninterrupted Solace of all their Sighs. The amorous *Dryad* permits herſelf to be ſurprized, without ſuſtaining the leaſt Apprehenſions. An Enchantment, which can never be ſufficiently admired, makes the fugitive Nymph incapable of directing her Speed to any other Place; and Love, who glides before her, and dazzles her Eyes with his beamy Torch, conducts her to the very Grotto ſhe would avoid. The Infantas, in all probability, being

being fatigued with their long Walk, will be desirous to repose themselves in that sequester'd Scene: There you and *St. Far**** may disclose to them the Pangs you sustain. The Sight of that charming Retreat will animate your Desires; and Heaven grant that it may inspire the Lovers with as much Discretion, as it may possibly infuse Weakness into the Ladies; and may they, at least, learn to profit by the Example of those Swains, who, when they quitted that Grot, did not leave in it any Monuments of their Felicity. When you retire from that Place, your Presence will be desired in a noble Hall, where you will find a Table covered with all the Delicacies that Imagination can represent to be most exquisite; and a Flow of the richest Wines will sparkle in Vases more transparent than Chrystal: Gay *Frenzy* will be invited to the Festival, and *Bacchus* will endeavour to finish it with as much Perfection as it was begun by *Love*. But, as soon as you discover the Dawn of *Aurora*, the Charioteers will be order'd to prepare their Horses: You will then depart; and, after a long Journey, will find yourselves at the Gates of *Paris*. There you will take leave of the Infantas, not without some Sighs on your part, and they will be as liberal of theirs. One of you two will be obliged to utter Protestations of Constancy, from which the

the other will, at prefent, be difpenfed. You will then afcend your Car, and, before *Morpheus* fheds his Poppies on your Eye-lids, you will talk of the Object of your Flame, and addrefs a mental Prayer to her, as you ought. Adieu my Lord.

BILLET.

Return to this Place. You are not worthy of an Invitation from me; for which reafon I am only difcharging the Office of a Secretary; but don't you imagine that Love dictates the leaft Endearment for you. I once more affure you, that I am not writing for myfelf. 'Tis true, I might make ufe of the Opportunity; but I am not fufficiently fatisfied with you, to have Recourfe to any fuch Pretext. You doubtlefs imagine that I am difcompofed at your Abfence; you may think fo, if you pleafe, and be deceived at the fame time. I go where my Inclinations lead me, am attentive to all I hear, and anfwer what I think fit. I divert myfelf at Play, and am a Lofer. I go to the Theatre, and am diffatisfied. I have Lovers, capable of amufing me, if I am fo difpofed. Are not thefe fine Refources; and can you believe that while I enjoy them, I can have any Time to be defirous of your Return? I likewife fee my Husband every

*every Day: He loves me beyond Conception; and, whatever you may think, a ſedentary Husband is preferable to an abſent Lover. The Signification of all this is, that you may continue where you are, if the Nuptials of Lady *** and* St. Far **** don't oblige you to quit your Solitude. She has form'd this Reſolution at laſt, and hopes to fix* St. Far **** entirely by this Proceeding: You may frame a Judgment of her Indiſcretion, by this Inſtance. If the Oaths of a Lover are of no Validity; of what conſequence are thoſe of a Husband? She promiſes herſelf much Fidelity, Complaiſance, and Tenderneſs from him; and, though theſe Expectations were all diſappointed in her former Marriage, ſhe is willing to believe St.* Far **** will not be defective in the leaſt Particular. Adieu, my Lord; the Nuptials are to be celebrated next Monday, and all the Company will be very well ſatisfied to ſee you arrive in the Evening. You may viſit me when it ſuits with your Conveniency; but, however, you ſhall not tax me with being incommodious to you; and will you now ſay, that I love you?*

LETTER LII.

AH me! my Apprehenſions were but too juſtly founded, and how happy ſhould I now be, had they always guarded me againſt your Deſires! Do you yourſelf then confirm to me, the Certainty I had of loſing you, which coſt me ſo many Tears, and from which you endeavour'd to relieve me, by ſuch numberleſs Proteſtations! Can you conſent to abandon me, Ingrate as you are! Have you conſidered what your Barbarity will coſt me, and are you reſolved to kill me with agonizing Deſpair? Could you ſo ſoon forget the Tenderneſs with which I adored you? You are determin'd to eſpouſe Lady *G****; Inhuman Man! And I am reduced to the Neceſſity of loſing you, without daring to complain of your Perfidy. But why am I not to be inform'd of my Fate from your Lips? Do you want Reſolution to acquaint me with your Happineſs; and, tho' it will infallibly deprive me of mine, can you be ſo unjuſt to me, as to believe I will not ſacrifice it all to your Welfare? My Heart has never reproached me on your Account; but I ſhould think myſelf altogether unworthy of your Eſteem, were I to indulge the Emotions with which it inſpires me on this Occaſion. And muſt I then tear you

you from that Heart, and renounce you for ever! For ever, did I ſay! Can I then pronounce ſuch a Sentence, which perhaps you yourſelf would refuſe to utter! Shall thoſe Days, which you paſs in repeated Vows of perpetual Tenderneſs, be loſt to me for ever? You reſolve then to live for another, and intend to extinguiſh, in her Arms, the Remembrance of my Love and diſconſolate Sorrows. You will no more tell me, that you adore me, and are determin'd to be as inſenſible as you would repreſent yourſelf. Who ever compelled you to love me? Did not you yourſelf ſelect me from the reſt of my Sex, to render me compleatly wretched? Ought you not to have been ſenſible, that your Heart would one day ceaſe to be my Property; and, when my Paſſion has ſo perfectly correſponded with yours, can you forbear to reproach yourſelf, for the mortal Anguiſh I ſhall ſuſtain by loſing you for ever? To love you to Adoration, and to be conſtantly convincing you of that Truth, were my only Cares; and who will now afford me any Compenſation for their Inefficacy? With what delightful Tranſports did I always behold you! but alas! I muſt now behold you no more. Ah! moſt perfidious Man, had your Paſſion been equal to mine, who could ever have robb'd me of your Heart? But what do I ſay, miſerable Crea-

ture

ture that I am; my Love was too inconſiderable for your Merit, and I muſt now be only ſollicitous to preſerve your Eſteem! Be not apprehenſive of diſpleaſing me, by compleating your Nuptials: I foreſaw the fatal Sacrifice, and ſubmit to it without a Murmur. You love me at preſent; but who can convince you that your Paſſion will never diminiſh, and that you will not hereafter repent, that you rejected a ſolid Eſtabliſhment, in favour of an Union that might ſoon be diſſolved, and which one Moment, either of your Caprice or mine, would poſſibly deſtroy for ever? I loved you for your Merit alone; and the Satisfaction of beholding you happy, ſhall requite me for the Loſs of all other Enjoyments. You were but little acquainted with the Temper of my Soul, if you imagined it capable of any other Diſpoſition. Conſign me to eternal Oblivion; or let us only be ſollicitous to cheriſh a mutual Eſteem. You ſhall be for ever dear to my Remembrance. Had I been capable of Inconſtancy, you would have deſpiſed me for my Levity; and, had you abandon'd me, I ſhould have hated you for your Ingratitude. Let us, at leaſt, have no Reproaches to caſt on each other. It is reaſonable that I ſhould aid you to eraſe me from your Heart; ſubmit then to this fatal Neceſſity, with the Reſignation I diſcover.

Don't

Don't imagine, however, that this Propofal has not coft me many a Pang; or that it will not yet coft me many a Flood of ftreaming Tears. I never loved you with more Tendernefs than I experience at this Moment; and I even conjure you, by all that Profufion of Tendernefs, not to forget me for ever! This indeed is a Compliance, in which you will find it difficult to indulge me; but ought you not to grant me fome Confolation in my prefent State, and have you no Sentiments of Humanity to afford me? You may reafonably believe I am overwhelmed with a Weight of Woe; and can you refolve to abfent yourfelf from me, at fuch a Time? Ah! give me not the full Profpect of all my Mifery, but permit me, at leaft, to flatter myfelf that you lofe me with fome Regret! Can a Love, like mine, merit fo much Indifference? Will a fingle Line of Sofnefs; will one tender Expreffion coft you fo dear? Alas! I am not intreating you to quit the fatal Object that deprives me of all I love. If you refufe me a few Moments of your dear Prefence, forbear, at leaft, to torture me with the Proofs of your Difdain. A little Compaffion for me, will be no Injuftice to her: It will only increafe her Triumph, at the fame time that it affords me fome Alleviation of my Sorrows. But with what Language could you comfort me, in your present Situation? You would reproach yourself for all your past Expressions of Tenderness; your Eyes would retract them; I should be convinced that no Hopes remained for me, and might possibly be guilty of some Frailties, for which I should infallibly reproach myself. No, my Lord, let me intreat you to see me no more. I will preserve the Remembrance of our Passion, to my latest Breath, and may you endeavour to retain the same Disposition. Return me my Letters and my Picture, and keep nothing that can be capable of recalling my Idea to your Imagination; and yet, if it be possible, forbear to banish me entirely from your Thoughts. Pity me, in some tender Moments; for I cannot presume to require, from you, any Sentiments that are more ardent. Adieu! The Tears that moisten this Letter, ought to afford you a faithful Proof of the Anguish I feel in writing that fatal Word. Let me never see you more. I am too well acquainted with the Torture of loving without a mutual Return, to be willing to give that Inquietude to Lady *S* ***. She merits all your Attention but too well. We are now separated for ever. Adieu. Ah! do not intirely chase me from your Remembrance! Condescend sometimes to recollect how much I lov'd you; but

but forget that I love you ſtill, and ſhall be for ever incapable of changing.

LETTER LIII.

I Am convinced of your Diſpoſition, my Lord, by the Ideas you have conceived: They demonſtrate your Contempt of my Perſon, and ſufficiently aſſure me of your Indifference. You may reſt perſuaded then, that my Paſſion for you, is entirely extinguiſhed, and that all my Alarms, at the Report of your Marriage, were only fictitious. I affected them with no other View than to conceal my new Paſſion; and they furniſhed me with a Pretext for diſcarding you in the moſt effectual manner. You are the only Perſon who could form, in ſuch a Caſe, the Imaginations you entertain. You tell me you have no ſuch Thoughts; why then did you aſſure me to the contrary in your Letter? Do you think I am not ſufficiently miſerable already? Don't I ſuffer enough by loſing you; but when your Paſſion is extinguiſhed, muſt it be immediately ſucceeded by Contempt? Am I then deſpiſed! O Heavens! and is it from you, Ingrate as you are, that I ought to receive this Treatment! I, who have ſacrificed my Love itſelf, to your Repoſe; I, who was al-

 ways

ways ſollicitous to convince you of my Tenderneſs, and have lately given you ſuch a Proof of it, as you might in vain have ſought in any other Breaſt. If the Loſs of me really affects you in the manner you repreſent; is the odious Character you afford me, any Evidence that I continue dear to you ſtill? If you ſuſpect me of Infidelity, you might complain of your Miſfortune, without offending me; but in what Particular would you be thought an Object of Compaſſion? Is it becauſe I have loved you with too much Tenderneſs? You ought to be ſenſible, if you can really be ſenſible of any thing, that I merited Pity, and not an Inſult. Did any Mortal ever love like you? I perceive, by your manner of Writing, that I begin to be odious in your Thoughts, and yet you have no Intention to eſpouſe Lady *S****. How can you reconcile ſo much Love and Averſion? With what Coldneſs do you aſſure me, that you will be ever conſtant to me alone? Ah! how different is the warm Language of a real Paſſion! But I find you are diſpoſed to deceive me. My Apprehenſions were once dear to you, and you endeavoured to diſſipate them, by all the ſoft Expedients you could poſſibly exert, and you dreaded to behold my Tears. You are determined not to eſpouſe Lady *S****; but had you rejected

jected her for my sake, you would have been impatient to repeat to me, your Protestations that you continued to love me alone. I consented to lose you, for your own Welfare, and sacrificed myself to your Happiness, without a Moment's repining: But I should die with Despair, were you to lose the Remembrance of that Sacrifice, in the Arms of a new Mistress. I may possibly be unjust; but what Satisfaction can I derive, from your Insensibility to the rest of my Sex, if your Passion for me be extinguished? I consider your Coldness and Inconstancy, in the same Light, since they equally deprive me of your Heart. You undoubtedly condemn my Apprehensions; but would any one, in my Condition, be less sensible of their Impressions? Is a Letter then a sufficient Satisfaction; and would it be too much if you came yourself, to calm my Inquietudes? How are your Thoughts employed, while you continue absent from me? You suspect me of Inconstancy, and I am apprehensive that you are perfidious: Can we possibly be serene with these Ideas? and, if you interested yourself, never so little, in my Heart, would you not come, and either convince me of my Infidelity, or share, with me, the Pleasure of being sensible that I am constant? Pity the Condition to which I am reduced, and only condescend to relieve me from my Fears, and clear up your own Suſpicions. Let me know, whether I ought to love you ſtill, or reſolve to hate you for ever.

LETTER LIV.

CAN you be the Object of my Averſion, my deareſt Count, when you afford me ſuch convincing Proofs of your Tenderneſs; and don't you rather hate me, for my Injuſtice to you, at a time when you were removing every Obſtacle that might have prevented you from being entirely mine? I have all imaginable Conviction of your Fidelity; and can you image to yourſelf then, the Ecſtacy of my Joys? I can no longer be doubtful that you love me; but are you ſenſible of all the Impreſſions this Certainty ought to produce in my Heart? Could I have any Cauſe to complain, if you had abandon'd me in reality? You would only have acted in obedience to my Deſires; but you was ſenſible how much it coſt me to urge them. You was touched at the melancholy State to which my Apprehenſions of loſing you, had reduced me; and I hope you will endeavour not to repent of your Compaſſion. Do you believe my Heart can make you any Compenſation

tion for what you have acted on my account? I now am certain that you love me, and you may depend on the softest Returns my Passion can possibly offer you. Why had you not the same Confidence in me, as I repose in you? Would not the Days we employed in giving new Torments to each other, have been better devoted to the mutual Proofs of our Ardours; and when we are neither troubled with the Jealous or Impertinent, should we occasion more Calamities to ourselves, than they could ever create us? Have we any need of Reconciliations, to secure us from lifeless Languors? Frequent Ruptures naturally disgust the Heart, and never contribute the least Ardours to Love. Would not the voluntary Absence, to which we condemn ourselves, prove an insupportable Punishment, were it to be inflicted by any other Person? and are we not very irrational, to subject ourselves to so many Inquietudes; or have we any superfluous Moments to lose? Let me intreat you not to love me with these immoderate Emotions you sometimes disclose; for they are always succeeded by too much Indifference. I am not ambitious of your Transports, and would only be sollicitous to possess your Heart. There are many tender Inclinations in the Soul, to which we may resign ourselves without any Violation of our Virtue. I am desirous of that Love, which they say was so familiar to *Plato*, and of which we have had so little Experience: A Love refined from all Impressions of Sense, and yet not easily wrought into a Habit, since we find it so difficult to be comprehended. Adieu! Let us, without discomposing ourselves with these Particulars, continue to love as we began. This will be sufficient for us, and I am inclined to think we shall be lost in our Researches after any other.

Gracious Heaven, how inconsiderate am I grown! I have entertain'd you with Trifles for these two Hours, and forgot to acquaint you that Lady *** desires a Visit from you at Noon. She intends to pass the Remainder of the Day at ***; and, as I have a thousand things to tell you, I am persuaded that I shall attend her. Ah me! —— Have you not the Curiosity to ask me why I sigh?

LET-

LETTER LV.

POOR Lady *G**** has loſt her Lover, after four Years Conſtancy; and, notwithſtanding all my Diſſuaſions, the Charms of little *I**** have compleated the Paſſion which his Diſguſt for his other Miſtreſs had ſketch'd out. Yes Madam, ſaid this Gentleman to me a few Days ago, the Affair is finiſhed, and the Aſſiduities I paid her, for a conſiderable time paſt, only flowed from Gratitude; and, if I except a trifling Idea that ſtill torments me, we have lived for theſe two Years paſt like good Friends, and nothing more. Her Senſibility makes me apprehenſive that ſhe will die with mere Grief, when ſhe diſcovers my Inconſtancy. I have not omitted any thing that might incline her to deſire a Rupture, which daily became more neceſſary to us both. I have counterfeited a Paſſion for other Women, and ſhe impatiently expected my Return to her. I have been to viſit her, a hundred times, with an Intention to tell her that my Paſſion was extinguiſhed, and it ſhould ſeem as if ſhe ſelected thoſe Moments, to confound me with the ſtrongeſt Proofs of her Tenderneſs; ſo that I was obliged to quit her, without adjuſting the Affair as I could have wiſhed. Thoſe Converſations, that were

were once animated, are now languid, and unproductive of any pleasing Effect; and all the Moments that Love, and her Pretence, formerly render'd so charming, are entirely disagreeable to my Remembrance. In vain do I endeavour to reason myself into Constancy, since my very Want of those Lectures, makes me sensible of their Inefficacy. I have sometimes the Curiosity to trace the Cause of my Disgust. I see an amiable Woman, graced with all the Charms of Youth and Wit, but her Attractions no longer affect me. My Reason continues to assure me she is lovely, but my Heart no longer confirms me in that Persuasion, and every other Circumstance pleads ineffectually in her favour. Ought she not to be sensible, by my Indifference, that I no longer love her; and, can a Lady be deceived by studied Transports, after she has experienced all the Ardours and Enthusiasms of a Lover. In spite of all my Efforts, we must come to a Rupture; and, in my Opinion, it gives a Man more Torment to feign a Passion for a Woman he never can love, than he can receive by practising that Dissimulation, with a Woman he never did love.

The Gentleman concluded this fine Discourse, with intreating *St. Far****, who professes a Friendship for Lady *G****, to insinuate

ſinuate ſome Suſpicions into her Mind, and to aſſure her that ſhe was no longer belov'd; and he promiſed not to contradict any one Particular. But your Lordſhip does not conſider, replied *St. Far* ***, that her Deſpair will prove fatal to her. Ah! rejoin'd *P* ***; were I not perſuaded of that Effect, I would not deſire you to inform her of my Inconſtancy. Conſent, in mere pity, to ſave me: She is deſirous I ſhould eſpouſe her; beſides, a Diſcovery, of this nature, is more ſupportable when imparted by another, than it can be, when it proceeds from a Lover, who has been accuſtomed to ſpeak a different Language. *St. Far* *** poſitively refuſed to charge himſelf with this Commiſſion. 'Tis well, replied the other, I ſhall ſollicit you no more; but remember that you compel me to plunge a Dagger into her Boſom. At this, he abruptly ſtarted away, and we continued in the *Thuilleries*, reflecting on this unuſual Conſtancy of Lady *G****, when we ſaw him advancing to us, with a wild and diſorder'd Aſpect. 'Tis done, ſaid he, and I am now content, if one can poſſibly be ſo, by driving a Lady one tenderly loves, to Deſpair. When he left us, he immediately went to her Houſe, where ſhe expected him with the utmoſt Impatience, and the Day was fix'd for compleating the mutual Proofs of of their Tenderneſs. The Conjuncture was preſſing; he was confounded at the Proſpect of the Danger; he ſtopp'd; he heſitated. She began to importune him; he was offended, and ſhe was ſeized with Deſpair; while he very frankly acquainted her with the Cauſe of her Calamity. She then ſunk down in a Swoon; *P* * * * tender'd his Aſſiſtance: She at laſt revived; threw herſelf, in a Flood of Tears, at his Feet, and utter'd the moſt affecting Language that was ever expreſs'd. *P* * * * likewiſe melted into Tears, and intreated her to arm herſelf with Reſolution; but the Softneſs of her Paſſion was ſucceeded by Rage: She ſnatch'd his Sword, with an Intention to plunge it into her Boſom: He wreſted it from her Hands, and diſengaged himſelf from her, as well as he could; and, that ſhe might have ſufficient reaſon to be convinced he was in earneſt, he writ her his laſt Farewel, in the *Swiſſe*'s Lodge. This Adventure he related to me, with an Air of Triumph, and gave me repeated Aſſurances, that ſhe would infallibly die with Deſpair.

The unfortunate Lady, upon his Departure, took to her Bed, and paſs'd the Remainder of that Day, and the enſuing Night, in Sighs and Faintings. She roſe in the ſame Extremity of Sorrow; and, as the Day-light was grown deteſtable to her Eyes, ſhe drew the

the Curtains of her Chamber, and with a languiſhing Recline under her Canopy, lamented the Loſs of her Lover; after which her Health became ſo impaired, that there was reaſon to be apprehenſive her laſt Moments were approaching; and in all probability, ſhe would ſoon have expired, if the young Duke of ***, who enter'd her Apartment, the Moment ſhe was receiving the Aſſiſtance of thoſe about her, had not reconciled her to Conſolation, within half an Hour after her Attendants imagined ſhe was breathing her laſt. The Duke, who thought this Adventure very entertaining, immediately related the Particulars to his Friends; and one of theſe, who was intimate with *P****, inform'd him of every Circumſtance. *P****, amidſt his Deſpair that ſhe was ſtill living, and had been ſo ſoon prevailed upon to receive that Conſolation of which he thought her incapable, found his Paſſion rekindled, by the very Circumſtances that ought to have extinguiſhed it for ever. He has been extremely ſollicitous to reinſtate himſelf in the Favour of Lady *G****; but you know the Diſpoſition of a Perſon who has condeſcended to be ſoothed in her Affliction; ſhe entirely deſpiſed him; and he has had all the Difficulty in the World, to forget her, as well as little *I****, whom he had loved to deſperation till then.

 Adieu,

Adieu, my Lord, and before you are disposed to treat me with any Instances of Perfidy, recollect the Adventure of your Friend, and the Manner by which Lady *G**** attained her Consolation.

BILLET.

*I have, this Moment, received a Visit from that egregious Prude Lady ***, attended by a couple of Wits, who will distract me with their Ingenuity, if I don't find some Expedient for my Relief. She has given me an Invitation to sup with her, and I am undone if you neglect to be there. Bring* St. Far*** *with you, I conjure you; he is fond of Disputation, and will afford these Men of Genius some Employment. I shall then enjoy your Conversation, or at least shall be so happy as to see you. Perhaps you may not conceive to what degree these Gentlemen are capable of being insipid. They talk eternally, and I have not Capacity enough to understand a Word they utter. You may judge then, what Satisfaction I am like to enjoy. Be so generous therefore, to deliver me, by your Presence, from the Persecution I must otherwise sustain; and be sure to come, though you should imagine I only form this Pretext to see you. The Service you will render me on this Occasion, shall be received with suitable Acknowledgments:*

ments: The Chagrin you may suffer, shall be requited, by my permitting you to see me fifteen Days successively, and with all the Privacy you please. Will you really come?

LETTER LVI.

CAN any thing in nature be so unaccountable as your Jealousy? and, can you think so meanly of my Conduct, as to believe me capable of loving the Man who gives you so much Inquietude? If you must needs torment yourself with Rivals, let them, at least, be such as may not dishonour me by their Unworthiness. But why should you create yourself imaginary Competitors, when every Part of my Conduct is such an evident Proof, that I am devoted to you alone! I would not have you suppose that I intend to clear myself from the Imputation of that Inconstancy with which you charge me: I should injure you too much, were I to persuade myself that your Jealousy is real. I am well acquainted with your capricious Turn of Mind, and you give me a singular Instance of it, by your present Suspicions. Your Delicacy is not so refined, as to be shock'd at my Conversation with a Man, from whom I never received a Visit, nor ever shall, whatever Imaginations you may pleaſe to entertain; and I am ſenſible you can never ſuſtain any real Uneaſineſs, from a Perſon who is not form'd in ſuch a manner as ought to give you any Apprehenſions. This modeſt Opinion of your own Merit, would ſurprize me, were I unacquainted with the Cauſe The Truth is, you allow me no Share in your Eſteem, but engroſs it all to yourſelf; and amidſt the Severities you launch againſt my Sex, you have not the Goodneſs to make any particular Exception in my favour. You are ſenſible of my tender Affection for you, but never conſider it as any Obligation. You believe I have an abſolute Propenſity to love, and if you ſometimes flatter yourſelf, that your Merit created a Senſibility in my Soul, you more frequently impute that Impreſſion to an Effect of Caprice, that might have diſpoſed me to have been as favourable to another, as I have prov'd to you. You may remember, however, that the Heart you ſo much deſpiſe at preſent, was not ſo eaſy to be gained. You was obliged to employ all your Artifice to conquer it, and would never have ſucceeded, if you had not diſguiſed your natural Diſpoſition, when you began to attack it; or if I had ſuffer'd the Dictates of my Reaſon to perſuade me that you reſembled thoſe Men, for whom I had conceived ſo much Horror. You may poſſibly

ſibly alledge to me the Continuance of your Paſſion, and I am willing you ſhould derive from it, all the Honour it can afford you. But, alas! how many Inſtances of your Perfidy to me; and what a Variety of your Attachments to other Objects, have I not been obliged to pardon! How many Pangs and Tears has it coſt me to reclaim your Heart; and how ſoon would your Paſſion have expired, if my obſequious Indulgence had not prevented you from extinguiſhing its Flame! How wretched would you have render'd me, by your Infidelity, had I not oppoſed your Coldneſs with ſo much Conſtancy, that you could not preſume to tell me I had loſt you for-ever! Your Paſſion would have been much more ardent, had I affected to treat you with an Indifference, equal to the Love you have experienced. Had Variety been my ſeeming Inclination, I could have created you a conſtant Perplexity, by leaving you uncertain of the true State of my Heart: The Arts of Coquetry and Diſſimulation, would have waked your Paſſion from thoſe Languors into which you have ſuffer'd it to ſink; and you would have dreaded my Inconſtancy, the moment you thought me capable of changing. But I can aſſure you, I ſhould bluſh to be indebted to ſuch degrading Arts, for the Poſſeſſion of your Heart. I am ſensible that I am fated to lose you; but, instead of making me the Victim of your Levities, be so generous as to confirm to me, at once, the Reality of that Loss. As miserable as it may render me, it can never be more tormenting than the cruel Uncertainty in which I now live. I only request you to declare, you no longer love me; and, can you think a little Sincerity too valuable a Return, for all the Tenderness you have experienced from me?

LETTER LVII.

WHEN your Passion, for me, was in its utmost Warmth, I foresaw that you would, one day, prove inconstant. I have now experienced the Truth of that Presage; and though it afflicts me too severely, yet it gives me no Surprize. Could I have any reason to flatter myself, that you would always continue to love me, and if I was assured of my own Constancy, by the Disposition of my Heart, what Security could that afford me for yours? You are, at last, determin'd to forsake me, and perhaps for another Object; or you may possibly be so satiated with Love, as to condemn yourself to an eternal Indifference. But I shall not pretend to enter into the Reasons by which

which you have suffer'd yourself to be conducted. A Lover would be too unfortunate, were it necessary for him to be always attached to the Object he once pretended to adore; and, for the sake of a Conquest he no longer esteems, should decline all Opportunities of making those that are new. I shall not trouble you with any Complaints, since it is not your Fault, if I continue to love you; and you have practised every Expedient, to extinguish a Passion you no longer had an Inclination to cherish. You never promis'd me an unchanging Love; but if you had really made me any Protestations of that nature, yet I should not be astonished to find you perjur'd. You once thought me amiable, but are convinced that I cease to appear so now; and since the few Charms of my Person were the only Motives to your Passion, it may justly be extinguished with those. My only Request at present is, that you would see me no more; and I am the more inclin'd to urge it, because I am sensible it will cost you nothing to grant it. I am conscious that I love you still; let me then habituate myself, by your Absence, to consider you with Indifference. The Sight of you would plunge me into new Despair. You could only repeat to me the Language of your Letter, and it would be ungenerous in you, to behold the Flow of those Tears,

which

which you have no Inclination to check. But is it poſſible then, that you ſhould reſolve to abandon me for ever! And have I no more Intereſt in that Heart, that perjur'd Heart, that pretended to derive all its Felicity from our Union! Ah! how tormenting is the Loſs of that Enjoyment, which was once the Source of our deareſt Delights! Notwithſtanding all I have ſaid of your Inconſtancy, alas! I was never in a Diſpoſition to preſage it! I had ſuch an implicit Confidence in your Proteſtations, and flatter'd myſelf that my exceſſive Paſſion had ſo effectually ſecured me from the Loſs of your Heart, that I never imagined you capable of any perfidious Conduct. I was conſcious that nothing could ever rend you from my Soul, and have ſometimes deluded myſelf into a Belief, that I ſhould be the only Object of your real Paſſion. I was delighted to think, that my Death alone could reſtore you to yourſelf; and that even in my laſt Moments, I ſhould enjoy the Felicity of beholding myſelf regretted, and beloved by you. Why do you envy me the only Conſolation that was left me! Come then, inhuman as you are, and be ſedulous to overwhelm me with your Indifference. Perſuade yourſelf, that you would treat me with too much Barbarity, ſhould you permit me to live any longer! I am now to loſe you eter-

eternally; for ſuch is the Reſolution you have taken! You are not prepoſſeſſed in favour of another, and yet you are determin'd to forſake me. Were the Expreſſions of your Letter, written with Deliberation; and did you ſeriouſly conſider their Importance? Reſt perſuaded then, that our Intercourſe expires from this Moment; and that ſince you have deſerted me in this manner, ſhould you hereafter throw yourſelf at my Feet, with more Tenderneſs than you ever yet diſcovered, and ſhould I even be conſcious of thoſe Sentiments in my Soul, which have ſo long conſtituted our Happineſs, I would reſolve to conſider you as the Object of all my Averſion for ever. Adieu; I have acquainted you with my Reſolution, and have nothing more to ſay to you.

LETTER LVIII.

I Deſired you, in my laſt Letter, to ſee me no more; for I am ſenſible that the Sight of you would revive thoſe Sentiments in my Soul, which it is my Intereſt to extinguiſh. But ſuch is the cruel State to which you have reduced me, that your Abſence is the greateſt of my Calamities. I no longer aſk you for any Returns of Tenderneſs; but, at the ſame time, I am certain that

that I have not merited your Reluctance to see me. Be not apprehensive that I intend to make you any Reproaches; for I am persuaded they would all be unavailing, and am more offended with myself, than with you. Had my Eyes not been so fatally closed, and had my Passion been so discreet, as to have permitted me to reflect on your Conduct, and to discover, in every Part of it, your Insensibility of my Condescensions in your favour, you should never have found it necessary to acquaint me with your Inconstancy. But alas! my Judgment was so obscured, at that time, that I believed you to be as perfect as I could wish. However, I shall not enter into any Detail that may displease you; and I have no Intention to reproach you, tho' you have been so cruel as to forsake me. But, in what Particular have I merited your Contempt? You are sensible that I am indisposed, and yet you absent yourself from me. What Offence have I committed, that obliges you to treat me with so much Barbarity? You are still apprehensive of my Passion; Ah! cease to entertain any Fears of that nature! As violent as it yet continues, your Insensibility, and my Loftiness of Soul, will preserve me from all its former Effects. You no longer shall see my Eyes overflowed with degrading Tears; and shall no more behold me descend-

descending to despicable Intreaties. But, tho' we cease to be Lovers, have we renounced the Pleasures of Friendship? This is the utmost I can possibly ask; but Inconstancy would not be sufficiently agreeable to you, were you not to aggravate it with Contempt. In what Circumstance of my Conduct does my Guilt consist? You alone have occasioned all my Crimes: Had it not been for you, I might still have enjoy'd—— Ah! to what purpose do I torment myself with such cruel Reflections! They only point out the Misconduct they were unable to prevent, and officiously redouble my Despair. I should be less afflicted at your Indifference, if, while I cease to be beloved, I could reinstate that Repose in my Soul, which you have banish'd for ever. But, alas! your Coldness, instead of extinguishing my Passion, seems to rekindle it with greater Violence! To what Unhappiness am I fated! I love you, even to Madness, when you only dissemble a Tenderness you never experience; and I die with Despair, when you cease to delude me. Pity the Condition to which I am reduced. I am only sollicitous to see you, and I will oblige you so far, as not to be alone when you visit me. Let me accustom myself, insensibly, to lose you for-ever. Tell me each Particular that can afford me the Confirmation of my Misfortune;

tune; it would be an Excefs of Cruelty, to conceal any Circumftance from me. Confider likewife, that if you abruptly difcontinue your Vifits, you may create fome Sufpicions in my Hufband, and you furely are too polite, to give him any Caufe to entertain them. Adieu, my Lord; I am not defirous that your Complaifance, for me, fhould be of a long Continuance, and I fhall be able, by a fudden Abfence, to free you from the Embarrafment of repeating it much longer.

LETTER LIX.

CEASE, for Heaven's fake, to write to me any more, and fave me from the Mortification of defpifing a Perfon I once thought worthy of my Efteem. You have come to a Rupture with me, and I am not difpofed to complain of your Proceeding. I entertained fuch a favourable Opinion of you, as inclined me to believe you would not treat me with Injuftice, nor ever abandon me, without fufficient Reafons. I have even efteemed you for the Sincerity with which you acquainted me with your Change; and you now prefume to intreat my Pardon! You can affure me, that your Eftrangement was the Effect of your Caprice, and are

are capable of plunging a Dagger into my Boſom, with all the Calmneſs imaginable. Do I, then, deſerve this Treatment, who lived for you alone; and can you entertain ſo contemptible an Opinion of me, as to imagine I can ever reſtore you my Heart for the future! Barbarous Man! who from no Inducement, but the Satisfaction of overwhelming me with Deſpair, have treated me as if I had been the moſt criminal of my Sex. Had you determined to devote your Paſſion to another Object, and only quitted me to reſign yourſelf entirely to her, I could have excuſed your Inconſtancy, and ſhould even have had the Generoſity to believe I had given you ſome Cauſe for the Change I have experienced in you. I would have conſider'd your new Paſſion, as altogether involuntary on your part, and might poſſibly have derived ſome Conſolation from that Thought: But that you ſhould thus pretend to forſake me, without the leaſt Regard to Decorum, and with no other View than to ſatisfy your Curioſity whether the Loſs of you will affect me, gives me a Pang I am incapable of ſuſtaining. As ſhort a ſpace of Time as ſuch a Feint may continue, it will always be too long, and nothing but ſuch Inhumanity itſelf could have Recourſe to an Artifice. I, however, could have pardon'd you that Diſſimulation, and ſhould have loved you so ardently, as to have flatter'd myself that your Proceeding had resulted from an Excess of Delicacy; and as peculiar as the Proofs may be, by which a Lover would assure himself of his Interest in our Heart, they are always charming, when they are so many Demonstrations of his Passion. Had my Idea of you been of this nature, one Day would have sufficed for your Satisfaction, and my Torment. You would not have refused me the smallest Instances of Complaisance, nor have absented yourself from me, for fifteen Days; and when you had afterwards seen me, you would not have added the most inhuman Insults to the Injury you had already offer'd me. And can you still presume to write to me! Can you recall my Idea to your Soul, without expiring with Confusion! You tell me that you love me; Ah! how happy should I be, were that Acknowledgment sincere!

May that Passion, then, be your eternal Torment; and may I, one day, give you as many Proofs of my Aversion and Contempt, as you have received of my Tenderness, and of which the most detestable of your Sex would have been more worthy than yourself.

LETTER LX.

IT would really be very ſingular, ſhould I ſtill continue to love you; and I agree with you, that my Conduct, in that Particular, would be extremely pleaſant. But I can aſſure you, my poor Count, that my Mirth is much abated, and I had reaſon to acquaint you, that you would not find the Concluſion of the Comedy ſo agreeable as you might imagine. Were you truly ſenſible what a ridiculous Part you act at preſent, you would not have any Power to perſonate it much longer. You are extremely languid and diſengaged, I confeſs; Lady *** had rejected your Aſſiduities, and I am diverted at your Surprize. What a number of Mortifications muſt you needs ſuſtain! Comfort yourſelf, however, for moſt Men have experienced the ſame Fate: But how could it poſſibly happen to you; and that, as amiable as you are, you ſhould be repulſed from two different Quarters? But you have one Reſource, after all; for it ſeems you once have loved me, and have been ſo ſucceſsful as to deceive me; have Recourſe then to your fruitful Imagination for ſome new Method of deluding me. I am perfectly acquainted with your diſconſolate Air, on thoſe Occaſions; but neither that, nor the affected Sighs you breathe from the bottom of your Heart; the little Flows of Language you expreſs with ſo much Delicacy; the Letters you pen with ſo much Elegance; the weeping Languor of your Eyes; your dejected Mien, nor all the Arts you have already aſſumed, will ever touch me for the future; and I believe theſe are the only Dexterities you can practiſe, to regain me. Even your Wit is all ineffectual, ſince it will be unobſerved by me: You therefore judge very properly, that all theſe polite Attractions will be unavailing. What ſtill contributes to your Misfortune is, that you paſs for a Deceiver, and that few Women of tolerable Underſtanding ever credit your Proteſtations: And, as you are not fond of Conqueſts that are too eaſy, I doubt your Sighs will not be ſo ſoon rewarded as you may wiſh. You ſee how unhappy you are! Your Paſſion for me began to diſguſt you; I was no longer capable of inſpiring you with Tenderneſs; and you forgot that you ever thought me amiable. You treated me in a perfidious manner, and endeavoured to render yourſelf happy with other Objects; but when you had the Mortification to be diſappointed, you grew deſirous of returning to me. I received you with ſome Severity, and you are now more amorous than ever. What a charming Heart is yours, and how

how delightful muſt it be, to have the Diſpoſal of all its Emotions! You, however, have ranged the Circumſtances of this Adventure, with great Judgment: According to your Plan I muſt needs continue to love you; and you think that Paſſion would be natural to me, were it not a little diſconcerted by Caprice: But you thought yourſelf confident that my Sentiments, in your favour, could not long be diſcontinued, and I cannot blame you, if you are ſurprized to find me ſo different from what you expected. You are not able to comprehend this Incident, tho' it proves more important than any other. But it is time for me to finiſh this little Pleaſantry, and anſwer your Letter. I owe you ſome good Advice, as well as a free Confeſſion of the Sentiments I entertain on your account. I muſt therefore acquaint you, that my Paſſion is entirely extinguiſhed: I could have told you the ſame, in the Height of my Reſentment, but not with ſo much Sincerity as at preſent. When our Minds are agitated to an extreme Degree, we may eaſily impoſe upon ourſelves; but as ſoon as the firſt Emotion is over, we conſider Things with Calmneſs, and are not ſo liable to be deceived. You may therefore receive it, from me, as an infallible Truth, that I neither love you at this time, nor ever ſhall for the future. Your Repentance may poſſibly be ſincere, but it will never affect me. We ſeldom grant our Pardon, but when it affords us ſome Pleaſure to offer it, and when the Injuries we have ſuſtain'd have not been ſo conſiderable as to extinguiſh our Affection. You are ſenſible of the Injuſtice I have ſuffer'd from you, and I ſhall not condeſcend to repeat the Particulars. Let your Heart be its own Judge; may it overwhelm you with all the Reproaches you merit, and place your Conduct before you, in ſuch an odious Light, as may prevent you from afflicting any other with the Injuries you have offer'd me. I once lov'd you to Adoration, and my Paſſion was incapable of a Moment's Inſincerity; but you have, at laſt, caus'd it to expire. You aſſure me, at preſent, that I am the only Object of your Tenderneſs; but you will be too unhappy, if you entertain any Sentiments, with which my Heart is unable to correſpond. But were even this poſſible, you ought to be cautious of indulging any flattering Thoughts. Render Juſtice to yourſelf, and renounce all Hope: Perhaps you may not have Diſcretion enough to diſcontinue your Viſits to me, and therefore I ſhall make it my part to prevent them. Abſence is our only Cure on ſuch Occaſions, and when we ſuffer by unfortunate Paſſions, the Sight of the Object that created them, gives us the ſevereſt Torments.

Torments. However, if your Departure is to be so sudden as you inform me, I grant you my Permission to visit me, in order to take your final Leave. I neither am, nor ever intend to be your Enemy; and it is equally certain, that I shall never be your Lover. Let not my Goodness betray you into any false Expectations; were it less than it really is, you might entertain what Hopes you pleas'd; but you ought to regard my Consent to see you, as an infallible Proof of my Indifference.

BILLET.

If it must be so, my Lord, I permit you to be at the Opera, and am infinitely obliged to you for your Industry, to be inform'd what Box I shall appear in; and since you so much desire it, I shall take care to have you accommodated with a Place: But, as tender as the Musick may be, all Opera Nights are not alike; and whatever soft things you may tell me, with relation to Armida *and* Rinaldo, *I shall remember too well that I have been the one, ever to allow you to be the other.*

LET-

LETTER LXI.

I Always thought till now, that Expoſtulations of Jealouſy were only the Privilege of one beloved, and can never be enough ſurprized at the Diſcourſe you entertain'd me with yeſterday. Every Circumſtance from you offends me, when I obſerve that Love, or rather Vanity (for you certainly have more of this than of the other) is intermixed with all your Conduct. Have you any Reaſon to believe, that the Perſon who is more indifferent to me than any other of his Sex, ſhould be more ſucceſsful in my Heart, than you, whom I have loved with ſo much Tenderneſs? What have you to demand of me, at preſent, and on what do you raiſe your Pretenſions? If you had diſcovered any Charms in my Tenderneſs, you would have been more ſollicitous to preſerve it, and would never have compelled me to change it into Indifference. I am not ſurpriz'd that you ſhould ceaſe to love me, ſince I no longer can affect you with any pleaſing Impreſſions; and it was natural for you to diſcontinue an Intercourſe, which could afford you no more Satisfactions. Whatever may be ſaid of Conſtancy, it always expires with Love, and ſeldom ſubſiſts longer than the Gratifi-

Gratification of thoſe Deſires it created. I was ſenſible, when I reſign'd myſelf to your Ardours, that they would ſoon diminiſh, and I ſhould be condemn'd to loſe you; but as I ſuffer'd myſelf to be betray'd by thoſe Sentiments that extinguiſhed my Reaſon, I had no Power to guard againſt the Danger, tho' I ſo well knew myſelf obnoxious to it. I have obſerv'd you, for ſome time, more tender than you even appeared before I gave you the utmoſt Proofs of my Weakneſs; and whatever they may have coſt me, they can never create me any Diſſatisfaction, while they contribute to your Happineſs. But alas! this delightful Time will ſoon come to a Period! your Deſires will grow languid, and you will be leſs attentive to pleaſe me: My Paſſion will ceaſe to preſent you with its former Charms, and you will find it difficult to afford it any ſuitable Returns. Some Conſiderations may, perhaps, prevent you from aſſuming an ungenerous Air of Coldneſs; but my Preſence will become diſtaſteful to you; you will receive, with Reluctance, the repeated Proofs of my Frailty, and every Circumſtance, on my part, will give you ſome Diſquietude. What would have been your Condition, if you could have had no Recourſe to Inconſtancy for your Relief? But it ill becomes me to complain of your Con-

duct;

duct; you are entirely Maſter of yourſelf, and can extinguiſh your Paſſion when you pleaſe. You imagine you continue to love me, and are even affected with Jealouſy: But is it poſſible you ſhould forget the Value you entertained for your Liberty; and do you no more remember that you ſacrificed me to the Pleaſure of enjoying it? You intreat me to afford you ſome obliging Inſtances of my Regard for you; and are not my Letters ſuch Favours as may induce you to hope for more? I obſerve, with Regret, that they inſpire you with Ideas, which, for the ſake of your Repoſe, you ought to have extinguiſhed long ago; and, if you would think juſtly, you ought to be ſenſible, that a Diſinclination to wiſh any thing to your Diſadvantage, may as naturally proceed from Indifference, as it can from Generoſity. Hatred may be ſucceeded by contrary Impreſſions; and tho' I will not pretend to anſwer for myſelf in every particular, yet I can venture to declare, you are not the Object of my Averſion. With reſpect to your Apprehenſions, you have Reaſon to imagine that I am not diſpoſed to relieve you from them; and that, if I really continued to love you, I ſhould not conſider your Jealouſy as any Obligation, ſince I am perſuaded it rather proceeds from the degrading Opinion you entertain of me, than

than from any Diffidence of your own Merit. But ſhould I really indulge a new Paſſion, I ſhould only act by your Direction, and this, at leaſt, would be an Evidence of my Regard for your Counſels. Adieu, my Lord; my Affairs will not permit me to ſee you do-day; my own Inclinations will oppoſe your Viſit to-morrow, and I ſhall not be able to anſwer for the reſt of the Week: You may therefore, adjuſt either your Pleaſures or Affairs accordingly.

BILLET.

You may well congratulate yourſelf for your Dexterity, in cauſing the Marquis my Husband to reproach me for my Incivility to you. You remember, I ſuppoſe, that in a former Circumſtance, of the like nature, you had Recourſe to the ſame Thought, and that it proved very ſucceſsful: But you muſt conſider that I ſincerely lov'd you, at that time, and was willing to improve any Pretext for accompliſhing a Reconciliation between us. As our Affairs are otherwiſe ſituated at preſent, you ought to have ſtudied ſome new Contrivance; but when one is not extremely amorous, one's Invention happens not to be very fertile. Such extraordinary Schemes will exhauſt your Imagination, and I adviſe you to reſerve them for Lady N***. *She aſſures me,* *me, you are very desirous to render yourself agreeable to her; but I fear it will be difficult for you to make her retract the Opinion she entertains to your Disadvantage: But I promise you to employ my best Endeavours to inspire her with more favourable Sentiments: For, as I am but too happy in beholding you devoted to another, I shall try all manner of Expedients to soften her Rigours. You will soon receive my Answer, by the Marquis; but I must intreat you not to employ him, in Messages of this nature. I reproach myself for ever consenting to such a Proceeding, and should be inexcusable, were I to suffer it any longer.*

LETTER LXII.

THE Prince of *** certainly loves me; but it is not equally true that I have any Aversion for him. The Manner in which you have seen us together, will not permit me to dissemble; and besides, it is so natural to be in love, that I cannot think any Denial of it necessary on this Occasion. Yes, my Lord, I really love him, and am surprized that you, who were always so jealous, can possibly doubt it. Do you forget then, that my Heart is so extremely tender, that were it even favourable to thirty Lovers,

Lovers, I ſhould have a Reſerve of Senſibility for thoſe who might ſtill preſent me with their Addreſſes. One Sigh alone is ſufficient with me. I can aſſure you, however, the Prince has not offer'd me any as yet; and I have taken the utmoſt Care not to render them neceſſary. He is too illuſtrious a Conqueſt, not to merit all imaginable Attention; and I am not able to conceive, why you ſhould fancy that he would find me inflexible. 'Tis true, his Wit is not altogether miraculous; but, whenever he pleaſes, he can be complimented with that Quality, by ſo many Perſons who really enjoy it, that his own Want of it will be leſs viſible. He muſt be very deſtitute indeed, if he has not Genius enough to amuſe a Woman; and, whatever you may pleaſe to think, he tells me the ſame fine things, you have utter'd yourſelf. He makes me ſolemn Proteſtations that he adores me, and delivers himſelf in ſuch a moving Tone, as extremely becomes him; while his Eyes, more eloquent than his Words, are conſequently more perſuaſive. His ſoft and ſedulous Air convinces me, that his Sentiments correſpond with his Expreſſions; though he never aſſures me of the Violence of his Paſſion, by ſuch inconſiderate Sighs as you affected yeſterday, and which drew upon you the Attention of a whole Aſſembly. His

Modefty is much fuperior to yours, and I difcover, in his Timidity, more Paffion than I ever obferv'd in your Self-fufficiency. He loves me without indulging the leaft Hope, and I fhould be pleas'd with the Appearance of fo difinterefted a Conduct, were it lefs a Reality. What other Declaration do you expect from me now? Perhaps he may impofe on my Credulity; but then he is careful never to difpleafe me: And, as I have made half a Conqueft in fifteen Days, I efteem it a confiderable Progrefs, for one fo difgufted with Love as myfelf. However, I am apt to think I fhall not amufe myfelf much longer, with thefe extraordinary Qualities. The moft amiable Lover may eafily ceafe to be fuch, and the Affurance that he has already pleafed, foon renders him incapable of that Power for the future. I am fo convinc'd of what I fay, that I am refolv'd to difmifs my fighing Admirers, before the weak Moment appears. We never act fo difagreeable a Part, as when we value ourfelves for our Fidelity to your Sex. Conftancy is no more than a Chimera; it no longer fubfifts in Nature, and is the moft abfurd Effect that can refult from the whole Courfe of our Reflections. Shall a vain Principle of Honour, which even eludes our Conception, when we fubmit to its Dictates, prevent us from changing, when we

are

are diſſatisfied with our Choice! Why ſhould we be ſubſervient to the Caprice of a Lover, who would make his own Inclinations the Rule of our Conduct; and oblige us to experience that Diſguſt which is created in him by a long Paſſion! For what reaſon ſhould we bear the Auſterity of a Maſter, from the Perſon we imagined would be our Slave? or why ſhould we think it meritorious, to love one who ceaſes to inſpire us with Tenderneſs! Can any thing be more ridiculous than ſuch a Proceeding, and am I not very happy, ſince you have freed me from ſo painful a Situation? But though you have favour'd me with ſo many Obligations, I muſt intreat you not to viſit me ſo often. You would, for-ever, entertain me with your Converſation; but, I think, I have already aſſured you I have no Anſwer to return you. You are likewiſe ſenſible, that when I permitted you to ſee me, I imagin'd your ſudden Departure would place us at a ſufficient Diſtance from each other: But you ſtill continue in Town, and I am not diſpoſed to be eternally complaiſant to your Deſires. Adieu, my Lord; the Goodneſs I have diſcover'd, by unfolding my Heart to you, without Reſerve, is not ſo advantageous to you as you might poſſibly wiſh; but it was neceſſary to reſtore me to my Repoſe. You would interrupt it, by engaging me to renew my Paſſion; and I believe the moſt effectual Method to diſſuade you from that Attempt, will be to convince you that my Sentiments can no longer correſpond with yours.

BILLET.

It ſeems you are indiſpoſed; and am I the Cauſe? thou artful, perfidious Man! I ſuppoſe then, I muſt likewiſe be accountable for all the Diſorders you may hereafter ſuſtain. In what a Variety of Shapes do you aſſault my Weakneſs! At our laſt Interview, you had Recourſe to Tears; and what have you not attempted to-day! Does your Recovery depend on me? Believe me, you rate your Health at too great a Price. You are deſirous to find my Heart as favourable to you as ever; but I am ſenſible, the Pardon I am inclin'd to grant you, would only afford you an Opportunity of inſulting me a-new. The happy Time you ſtill deſire, is already paſs'd; you have almoſt eraſed it from your Remembrance; and why ſhould I ſigh, when I recall it to my Thoughts! All the World aſſures me that you ſtill continue to love me; but they certainly miſinform me, ſince I find it ſo difficult to believe them. Regain your Health, however, that I may have the Confirmation of what they ſay, from yourſelf; for I deſire nothing more than a Conviction

of

of that nature. I am ſenſible, that you already inſpire me with abundance of Compaſſion; the reſt I ſhall reſerve till I ſee you.

LETTER LXIII.

MY Pardon has been only too extenſive, cruel as you are! You yeſterday beheld my Tears, and Weakneſs; what can you deſire more? I am not diſpleas'd at your Fears, but am unwilling to indulge you in too much Security. Were you entirely convinced of my Paſſion, it would be leſs pleaſing to you than your preſent Uncertainty, which proves to me, that, as yet, you are unacquainted with all the Wrongs you have offer'd me; for your Suſpicions that you are not beloved, are ſo many Confeſſions that you hardly merit that Favour. But do you intend to continue long in that doubtful State? Will your Heart be really devoted to me again; and are you ſenſible of the Gratitude and Tenderneſs you owe me? I have ſeen you affected with Tranſports that ſeem'd ſincere: But ah! how apprehenſive am I, that Vanity was their Source! You caſt your Eyes on a Rival, and never thought me worthy to be loved, till you loſt all Hopes of regaining my Heart. It rais'd your Indignation to ſee yourſelf on the Point of loſing an Enjoyment you ſo long poſſeſſed, and you was more ſollicitous to make the Prince * * * ſenſible of the Power of your Charms, than to afford me any Evidence of your Paſſion, when you endeavour'd to deprive him of the Heart he wiſh'd to inſpire with Impreſſions in his favour. Yóu imagin'd I was not diſpleas'd with his Addreſſes, and you conſider'd the Loſs of my Heart, as a Circumſtance that might tend to your Diſhonour. I needed not the Aſſiſtance of your Idea, to guard me againſt any Tenderneſs for him. When I was even oppreſs'd with my utmoſt Sorrows, you were as dear to me as ever. My Reaſon would indeed declare againſt ſo extravagant a Paſſion, and endeavour'd to diſguiſe the Emotions that roſe in my Breaſt. I imagin'd I could prevail on myſelf to hate you, but ſoon found that Sentiment too painful to be true. I then wiſh'd to conſider you with Indifference; but alas! that very Deſire convinced me of my Incapacity to accompliſh it. I was tortur'd by theſe Agitations of my Soul, and they only abated when I beheld you. Love then employ'd all my Thoughts, and your Senſibility was the only Subject of my warmeſt Deſires. Happy ſhould I have been amidſt the Anguiſh that oppreſs'd me, could I have conceal'd it from your Obſervation, and been capable of a Reſolution only

only to ſee you in publick. How dearly did it coſt me to avoid your Preſence; and what Confeſſions ſhould I not have made you, had I reſign'd myſelf to the natural Propenſity of my Soul! How have your Tears cauſed my Eyes to flow; and how deſirous was I to eaſe you of the Share of Anguiſh you ſuſtain'd! Did I aſſure you in my Letters, that I ceas'd to love you; and could you poſſibly credit ſuch a Declaration? Could Indifference be well expreſs'd by the Paſſion that conſum'd me? Should I have writ to you at all, if I had not been as much intereſted in your Affection as ever. But if you miſapprehended my Letters, did not my Eyes rectify your Miſtake? They, indeed, were the faithful Expoſitors of my Heart, and Love was for-ever legible in all their Glances. Your Sighs were always ſucceeded by mine, and the Torments I ſuſtain'd, were more agonizing than yours, ſince I durſt not acquaint you with my Alarms. I was jealous, even to Madneſs, and imagin'd your Eyes never diſcloſed the leaſt Indifference to the reſt of my Sex. You ſeem'd to be inſpir'd with Tenderneſs for every Object but myſelf; but whatever Reſentment that Imagination might infuſe into my Soul, the moment I recall'd you to my Remembrance, I forgot each Subject of Complaint you had ever given me, and my

Memory

Memory had no Traces that were pleaſing, except thoſe that prevented me from baniſhing your Idea. My Eyes were rivited to your Picture, and in vain did I endeavour to call it the Image of a perfidious Creature. I only beheld thoſe Features which all my Reſentment could never eraſe from my Soul. Barbarian as you are! why is your Heart unaffected with the Tenderneſs that perpetually ſoftens mine! You can declare you love me, in all the Rapture of Language; but why ſhould your Imagination aſſume the Province of your Heart! How do you injure me, if you utter what you never experience; and yet how could you ſo well repreſent thoſe Emotions, did they affect you but faintly! As I am now ſatisfied with your Sentiments, be it your Care to perpetuate that Impreſſion. Reſolve to be mine, as entirely as I determine to be yours. Live to give me all thoſe Proofs of your Paſſion, which I have a Right to demand, and receive them reciprocally from me. Let our Union be eternal; and may we forget, amidſt our Tranſports, that any Accident can have Power to effect our Separation. Why, in ſome ſequeſtred Part of the Univerſe, ſweetly contented with ourſelves, remote from every Care, and utterly unknown to the reſt of the Creation; can we not behold our Days renewing for no other

End,

End, than to preſent us with the Pleaſures that flow from a warm and delicate Paſſion! As we ſhould then be ſure to paſs the ſucceeding Day in Love, we ſhould the leſs regret that, whoſe Portion of Hours was expired. The agreeable Remembrance of the paſt, would only animate us to improve the future; and, amidſt the Charms of a Paſſion for-ever new, our after-Periods of Time would only preſent us with the Certainty of our mutual Love. Were I alone to converſe with you, in ſome ſerene and bliſsful Solitude, I ſhould no longer be apprehenſive of beholding you ſeduced from my Ardours; and as they would be always increaſing, they would render you incapable of entertaining an Inclination to forſake me. But ſince I am not to expect ſo compleat a Felicity, endeavour, at leaſt, to conduct yourſelf in ſuch a manner, that amidſt the Tumult of the Word, you may only be ſenſible of Solitude, when you are abſent from me; and that all the Objects around you may increaſe your Wiſhes for a Reunion with that from which you are then divided. And when you attract the Glances of all the Fair, be only ſollicitous to diſtinguiſh mine, and believe me to be alone worthy of your Preference, when-ever you are tempted to Inconſtancy. Your utmoſt Profuſion of Love can never repay me, too amply, for the

the Sufferings you have caused me to sustain; and I should die with Despair, were I to see you devote that Tenderness to another, which ought to be my peculiar Claim. Could you possibly believe that I lov'd the Prince * * *? And tho' your Conduct had extinguished my Passion for you, are you so little acquainted with my Disposition, as to believe me capable of a new Commerce with any of your Sex; or that I could possibly desire a Continuance of my Dishonour? I then should justify your Inconstancy and Contempt, too well. You know, by Experience, that my Favours are not easily accorded: You are sensible there were certain Moments wherein my Loss of you would have been insupportable, but that I hoped it would reconcile me to my Duty, and teach me, by a better Conduct, to discontinue the Reproaches I made myself, and which, perhaps, I suffer'd from all the World. You never presumed to sollicit my Sacrifice of this Rival to your Repose; and how happy should I be, would you prove so just to me, as to believe any Request of that nature would have been unnecessary! But you shall never see him, for the future, in my Apartment; and would to Heaven, he had been Master of more Merit, that your Triumph might have been as glorious as I could wish. Adieu; I begin to perceive

ceive my Letter has a very frightful Length, and that I have not been very punctual to my Promiſe: But it has been ſuch an Age ſince I gave you any Aſſurance that I lov'd you, that I can eaſily pardon myſelf, for repeating that Expreſſion a little too often to-day; and if you ſhould not likewiſe forgive me, I can only reproach myſelf for not having expreſs'd the half of what I experience. I ſhall no longer give myſelf the Trouble to abridge your Viſits. Adieu.

You will hardly gueſs at the Misfortune that has happen'd to me. The Marquis my Huſband has juſt now inform'd me, that my Aunt is very much indiſpos'd, and I muſt be gone this Moment, to paſs the whole Day with her. I ſhould be inconſolable at this Accident, if I did not hope to have ample Amends to-morrow, for the Pleaſure I muſt loſe this Day. Can there be any People in the World more unfortunate than ourſelves?

BILLET.

I was preparing to write to you, when I received your Letter; and tho' I thought I had a number of things to tell you, yet I find myſelf at a loſs for any Particulars at preſent. I could not imagine it would be ſo dif- *ficult*

*ficult for me to anſwer your Letter; however, I am very ſenſible that I deſire to ſee you: But don't you think my Cloſet too ſolitary a Place for a Viſit? Since I have remov'd my Books from it, we have no Excuſe for being there; and ſince——Good God, what a number of perplexing Circumſtances am I creating myſelf! Of what Conſequence is my Cloſet to you? I had an Inclination to attend Lady *** into the Country, but was unable to fix that Reſolution without your Conſent: Come and free me then from my Uncertainty.*

LETTER LXVI.

SINCE you have retir'd into the Country, ſeveral extraordinary Particulars have happen'd in Town. Lady *** is become a Devotee, and *T**** is grown a mere Libertine; ſhe has quitted her Lover, and he his Benefice; but 'tis thought they, each of them, will repent of their Proceeding. Count ***, tho' as diſagreeable as ever, is extremely fortunate with my Sex, and the ſerious prude Lady *** begins to amuſe herſelf with amorous Inclinations. The inſipid Marchioneſs is altogether as cenſorious as ever: She is eternally at play, and preſerves her Reliſh for lively *Champaign:* She likewiſe continues to be extremely fond of her

her flushing Complexion, her ridiculous Shape, her eternal Prattle, her Vanity, her Vapours, her Rage, and her old Lovers: In short, she is a most immutable Lady. Inconstancy reigns to a prodigious degree at *Paris*, and is grown an epidemic Distemper. Heaven preserve us from its Effects! Amours were never of so short a Continuance as now, whether it be that Favours are refus'd with too much Severity, or granted with too little Hesitation, I am uncertain; but the whole Affair is commonly finish'd in fifteen Days. *D* * * * was yesterday in the good Grace of Lady * * *; but she has entirely discarded him to-day; and he, in revenge, has devoted himself to the old Countess, whose other Gallant has forsaken her; but the two good Ladies are not destitute of Lovers. I was yesterday with * * *, and you had Reason to say we were treated a little censoriously in that Place. The charitable *N* * * * has inform'd me of all the Particulars; but why should we be chagrin'd? Do you imagine that, in what manner soever we live, it will be possible for us to escape Detraction? What will then become of those gay Ladies, who are obliged to withdraw from the Gallant World, to make themselves Devotees out of mere Necessity; and who are criminal from their Constitution, and censorious by Choice? A certain Lady can have a thouſand Lovers, and be leſs diſhonour'd by their Number, than her Choice; and will yet think it unpardonable in me, to have only one. Old Lady *** is implacable againſt us; but of all our cenſorious Enemies, I regard her the leaſt. I am ſure ſhe will ſometimes talk ſo much like a Prude, that ſhe is perfectly unintelligible; and it might juſtly be ſaid of her, if one pleas'd, that a certain ſprightly Marquis, who conſtantly viſits her, and is for ever publiſhing the Goodneſs of the adoreable *Climene*, is more obliged to her Conduct, for the Particulars, than to his own Imagination. She may detract from my Charms, without ceaſing; but I ſhall never believe myſelf diſagreeable, till you ceaſe to love me. Little *D* *** has been extremely pert; but can you prevail upon yourſelf to chaſtiſe him? His Paint, his effeminate Voice, and his ridiculous Airs, render him the Jeſt of *Paris*. Let him live therefore, and we ſhall be ſufficiently aveng'd. Young Lady *** begins to appear more ſparkling, and leſs formidable than ever: She has improv'd by the Abſence of her Lovers, and perhaps is the only Perſon of her Sex, who can preſerve ſo many Charms, amidſt ſuch a Variety of Pangs. But her Gallants are now returning in Crowds: Thoſe whom ſhe has formerly treated with Diſdain, remember

ber it no longer, and others are not at all apprehensive of her Rigours. Lady *D**** who has never experienc'd such Fortune, is persuaded its Continuance will be short, and that amidst the Number of her Conquests, she will have some Losses to sustain. Lady *S****, and the old Marquis of ***, whose Amours were only in Imagination, have lately conceived a real Passion for each other, which surprizes all who know 'em. Her Ladyship is a Prude, but extremely tender; and the Marquis is amorous, but in the old Fashion She is fond of the modern Taste; but his Lordship is devoted to the other, because it proves so commodious to decay'd Lovers. You would be infinitely diverted, were you to hear the melting Conversation of these little Persons; and indeed it is quite hideous. Ever since the Lady has been so generous as to admit the Marquis into her Service, all the Discourse at her House turns upon the Delicacy of Love. His Lordship daily sends her his Remarks on each Book in *Astrea*, and moderates the Lady's Self-sufficiency by his learned Speeches. She vows that she never saw Love made in such a manner as it is in these Times, and is offended with the young People at Court, who introduc'd it. The Marquis, however, finds it necessary to be thought a fortunate Man with our Sex; and notwithſtanding all his Diſcretion, he never viſits Lady *** without looking as myſteriouſly as if he had ſome real Affair to tranſact with her. She aſſumes an Air of perfect Satisfaction, and believes it will be favourable to her Reputation. It is reported, however, that ſhe would be more diſſatisfied with an Amour of this nature, than ſhe really ſeems, were it not for the young Lover ſhe keeps about her. He is a mere Child, but extremely complaiſant, and he fills up thoſe Spaces of Time which are not devoted to the Marquis. Mercy upon me! I have furniſh'd you with Detraction enough, or I am much deceived! But I am piqued, and could proceed for ever. I believe I could even rail at you. Good Morrow.

BILLET.

You are entirely irregular in all your Conduct. I yeſterday expected you at ſeven, but was not favour'd with your Company till nine; and you was ſo provoking as to think this a Circumſtance of no great Importance, in an Aſſignation. You oblig'd me this Morning to wake from a charming Slumber, to read a Letter which was not worth the leaſt Particular of my Dream. Be inform'd, once for all, that one never truſts another to wake the Perſon one loves, when that Office can be perform'd perform'd by one's self; and you had no Expedient, but this, to prevent my regretting the agreeable Dream you interrupted. I suppose you will ask me what this agreeable Dream could be? I fancied myself in a most delightful Garden, and, if I am not mistaken, I was Flora *herself.* Zephyrus *did not much resemble you, and yet I thought him the most amiable Deity I had ever seen. He had committed some little Offence, and intreated me to pardon him; and as you have accustom'd me to these Condescensions, I comply'd without the least Hesitation, and he was preparing to thank me, when your Letter disconcerted the Flow of his Gratitude. I must confess, I was not much offended at this Interruption: And tho' you may be unworthy of the Favour, I can't help acquainting you, that you have my Permission to begin and end my Dreams. Adieu; you shall be inform'd when I am dispos'd for my next Slumber.*

BILLET.

I can no longer pardon your Negligence, and you are not to imagine that my Apprehensions are trivial. The Conduct of the Marquis my Husband, his frequent Continuance at V * * **, the Conjuncture that makes it necessary for him to be advanc'd to the Place that is now vacant; the secret Preparations* *he has been making this Month; his Rank, his Fortune, and his Attention to Things he never thought of before, are ſo many Inquietudes to my Soul. I have imparted my Fears to* St. Far ***, *who finds 'em juſt, and you alone are incredulous. I foreſee ſuch Misfortunes as make me tremble, and even thoſe that are more fatal preſent themſelves to my View, ſince you will not condeſcend to ſhare my Diſquiet. Continue then where you are at preſent; you will ſoon hear of my Departure, which will be render'd leſs diſagreeable by your Indifference. But if my Apprehenſions ſhould really happen to be ill founded, is not my Intimation of them ſufficient to make you ſympathiſe in my Affliction? You would dread the Event that threatens me, as much as myſelf, had Love taught you to ſhare my Torments. So much Security is too evident an Indication of Coldneſs; and, if we muſt be ſeparated, no Tears will flow, but mine. However, you ſhall not enjoy the Satisfaction of beholding them; for you would be ſo inhuman as to triumph in my Sorrows; and I had rather ſuffer Death, than afford your Vanity that Gratification. But why do you continue at ſuch a Diſtance from me? I am ſenſible of your Averſion to Buſineſs, and am perſuaded you would have return'd, e'er now, were you not detain'd by ſome new Pleaſures. But however that may be, don't imagine that*

I

I sollicit you to leave the Country. Be assured likewise, that my Affliction is not to be calm'd by a Letter: Your Presence alone can excuse you, and cause me to acknowledge the Tenderness I yet experience for you, as ungrateful as you would willingly appear.

LETTER LXV.

OUR cruel Presages are at last accomplish'd! Our Unhappiness is but too certain, and the Ambition of the Marquis, my Husband, has plung'd a Dagger into my Bosom. He has, at last, obtain'd the Employment for which he sollicited, and is preparing to carry me into a Country, which, as amiable as it may be thought, will always have the Aspect of a savage Land to me. I am now expos'd to all the Torments that can be created by a fatal Passion. The Dread of your Inconstancy was once my only Calamity; but I am not certain at present, whether it would not be less afflictive to me, to find you false, provided I could always see you, than to lose you for ever, when your Constancy is untainted. Are you truly sensible of the Horror I experience in this Situation? I love you, beyond the Power of Conception; —— But, did I only say, love! Ah! how inexpressive of of my Tenderneſs for you, is that faint Syllable! And muſt I then quit you for ever! Alas! you likewiſe love me, and that Thought compleats my Deſpair! How can we poſſibly live, when we are thus to be ſeparated from each other! We have thought a Moment's Abſence inſupportable, and were then deſtitute of all Delight. But I muſt now leave you for ever! For ever! — O gracious Heaven! can I write that Expreſſion, and continue to live! Have we really merited the Calamities we ſuſtain! Am I then fated to trouble the dear Repoſe of your Life! I, who would ſacrifice my own with Tranſport, to render you happy! But alas! our Doom is ſign'd! we are now to meet no more; ſince Heaven has decreed that our Separation ſhall be eternal! Could we poſſibly believe that the Adieus we ſo lately exchanged, ſhould be our laſt! The Anguiſh of this Idea ſinks me to Deſpair! Muſt we then be parted for ever, and ſhall we be perpetually lamenting our Abſence, without one flattering Hope of Reunion! Each of my future Days, then, will afflict me with a new Portion of Woe; and I ſhall only live in a languiſhing Sollicitude for Death. I ſhall ſee thoſe Days of Horror roll ſlowly away, without enjoying one Moment of your charming Preſence; for alas! my weeping Eyes muſt behold you no more! Had my Misfortunes afforded me but one dear Probability of ſeeing you hereaſter, that precious Moment, which would always be preſented to my Imagination, with the delightful Hope of beholding you faithful, would ſoften the Severity of my Tortures. Can ſo exquiſite a Pleaſure be purchas'd with too many Tears? But I am not allow'd to entertain that pleaſing Expectation, and the Continuance of my Unhappineſs is the only Proſpect that riſes before me. As the Duties of your Station will oblige you to reſide in *France*, I can only be the Object of your Compaſſion, and you may poſſibly not afford me even that, for any Length of Time. Alas! I ſhall no ſooner arrive at the Place to which I am baniſh'd, than my Image will be effaced from your Heart; our mutual Love will then appear to you like a Dream, whoſe Remembrance will afford you no Satisfaction! But, can you indeed conſent to render me ſo wretched? Can you poſſibly forget with what Tenderneſs I lov'd you, and how infinitely dear to my Soul you ſtill continue? Pity me ſome Moments at leaſt, and let me intreat you to remember, that Love created all the Calamities of my Life, and will ſoon lay me in the Grave. Yes, my deareſt Lord! I ſhall not long ſurvive my Separation from you, for I have no

Forti-

Fortitude to ſupport me in ſuch a threatning Scene of Woe. Adieu; I fear I ſhall prejudice your Affairs, ſhould I deſire you to haſten your Return; but you are ſenſible how much I need your Preſence at this time. I behold the killing Preparations for our Departure; and perhaps when eight Days are over, I ſhall never be permitted to ſee you more. They are even ſo inhuman as not to allow me to weep; and while I am dying with Anguiſh, I am oblig'd to diſſemble a ſerene Aſpect to thoſe who congratulate me on the new Dignity that deprives me of your Preſence for ever. Adieu; let me ſee you, however, that I may, at leaſt, mourn, with you, over the Misfortunes that await me. I am ſenſible of the Tortures I am preparing for my Soul, by deſiring to ſee you; but I ſhould think myſelf happy, to expire in your Arms!

LETTER LXVI.

NO, my deareſt Lord; I can never conſent that you ſhould follow me to the Land of my Baniſhment. It would be impoſſible for you to behold me in my preſent Condition, without dying with Anguiſh, and mine would be augmented by your

your Preſence. My Soul likewiſe preſages that I ſhall never ſee you again. In vain did you flatter me with approaching Scenes of Bliſs, for I am certain there are none in reſerve for me. Theſe ſix Months have I ſuſtain'd a languiſhing Indiſpoſition, and am ſenſible it will ſoon be render'd mortal by my Sorrows. This Idea alone could make my Remains of Life ſupportable; for why ſhould I wiſh to continue in this World! I am overwhelm'd with a cruel Weight of Woe, and can entertain no Hopes of Relief, ſince I am fated to love you to the laſt Moment of my Life, and am convinc'd that we ſhall no more be reviſited by thoſe happy Days we paſs'd in mutual Vows of an eternal Paſſion. They are now for ever loſt to us, and the Remembrance of the Joys they afforded, will only contribute to our Deſpair. How can I poſſibly ſupport an endleſs Abſence! I am perpetually counting the Moments I paſs without you. But, could I have the Satisfaction to be aſſur'd of your Happineſs; could you really be inſenſible of our Separation, and would conſent to loſe me without Reluctance——Alas! I ſhould then die with Deſpair! I am unacquainted with my own Inclinations: I even wiſh you would ceaſe to love me; I cannot think of your Torments without Diſtraction; and yet nothing renders my Sorrow ſupportable,

able, but the Aſſurance that you continue to ſhare it. I recollect the Condition in which I beheld you, when we were oblig'd to ſuppreſs our Tears at the cruel Adieus we exchang'd, when the Eyes of thoſe, who obſerv'd our Actions, compell'd us to conſtrain them, and when the dying Languiſh of my Soul render'd me incapable of aſſuring you that I would never ceaſe to love you. But let me intreat you to preſerve yourſelf, for the ſake of all that's deareſt to your Thoughts! And ſhould I be that deareſt All, how infinite would my Happineſs then prove! Be careful of your Welfare, I implore you! Live in perpetual Felicity, but forbear to baniſh me from your Remembrance. Let my Idea be ſometimes preſented to your Imagination, you will ſoon receive the Tidings of my Death; for I ſhould be too miſerable, were I long to linger out ſo wretched a Life. I yeſterday thought myſelf expiring, when I approach'd the Manſion that is honour'd with your Name. We happen'd to ſtop there, and I alighted out of the Coach: Ah! how ſhould I have been delighted to have ſeen you in that charming Place! We viſited the Apartments, and I was ſhewn that where you uſually reſide: Your Picture was the firſt Object that met my Eyes, and I fainted the moment I beheld it. My Diſorder continued

tinued ſo long, that I was oblig'd to deſire them not to proceed in our Journey. I paſs'd the Night in your Bed: O that fatal, melancholy Night! No Imagination is able to conceive the Anguiſh it gave me. The next Morning I took a View of your Park, and thought, with a Sigh, that you would one day return to that Solitude, to lament my Abſence; and that you ſometimes would review, with Pleaſure, thoſe Places where I left you many an Evidence of my Love and Sorrows. What a Flow of Tears did I ſhed over your Picture! I thought myſelf in the laſt Moments of Death, when I kiſs'd it. Perhaps my Tomb may recall me to your Memory! But why do I entertain you with theſe melancholy Imaginations! Can I be ſo barbarous as to increaſe your Deſpair! I am ſure you love me, and I tremble for you, if your Condition has any Similitude to mine. I, at laſt, quitted that charming Retreat, where you muſt continue in my Abſence. There did your Picture preſent me with the laſt View of your inchanting Form that I ſhall ever obtain. O Heavens! you will there ſeek for me in vain! Our ardent Wiſhes will have no Power to unite us: But why ſhould I conſent to be the Cauſe of your Unhappineſs! Ah! when ſhall I be deliver'd from the Anguiſh of that Thought! Fatal Days! will you never come to your final Period! This is what I paſſionately deſire, and ſhould be delighted to die this Moment. You have intreated me to wait for happier Times; but do you imagine my Soul can riſe above the Woes that aſſault it? I am ſenſible that I ſink beneath their Weight, and I reſign myſelf to my Doom, without a Murmur. Adieu, my deareſt Count; you occaſion all the Calamities of my Life: Heaven grant that I may not be the Cauſe of yours! Devote ſome few Moments to the Remembrance of an unfortunate Creature, who lives for you alone. Once more Adieu; and O that it may not prove the laſt! Alas! I have loſt you for ever, and ſhould eſteem Death my greateſt Felicity.

LETTER LXVII.

THREE Hours have I vainly linger'd out, in expectation of a Letter from you: My Fears are too juſtly founded, and you love me no more. I am now deſtitute of every Enjoyment. I had no Reſſource, but the Hope of living in your Remembrance.——Ah! why was I willing to be ſo credulous! I deceiv'd myſelf, when

I

I imagin'd my Misfortunes would increaſe your Paſſion. Ungrateful Man! can you then abandon me in this inhuman manner, when you are ſenſible I am this moment dying for you! You will not long be diſquieted by me, and I am aſtoniſh'd that I can yet deſire to be the Object of your tender Affection. What are the Hopes I would entertain? In the unhappy Situation to which I am now reduc'd, the Certainty of your Paſſion would add to my Calamities. I am perſuaded I ſhall ſee you no more; why then do I cheriſh thoſe Deſires that can only torment me! Have you an Inclination to teach me to forget you? Reſtore me then to myſelf; reſtore me, if poſſible, to my loſt Repoſe. *Barbarian* as you are! is it not enough that your Abſence overwhelms me with Deſpair; but muſt you render me ſtill more miſerable, by convincing me that I have loſt you for ever! Are you then reſolv'd to abandon me! Ah! if you ſtill retain any ſlight Remembrance of me, let me intreat you to caſt your Eyes on my wretched Condition. Death would now be the leaſt of my Calamities: But, O merciful Heaven! what a Scene of Terror does it daily preſent to my View! How does it reproach me with all my Crimes! With what a dreadful Fatality does it recall your Idea to my Soul! You are incapable of conceiving the Tortures I ſuſtain, and they are not to be deſcrib'd by the utmoſt Power of Language! Tho' you ſhould ſtill continue to love me, and were as much rack'd at our Abſence, as myſelf, your Sorrows would have thoſe Mitigations which I muſt never expect. 'Tis true, you have loſt me for ever, but you can lament that Loſs without the leaſt Conſtraint. No Perſon interrupts your Sorrows, and you are not requir'd to unfold the Cauſe of your Tears. No one compels you to diſſemble a Tenderneſs to an Object you cannot love. You offer me all your Thoughts, and are at liberty to pour out the Anguiſh of your Soul, without Reſerve. You are not fated to any Subjection, and may have the Satisfaction of devoting all your Hours to Grief. But, O how unfortunate am I! Have I once enjoy'd a Moment's Tranquillity theſe ſix Days paſt! Ah! why am I not ſequeſter'd from the reſt of the World! My Sighs would, at leaſt, be allow'd me in Solitude,. and I ſhould then be ſo happy as to enjoy your amiable Idea without Interruption. But, is it poſſible that you ſhould exhort me to forget you? Tho' this Counſel ſhould be only ſuggeſted by your Generoſity, and that, in compaſſion to my Misfortunes, you ſhould determine to end

end them, by reſolving to be no more be- lov'd, what can you render me in the room of my Sorrows? Perhaps you will tell me, that I ought to forget you: But what would be the Conſequence, were I capable of obey- ing you? You! who are ever preſent to my Thoughts, as well in the Tumult of the World, as in the Calm of Solitude, and the Silence of Night. You! who are the ſole Cauſe of all my Woes: You! whoſe Indif- ference could never rend you from my Heart. The more you wound it, the ſtronger is it riveted to your dear Image. O Remem- brance too painful, of thoſe Moments that glided away in lovely Raptures! Fatal; pleaſing Moments, that are now loſt for ever! Why are you ſtill preſented to my Memo- ry! Vainly do I endeavour to baniſh 'em; they purſue me through all my Retreats. If Slumber at any time ſteals upon my Sor- rows, and cloſes my Eyes for a few Mo- ments, don't imagine it affords me the leaſt Repoſe. My Calamities then riſe before me in a ſtronger Glare; your Image dwells upon my Senſes, I behold you languiſhing with Love; you ſympathize in all my Anguiſh; I have the Pleaſure to intermix my Tears with yours; I hear the melting Muſick of your Voice, and all my ſad Ideas are then brighten'd into Extacies too great to be deſcrib'd. I ſeem to wander with you, in thoſe delicious verdant Scenes, where we once reſign'd ourſelves to the Ardours of our mutual Paſſion, and gave a Looſe to all the Softneſs that Love could inſpire. I then fancy that I am folded in your Arms; I liſten to the gentle Breathing of your Sighs; I indulge you with a Profuſion of the warmeſt Careſſes; my Tranſports are kindled by yours; I am loſt in extatic Bliſs; I faint; I die; —— and then the dear Illuſion is over: But the Torment it creates me, makes me believe the whole Scene a Reality. I ſearch for you all around; I call you with the Voice of Love, and would willingly imagine you are near me. My Deſires afflict me with painful Inquietudes; my Tears trickle a-new; and I paſs the remainder of the Night in thoſe cruel Imaginations, which the Day has no Power to diſſipate. I only view the riſing Dawn, to deteſt it, and my pleaſing Hope that you continue to love me, is my only Conſolation. One Letter from you, calms all the Anguiſh I have ſuſtain'd, and I read it without ceaſing. Why then do you refuſe me this reviving Solace! Do you imagine, that ſomething is ſtill wanting to compleat my Miſery; and muſt I receive it from your dear Hand alone? To whom ſhall I have Recourſe, in this my deſtitute

deſtitute Condition? Should you reſolve to forſake me; who will aid me to ſupport the Remains of a languiſhing Life? Perhaps ſome new Paſſion has for ever eras'd me from your Remembrance; be ſo generous then as to let me continue ignorant of your Infidelity. Endeavour to deceive me, in mere Compaſſion, that, if poſſible, I may never know to what degree you have cauſed me to be wretched. Let me breathe my Laſt, without complaining of your Barbarity. You deſire me, in your Letter, to forget you, and you may poſſibly hope that my Obedience will render your Ingratitude leſs viſible. Perhaps I injure you by that Suſpicion, and my Abſence may probably furniſh you with new Motives to love me with a conſtant Paſſion. But you neglect to viſit me, and no longer revive me with your Letters. Adieu! If I really continue to be dear to you, remember the Tenderneſs you owe me; but if you conſider me with Indifference, think how much I need your Conſolation and Pity.

LETTER LXVIII.

O Heavens! what fatal Tidings have you ſent me in your Letter! Is it poſſible, that after all the Unhappineſs I have already experienc'd, there ſhould ſtill be more Calamities for me to ſuſtain! Can it then be true, that Lady ***, that generous, conſtant Friend, is dead! You have then beheld her in the Condition that will ſoon be mine, and your Sorrows, e'er long, may have ſome Affinity to thoſe of the deſolate *St. Far* ***. How do I tremble at this diſmal Thought! Not that I am intimidated at the mere Approach of Death; but, O righteous Heaven! what Scenes of Guilt and Horror; what melancholy Subjects for Repentance riſe before me! I ſhall ſoon be join'd to my dear departed Friend: But alas! how little ſhall I reſemble her in the Circumſtances of my Death! She had no Convictions of Guilt to wound her Soul, and her laſt Moments were not diſcompos'd by thoſe cruel Reflections that will embitter mine. When ſhe beheld herſelf on the Point of being ſever'd from her deareſt Object, ſhe was under no Neceſſity to conſtrain her Sorrow. Her Tears were blended with Innocence; but, what will be my wretched State, since I ought to reproach myself for those Sighs which even my Calamities extort from my Breast! I am constantly haunted by the most criminal Ideas, and find it impossible to chase them from my Remembrance. My eternal Separation from you; the declining State of my Health; the near Prospect of my Death; the Conflicts of Remorse, that perpetually rend my Soul; my Passion, which neither a wasting Constitution, nor a trembling Soul can diminish, and which is even cherish'd by its own Torments; the Woes that afflict me at present, and my Apprehensions of those to which I may be fated hereafter; my Fears to recollect my past Conduct; my burning Impatience for your Return, and my Despair of ever beholding you more; these are the Entertainments in which I pass my forlorn Days. I am fetter'd by cruel Decorums, and, of all my Misfortunes, can only bewail the untimely Death of my Friend, and with which Lord *** seems to be as much affected as myself. His Inflexibility in tormenting me with his hateful Passion, and the sympathising Tears he devotes to my Grief, entirely compleat my Desperation. I should rejoice to be the Object of his Aversion, and wish he would for ever detest me, as much as I detest myself. My Soul is chill'd, chill'd, when-ever I behold him. In vain do I ſometimes endeavour to excuſe my own Frailties, by recollecting the Diſorders of Soul he ſo often diſcovers: I am ſenſible they can never juſtify mine, and I reſign myſelf to all the Horror with which my Crimes inſpire me. I am ſometimes inclin'd to flatter myſelf, that my Paſſion has been ſucceeded by Repentance; but alas! I find it impoſſible to forget you. And could I ſay, forget you! you reign triumphant, amidſt the ſevereſt Reflections that rack my Heart. I eaſily perſuade myſelf, that you regret my Abſence, and that dear Belief teaches me to ſubmit to Death without a Murmur. But, may I not be privileg'd to behold you once more? Ah! if you ſtill continued to love me, could I need to aſk you that Queſtion! Are you not ſufficiently ſenſible, that the Sight of you would ſooth my Torments, or, at leaſt, would cauſe me to die with leſs Reluctance? But alas! what would your Entertainment be in this Place! Why ſhould I be deſirous to pierce your Soul! What a fatal Spectacle ſhould I preſent to your View! You could only know me by my Paſſion, and I ſhould be acceſſary to the Encreaſe of my tormenting Remorſe. Adieu: Do not forget me, my Lord, but permit me to live in your Heart.

This is a Confolation you owe me, fince nothing could ever rend you from my Soul; and, if I had not lov'd you to Idolatry, I fhould not have fuftain'd the Calamities that fink me to the Grave. But, do not believe I reproach you for what I have fuffer'd; this may poffibly be the laft time I fhall be able to write to you. but if Heaven has not otherwife ordain'd, I will continue to affure you that I will be yours alone, to the laft Moment of my Life. Adieu: Let *St. Far**** have the Letter I have inclos'd; aid him to fupport his Defpair, but let him not be acquainted with my Condition. Alas! you yourfelf may poffibly have too much occafion for the Relief you offer him.

LETTER LXIX.

YOU are not fenfible, while you are fo intent on your Journey to this Place, and are affording me fuch endearing Proofs of your Tendernefs; I fay, you are not fenfible, that with all the Expedition you can poffibly make, you will only arrive time enough to fee me breathe my laft. Is not Death fufficiently doleful in itfelf; but would you add to the Horrors of mine, by your unavailing Prefence! Such a Sight will be too fatal for you to ſupport; for you cannot behold me in my deplorable Condition, without dying yourſelf. Fly then from an Object that would add new Anguiſh to your Deſpair, and leave me alone to ſuſtain the Severity of my laſt Pangs. We muſt now indeed be parted for ever! No more Hopes are in reſerve for us, and we ſhall never behold each other again. Receive this Stroke of Fate with Fortitude; and, ſince our Calamities are not to be eluded, ſubmit to them with the Reſignation I have acquir'd. Ever ſince I have been ſever'd from you, what could I wiſh for more, than to finiſh the remainder of a Life that was doom'd to ſuch Deſpair as knew no Intermiſſion! My Days have, at laſt, attain'd their final Period; and as you ſincerely love me, and can judge, by your own Experience, of the inſupportable Woes I ſuſtain, inſtead of wiſhing me to live, congratulate me on a Death that releaſes me from Tortures a thouſand times more dreadful than all its Terrors. Had I been permitted to ſee you once more, might I not have beheld you inconſtant? and would that racking Idea have comported with my expiring State? Ah! what are the preſent Diſpoſitions of my Soul! Great God! wilt thou then permit Death to ſurprize me in the unprepar'd Bloom of Life!

Life! How do I ſtill reflect, with Pleaſure, on thoſe Moments that ought to ſhake my Soul with Horror! What a fatal Confuſion of Thoughts crowds upon me! Ah why, my deareſt Lord, can I only think on you, when there are ſo many awful Subjects that ſhould engage my Attention! In a few Moments, I ſhall be yours no more; the Object you have lov'd with ſo much Tenderneſs, and who conſecrated all her Vows to you alone, till ſhe at laſt became the Victim to her own Paſſion; that Object is now preparing to expiate her Crimes and Frailties by Death. O the dreadful Image! To what State ſhall I now be conſign'd! What Compunctions of Soul do I experience! Great God! ſhall they be all unavailing! Adieu; let me intreat you to write to me no more. Live, my beloved Lord, and, if it be poſſible, live happy. My Fortitude begins to forſake me. Fatal, cruel Moments! Adieu. Forget me for ever, if it be neceſſary to your Repoſe. Alas! Death itſelf is leſs painful to me than that Requeſt!

LETTER LXX.

I Muſt now flatter myſelf no more with Life: The fatal Moment approaches, and I muſt leave you for ever; for Death has begun his Work! It is no longer the frail Perſon enſlav'd by a fatal Paſſion, who writes to you now. It is an unfortunate Creature, who repents of all her Crimes; who reviews them with Horror; who is ſenſible of all their Weight, and who yet is unable to refuſe you new Proofs of her Tenderneſs. Sad Remains of my Frailty, which, amidſt the Terrors and Apprehenſions of Death, ſtill preſent you to my Imagination! I have burnt your Letters, and began, by that Sacrifice, to diſengage myſelf from Life. I have depoſited your Picture in faithful Hands; and would to Heaven that I had likewiſe parted with all my Remembrance of the Original! What ſweet Tranquillity would then compoſe my Soul! With how much Calmneſs could I reſign my Life, had all its Moments been leſs devoted to you! I am an Object of Horror to myſelf; and how infinitely wretched ſhall I be, if I am not an Object of Compaſſion! How joyfully could I ſupport my preſent Woes, did not the Proſpect of greater preſent itſelf

to

to my View! And, muſt Death cloſe my Eyes for ever! What Pangs have I yet to ſuſtain, before this dreadful Scene be over! How little ſhould I regret the Loſs of Life, would its Period likewiſe end my Anguiſh! But, O great God, what Fate am I yet to experience! And what, my deareſt Count, will become of you! I behold, in an Hereafter which I am not permit to enjoy here, thoſe Agonies of yours, that now render me compleatly wretched. I ſee your Tears; I hear the killing Language of your Sorrows, and ſympathiſe in all your Deſpair. Ah fatal Idea! My Tears have already flow'd before yours, and I can no longer ſupport my Anguiſh. Adieu. May your Days be more fortunate than mine have prov'd! And oh, may all my Vows for your Welfare be heard! Adieu; I muſt loſe you for ever! Think of me ſometimes, at leaſt, but ceaſe to remember my Frailties. Aſſure *St. Far**** that I die his faithful Friend. Tender him your Aſſiſtance, and may he be ſo generous as not to forſake you in your Sorrows. Did he but know how much I have ſympathis'd with him in his Deſpair! Let me intreat both you and him to continue conſtant Friends. My Tears, and the Pangs of Death, render me incapable of writing more. Pity me, I beſeech you; but be careful of your own Welfare! Perhaps I ſhall be no more, when you receive this Letter. Adieu. I muſt endeavour to improve my few remaining Moments. I am now come to the laſt Period of my Days, and am preparing to end them with Fortitude. Adieu! Adieu! Adieu! for ever!

The End of the Second and Laſt Part.